T0155105

ZERO
Visibility

Georgia Beers

ZERO VISIBILITY

THIS TRADE PAPERBACK ORIGINAL IS PUBLISHED BY BRISK PRESS, BRIELLE NEW JERSEY, 08730

EDITED BY HEATHER FLOURNOY
COVER DESIGN BY STEFF OBKIRCHNER
AUTHOR PHOTO BY STEFF OBKIRCHNER

FIRST PRINTING: JANUARY 2015

ISBN-13: 978-098998956-5

By Georgia Beers

Anthologies

Outsiders

Georgia Beers
www.georgiabeers.com

ACKNOWLEDGEMENTS

Writing is a very solitary art, and as an introverted writer, I'm absolutely okay with being solitary. That being said, the creation of a book cannot be accomplished by the writer alone. Many other fingers are in the pie, so to speak, and *Zero Visibility* is no exception.

Thank you to my dear friend, Steff Obkirchner, for so many things. Not only does she serve as my webmistress, cover designer, and personal photographer, she is also a wealth of information. She reads over my work and makes suggestions. She offers up ego boosts and/or pats on the back when I need them (and conversely smacks me in the back of the head when I need *that*). And she introduced me and Bon to the stunning beauty of the Adirondack Mountains, which led me to write this book. She is irreplaceable in my world.

Thanks to my awesome niece, Allyson Whitney, who gave me a very quick crash-course in the rules of ice hockey. The girl knows her stuff and answered my text questions accurately and immediately. And just for her: Go, Preds!

My deep, heartfelt thanks and love to The Triumvirate. I don't know what I'd do without you. You keep me sane and make me laugh at the same time. I'm never letting you guys go; I hope you understand that.

To my editor, Heather Flournoy, thank you for your gentle yet knowledgeable hand. I think this may be the beginning of a beautiful friendship.

As always, thanks to Brisk Press for being so easy to work with. Everybody's path from writing to printing to publishing should be so smooth. You guys rock.

My eternal gratitude and love to my wife, Bonnie, who puts up with every quirk a writer could possibly have and then some (we are talking about me here), and does it with a positive attitude, some ridiculously good ideas, a sense of humor, and a boatload of love and support. I couldn't ask for a better partner, in business and in life. Boobs with a hat on, baby.

And last, but never, ever least, thanks to you, my readers. I'm a very lucky woman in that my readers stay with me no matter what path I choose to take. Please keep the e-mails and Facebook notes coming. They mean more to me than you know.

CHAPTER ONE

CASSIE PRESCOTT WAS A big ball of emotion as she drove home a day earlier than expected. The sporting goods conference had been an informative one. She'd come across several new items that would sell well in her store this ski season, and she'd been able to meet a couple of vendors with whom she'd spoken on the phone, but had never seen face-to-face. Texting and e-mail was all fine and good, but nothing beat actual personal contact. Cassie preferred it. A couple nice dinners and a fun happy hour in the hotel bar last night were highlights of the trip so far. She wasn't due to head home until tomorrow evening, but her mother had called her on her cell to deliver the news that Caroline Rosberg had passed away suddenly the previous night, and calling hours were tomorrow.

Missing the funeral or even the calling hours were not options. Cassie had immediately packed up her stuff, texted her apologies to the folks she'd made plans with for the remainder of the conference, and loaded up the car to make the five hour trek home to Lake Henry.

Normally, she would enjoy the drive. It was mid-October in the Adirondacks, and the mountains of upstate New York were a spectacular visual explosion of reds, oranges, and yellows. It was this array of color that brought the tourists to Lake Henry in droves and kicked off the busy season. The hotels and inns would be stuffed to the rafters until after New Year's, and even then, things would only slow down a bit. Cassie's sporting goods store would be filled with customers. Tourists would be milling along Main Street, visiting the shops, eating at some of the finest restaurants in the state, and getting ready to ski. It was her favorite time of year. She loved fall and relished its approach; the change in the scent of the air, the chill in the temperature. She loved unpacking her sweaters and warmer clothes. She loved the promise of winter, which meant roaring fires and hot chocolate and hikes in the snow with her dog. She loved the way the trees looked in all their blazing splendor. But today, the drive went by in a blur as Cassie's occasional tears mixed with her racing thoughts and prevented her from appreciating any of the beauty around her at all.

Dusk had fallen when she finally passed the sign that normally put a cheerful grin on her face.

You are now entering Lake Henry. We're glad you're here!

Lake Henry would be different without Caroline, a woman who was a fixture in their tight-knit community, somebody who'd lived in Lake Henry her entire life. Which, it turned out, hadn't really been long enough.

Cassie swallowed hard and made the right turn onto Main Street, which circled the whole of Lake Henry, a path she walked with her dog every morning. Thankfully, she was saved from further thoughts of sadness by a sight a bit too common during the busy season, but one that never failed to make her laugh. A woman, dressed in a business suit of jacket, pants, and heels, was trying her best to navigate the cobblestone sidewalk that ran all the way down Main Street. It was a scientific fact that cobblestones and high-heeled shoes did not mix well, and every third or fourth step the woman would stumble slightly, regain her balance, and continue on her way. Behind her, she pulled a large suitcase, which was obviously quite heavy, and the rhythmic bumping of its wheels over the stones was alarmingly loud.

Cassie glanced at her as she drove past, was able to make out short blonde hair, a very tall, lean frame, and a scowl that made the woman look as if she might kill the next person she came across.

Cassie smiled. "Good way to roll an ankle," she mumbled, and fought to keep from saying it loudly out her slightly open car window. Instead, she simply shook her head. "Tourists." Heels were *so* not the dress code for Lake Henry. Hikers? Sneakers? Boots? Skis? Snow shoes? All yes. Heels? Not so much.

At least her drive home didn't take her past The Lakeshore Inn. That was Caroline's place; she'd run it ever since Cassie was a kid, and Cassie had spent many a summer helping out with housekeeping and general maintenance to make some extra cash. She still popped in several times a week to see if Caroline or Mary, Caroline's right hand, needed anything. The Lakeshore Inn was, as its name suggested, right on the lake. But it was in the opposite direction of Cassie's store, and for that, tonight, she was grateful.

On autopilot, she waved at various people, smiled at others. She knew pretty much all the locals, and they all knew her. She'd lived here for all of her twenty-eight years—with the exception of the four miserable years she went away to college —and she couldn't imagine living anyplace else. Lake Henry was in her blood.

It was in Caroline's, too. Cassie knew that. They'd talked about it. Caroline had been given many opportunities to leave, to live someplace warmer, someplace hipper, but she'd always said the same thing to Cassie: "How can I leave? Lake Henry is in my blood."

And now she'd be buried here.

Cassie swallowed down the ball in her throat and tried to remember where she'd last seen her all-purpose black dress. She was going to need it.

"God damn fucking cobblestones," Emerson Rosberg muttered as she stumbled yet again on the stupid sidewalk. "Who the fuck uses cobblestones anymore? Is it still 1873 here? Have they never heard of cement? Concrete? Asphalt?" She glanced up and saw the big sign lit by an outdoor light aimed up from the ground. The Lakeshore Inn. "Thank freaking god."

Apparently, she'd been away too long, as she'd forgotten that parking in Lake Henry was at a premium, and The Lakeshore Inn was no exception. Every space was occupied when she arrived. She'd been forced to park down the street—a good half mile away—in a public lot that would end up costing her an arm and a leg if she had to stay there for long.

And what the hell had she packed? Bricks? Her suitcase seemed to have gained a good fifty pounds since she started pulling it behind her, these last few steps the hardest yet. The autumn evening had dropped in temperature, her blazer doing very little to keep the chill away from her skin. Without stopping to take in the building—or the larger one across the street that used to be part of The Lakeshore Inn—she dragged her suitcase down the walkway, letting it bounce roughly down the steps, following the signs to the office.

Inside, the atmosphere was completely different. Warm.
Inviting. The counter for the office overlooked a common area
set up like a living room, complete with leather couches,
bookshelves lined with classics, and a gas fireplace, which was
burning brightly now and filling the room with a pleasant
coziness. A young couple holding hands quietly excused
themselves as they sidled by her. Nobody else was in sight.
Emerson thought about just going behind the counter to the
kitchen and office she knew were there, but somehow it didn't
feel right. Instead, she gave the little silver bell on the counter a
soft tap.

"Be right with you!" The voice was pleasant, high-pitched,
and a little sing-song. Emerson scratched at her forehead and
waited. When Mary came around the corner and saw Emerson,
she stopped dead in her tracks, and her eyes filled with tears.
Not for the first time—or even the second or third—judging
from how red-rimmed they were. "Oh, Emerson!" Mary came
around the counter and before Emerson could take a step, she
threw herself into Emerson's arms and began to cry openly. "I
can't believe she's gone."

Those were the only words Emerson could make out
clearly as she stood holding the sobbing woman, awkwardly
patting her back and looking around the room for some means
of escape. Of course, there was none, so she stood, patted, and
waited in extreme discomfort until the older woman pulled
herself together and took a step back. She held Emerson at
arms' length with a shockingly strong grip.

"Let me get a good look at you," she said, and Emerson
took the opportunity to do the same. Mary O'Connor was at
least a decade older than Emerson's mother, which would put
her in the category of approaching seventy. She had always

been a huge bundle of energy, and she still made Emerson think of her as birdlike, the way she flitted around quickly, her tiny frame moving at a speed seemingly twice as fast as everybody else. She was still petite, but her usual peppiness had been tempered. Her eyes were sad, and it was as if the natural light she always carried had dimmed.

"My god, how long has it been?" she asked Emerson now, forcing cheerfulness into her voice.

"Five years," Emerson replied, trying to hide the embarrassment that now colored her cheeks.

"Five years," Mary repeated, and her feigned surprise said she knew *exactly* how long it had been. "My god."

Five years? Emerson thought, and the fact of it actually surprised her. Five years since she'd returned home. She had her reasons. Oh, she had lots of very logical reasons. But now that her mother was gone, none of them seemed all that important. In fact, they seemed downright ridiculous. She would never come home to her mother again.

I hate this fucking town.

"You must be famished." Mary's voice interrupted Emerson's thoughts, and the mere mention of food made her stomach rumble in response. "I've got some leftover chicken soup in the fridge. Come on back to the kitchen, and I'll heat you up a bowl. And we'll need to talk about the details for tomorrow." Her expression was somber as she gestured to Emerson's suitcase. "I assume you'll want to stay in your mother's place."

Emerson blinked in surprise as she followed Mary around the counter. "Oh. Actually, I thought I'd just crash in one of the rooms."

Mary glanced over her shoulder with a raised eyebrow. "Honey, it's October. We're booked solid."

Realizing she hadn't really thought it through, Emerson gave an embarrassed nod. "Okay," was all she could think to say.

The mouthwatering aroma of homemade chicken soup filled the kitchen within minutes as Mary said, "Your mother had most of the details for her funeral all written out and in a file, so I was able to follow it pretty well." She ladled the steaming soup into a big stoneware bowl and handed Emerson a spoon. "I remember her talking about how confusing it was for her when her father passed away, all the sifting through paperwork and looking high and low for forms and information. She vowed never to do that to you."

Emerson nodded as the first explosion of taste hit her tongue. The soup was amazing and she tried to focus on it instead of this conversation she really didn't want to have. But Mary continued.

"I chose her favorite outfit for her to be buried in. You can pick something else if you want," Mary added quickly as she took a seat across the table. "I don't want to step on your toes."

Emerson swallowed, then cleared her throat. "No, no. It's fine. I'm sure you made the right choice for her." *It's not like I'd have any idea what her favorite clothes were.*

"Calling hours are tomorrow from two until four and then again from six until nine. We can go over in the morning and take care of any leftover paperwork. I did what I could, but as Caroline's next of kin, you'll need to handle a few things. Obviously."

Emerson nodded, continued to eat, continued to listen.

"The day after tomorrow, there will be a quick service at the funeral home at ten, then we'll drive to the cemetery. John and Stella are closing the restaurant so we can have lunch there, then they'll reopen for dinner."

"Which restaurant is that?"

The first flicker of disapproval came then, but zipped across Mary's face so quickly, Emerson almost missed it. "Harbordale."

"Ah." Emerson nodded. She had no idea where Harbordale was. Must be new since her last visit. She finished her soup and vacillated between wanting a second bowl and wanting to fall face-down into bed and sleep for a hundred years. A quick internal debate and sleep won out. She took her bowl to the sink and rinsed it out as she spoke. "That was delicious, Mary. Thank you so much." She set the bowl in the drying rack and turned to face her mother's best friend. "Hey, is there room for me to park my rental someplace? I'm down the street in the lot."

"Well, Caroline's car is here in her spot. You can probably take your rental back and just drive hers."

Emerson nodded, immediately thinking what a pain in the ass that would be, but she was too tired to think of any alternatives. "Okay." They stood for a few awkward moments and Emerson said, "I am so tired. Flying just drains me. I think I'm going to hit the hay. If that's okay with you."

Mary jumped up. "Of course. Of course. Follow me."

Her bag rolling along behind her, Emerson trailed Mary out the kitchen door and along a stone pathway. It was too dark to see much at this point, but the smell of the leaves and the water, the sounds of the crickets and the bullfrogs lulled Emerson momentarily back into her childhood. Funny how you could be away for so long, and something as simple as the croak of a frog could bring back decades-old memories.

"Here we are," Mary said, fitting a key into the door lock of a small, weathered-to-the-point-of-charming cottage. She pushed the door open and reached around to hit the light switch, but didn't step in. "I had the sheets changed this morning, so they're fresh. It's your mom's place—er—was your mom's place, so...you don't need me to tell you anything about it. It's yours now." She dropped the keys into Emerson's hand as her voice caught, and she looked like she wanted to say more. Instead, she simply instructed. "Get some sleep. We'll talk tomorrow." With a quick spin on her heel, she hurried back to the main house, sniffling softly.

Emerson closed the door behind her, standing in the silence. She hadn't been in this cottage in a long time, not since her mother had moved in. That was before she'd sold the main building, the huge Lakeview Hotel across the street. She didn't want to think about that now. She didn't want to think about anything. She was so tired her eyes wouldn't focus, but she followed her blurry vision anyway. The layout of the cottage hadn't changed from when she'd been a kid, so she stumbled along to the bedroom, peeled off her clothes, and fell into bed, sleep claiming her before she had another conscious thought.

CHAPTER TWO

CASSIE BLEW HER NOSE one last time before she reached for the door handle and got out of the car. She slammed the door and gave a full body shake, as if she could rid herself of the awful feelings of sadness and grief simply by jiggling her clothes.

"Well," Jonathan Brickman said from the driver's side. He caught Cassie's eye over the roof of his silver Lexus. "That sucked in a big way." He looked even more dashing than usual, his toned, six-foot frame clad in a somber black suit with a lavender dress shirt underneath and a black tie accent. His dark hair shone with the copious amounts of product he put in it each morning, and Cassie knew if she touched it, she'd get pricked as if by a porcupine. Jonathan's hair didn't move; that was the point. But it looked damn good. Combined with his olive complexion, alarmingly precise goatee, and calming green eyes, he was a beautiful man.

Too bad he wasn't her type. She wasn't his, either, which was what made their friendship so perfect.

Cassie merely nodded at Jonathan's comment. She didn't trust herself to speak yet, the tears still a bit too close to the surface. Taking in a deep lungful of fresh Adirondack air she steadied herself, waited a beat or two, then gave another nod.

"Okay?" Jonathan asked, his voice laced with sympathy as he came around the car and dropped a comforting arm over her shoulders.

"Yeah, I think so. I hate funerals."

"We all do, sweetie."

"She was so young." Lake Henry was a small town, just about everybody knew everybody else anyway, but Caroline… she was loved by all. Every last one. She was one of those people. Visitors actually had to attend her wake in shifts, there were so many who wanted to pay their respects. And this morning, the funeral home had been packed. "Only a few years older than my mom. I can't imagine losing her already." A lump formed in her throat, and her eyes welled.

Jonathan squeezed her close. "Your mom's fine, Cass."

"So was Caroline before the blood clot. She had no idea she was even in danger. And then, bam! That's all she wrote." The tears spilled over. "It's so wrong, Johnny."

"I know, honey. I know." He turned her face into his chest and held her tight while she cried.

After a few moments, she pulled away, dried her eyes with a way overused tissue, and blew her nose yet again. "Okay. Enough." Another full-body shake and she felt better. "Enough. I've got things to do, Johnny. Why do you keep me here in the parking lot while you wallow? You're so needy."

Jonathan smiled, revealing a row of perfect teeth. "I can't help it. I'm such a queen." He slid his hand down her arm, clasped her hand in his. "Hey, speaking of royalty, did you notice the Ice Princess?"

Cassie rolled her eyes at the mention of Caroline's daughter. "You mean that she barely shed a tear? I think she was the only one."

"Some things never change." He kissed the top of her head. "Catch you later. Time to go to work." He headed toward the back door of his high-end gift shop, Boutique. Cassie watched until he disappeared inside, then turned to face the lake.

The back parking lot was a mere few steps to the water, which was calm and sun-glinted today. Just looking at the surface made Cassie feel more peaceful, so she stood there for several long moments. To her left was a long dock that reached twenty-five yards out into the water, and was used to help her customers give kayaks and canoes a test drive before they purchased them. The bottom floor of her store, the basement, was actually a walk-out, the whole wall that faced Lake Henry a bank of windows, and featured any water equipment you might need. She could see her mother inside behind the counter, ringing out a customer. The floor above her was the main one and housed general sportswear, jackets, and equipment for any team sports, plus the shoe department and the front door, where customers entered from Main Street. Frannie, Cassie's very first and most trusted employee (aside from her mother) was managing at the moment. The second floor was stocked full with winter apparel, ski equipment, snowshoes, snowboards, and anything else that might be needed for the coming months. She had two employees working up there today, as it was the beginning of peak season. A third would be in at noon.

With a deep breath, she turned and headed inside.

"Hey, Mom," Cassie said in greeting as the customer left with a large bag. Three more were milling about.

Katie Parker opened her arms to her daughter. Cassie stepped into them without further prompting. "How're you doing, sweetie?"

"Ugh," Cassie groaned into her shoulder, then breathed in the scent of Red Door, her mother's one and only perfume. "I'm glad it's over."

"Are you positive you don't want to go to the lunch at Harbordale? I'm sure we could get somebody to cover down here."

Cassie shook her head as a young woman approached the counter with a pair of sunglasses. "No. It's fine. I don't really want to go, but you and Dad should. Just let me go up and change, and I'll come down and relieve you, okay?"

She wasn't quite ready to deal with the rest of her employees, let alone customers, so she took the back staircase up to the top floor of the building where her apartment was. She barely got the door open before she was greeted by forty-one pounds of wiggling, wagging Australian Shepherd who let her know how displeased he was to be locked up at home rather than down in the store where he much preferred to be.

"Hey, Gordie," Cassie said softly. She opened her arms, and he leapt into them without any further prompting, a trick she taught him when he was still a puppy. Cassie buried her face in his soft, tri-colored fur and held him tight. Sensing her emotions—something at which her dog was frighteningly adept—he remained still in her embrace, allowing her to hold him as long as she needed to.

When she felt better, she let him down, checked her messages (none), and headed into her bedroom—Gordie right behind her—suddenly needing nothing more than to get out of the little black dress as quickly as possible. With a relieved groan, she kicked off her modest heels wondering, not for the first time, why women insisted on wearing such uncomfortable footwear. Trying not to dwell on the morning's activity of attending the funeral of a woman she'd loved and respected a great deal, she pulled off her dress and tossed it in a heap on the bed. Once in her wind pants and fleece pullover with The

Sports Outfitter logo embroidered on the left chest, she felt like a normal human again. Stopping by the bathroom, she gave her teeth a quick brush, wiped off her mascara and its subtle black smudges left under her eyes, and pulled her dark hair into a ponytail.

"Better," she said to her reflection, then gave one quick nod. "Okay, Gordie. Let's go to work."

Gordie had only a tiny nub of a tail, but his entire back end wiggled in happiness as he followed Cassie to the door and then down the steps. She kept a hand lightly on his fur as they descended, and though she felt a little better, she still couldn't shake the fact that she would never see Caroline again. It still didn't seem real.

Clearing her throat, she opened the door from the stairway to the shop, pasted on her happy business face, and greeted her customers.

If Emerson had thought she'd been bone tired two nights ago, she apparently didn't understand the definition because she was pretty sure she was about to drop tonight. It wasn't just the standing and the nodding and the small talk with people she didn't know. It was her overstimulated brain. It was the ache in her cheeks from forcing herself to smile. It was the throbbing of her knee, which only happened when she overdid it or was on her feet for too long, usually in the wrong shoes. She wanted nothing more than to soak in a hot bathtub in a room filled with silence, a glass of wine in her hand, and that's what she planned to do.

Consciously avoiding the rest of the cottage, she dropped her clutch, stepped out of her heels, and walked straight through the bedroom into the attached bathroom.

"Some things never change," she said with fondness to the empty room as she easily located her mother's stash of bubble bath and bath salts. Emerson got her love of soaking in the tub from her mother, who did so almost every night before bed without fail. As an athlete, Emerson found there was nothing quite as soothing to her aching muscles as a good soak. Choosing a lilac-scented bubble bath, she pushed the rubber stopper into the drain of the old-fashioned claw-foot tub and turned the tap on as hot as it would go.

Her clothes in a pile on the white tile floor, Emerson looked around the small room. She'd successfully avoided any close scrutiny of her mother's living quarters over the past two days by concentrating on the events that lay ahead of her. But now those events were over, and there was nothing for Emerson to focus on except her departure, which was uncertain as of right now. There was paperwork to deal with, not to mention her mother's possessions. There was no other family. Caroline had been an only child, and her parents passed away long ago.

There was only Emerson.

The bathroom décor was simple and tasteful, a white base with purple accents. On the wall was a framed photograph of Clark Mountain, the biggest peak in the area, blanketed with an eerie fog. *Must have been taken first thing in the morning*, Emerson thought, having grown up seeing the mountaintop— affectionately dubbed Mount Hank—every morning on her way to school. Still, it was a soothingly calm shot, and it brought back all kinds of memories Emerson had no desire to handle at the moment.

Shaking her head free of recollections, she stepped gingerly into the tub, wincing at the heat of the water and was suddenly hit with a memory so vivid it was like watching it on a movie screen.

Caroline, light hair piled atop her head, lowered herself into a tub filled with steaming water and bubbles, sucking a breath in through her teeth as she did so.

"Mom, why do you make it so hot if you can't even get in?" a young Emerson asked with a laugh as she set a clean towel and a glass of wine on the hamper within Caroline's reach.

"It does me no good if it's lukewarm. And it cools off very fast. You don't want me soaking in a cold tub, do you?" Caroline slowly settled herself all the way in and exhaled with relief. Waving a hand, she said, "Shoo. Let me soak in peace." Her eyes closed and a ghost of a smile played on her lips.

Emerson settled in now too. A glass of wine was also within her reach. Good wine. Her mother didn't skimp on many things, and wine was no exception. She took a sip of the rich Zinfandel, let it coat her tongue before swallowing, and stretched her left leg, propping her heel out on the rim of the tub. For the first time in several hours, the throbbing of her knee seemed to ease. She should have taken her pills before she got in the water.

So many people...

That thought had run through her mind over and over again today. Her mother knew so many people. And so many people obviously loved her. The wake had felt like hours of nonstop mourners; people she didn't know, people she vaguely remembered, people who expected her to know them.

Hundreds of handshakes. Countless hugs, many often awkwardly unwanted. Too many "I'm so sorrys" to count. She closed her eyes, slipped a bit lower in the water, and tried her best to soak the day away. She sighed at what lay ahead. Even though her mother was now laid to rest and Emerson had handled all the niceties with a controlled charm, there were some tough decisions to be made.

The Inn.

The rental property.

Caroline's possessions. Car, clothes, everything else.

All of it belonged to Emerson now. All of it. And the thing was, Emerson didn't want it. Any of it. She wished she could simply slap a big For Sale sign out front and fly herself back to L.A. Get back to her life, her job, warm weather.

She reached for the wine glass again, noticing that the blinking green light on her smartphone hadn't magically stopped blinking in the twenty minutes since she last looked at it. A too-large gulp of wine in her mouth, she set the glass down and picked up the phone.

Six missed calls, the screen told her. *Four new messages*.

With a growl of annoyance, she punched buttons and signed into her voicemail. She hated this age of electronics, of constant contact. Yes, it was convenient to be able to so easily find information or send an e-mail. But she hated that she could never get away, that she couldn't just disappear, be out of touch, unreachable.

The first two messages were clients just checking on their orders. Emerson saved them to return later. The third was a weirdly cryptic message from her coworker, Brenda.

"Emmy, call me back as soon as you can. There's some funky shit going down around here." It was just like Brenda to blow something out of proportion and then leave a frantic message. Emerson shook her head and deleted the message. The fourth message was a hang-up from a restricted number. Emerson shrugged, tossed the phone aside, and revisited her glass of wine.

There was so much to do tomorrow, but she didn't want to deal with any of it right now. Right now, she wanted to drink her wine, soak her muscles, and clear her head of all things that reminded her of one clear fact, the reason she was here.

"My mother is dead." Her whisper seemed loud in the silent room. A lump formed and she swallowed it down. "My mother is dead."

The air she pushed from her lungs created a channel through the bubbles closest to Emerson's face. Another sip of wine and she closed her eyes as a profound sadness settled over her.

CHAPTER THREE

IT TOOK A COUPLE DAYS for Cassie to resemble her old self again, and by Monday morning, she was ready to get back to life. Mourning had its place, but she wasn't the kind of person who could stay quietly solitary, crying alone in her apartment. She needed to get out, to share some conversation, offer some help, *do something* to keep her from feeling the pain of what she had lost.

Mary had to be having a difficult time. She'd held on to Cassie so tightly at the funeral. Caroline had been her best friend for years. Hell, they were more like sisters, and Cassie knew that running The Lakeshore Inn all by herself wouldn't be an easy task for Mary even if she weren't completely heartbroken. When she opened her eyes first thing that morning, Cassie made the decision to get a few quick things done in the store, leave it to her mother for a couple hours, and pay a visit to Mary, see what she could do to help.

Lake Henry was a very big tourist attraction, but the village itself was rather small, barely two miles square not including the water. The lake was an easy three-point-one miles around and had a lovely brick-paved sidewalk circling the perimeter. Cassie and Gordie walked it religiously.

The morning was sunny and beautiful with a definite scent of autumn in the crisp air. Cassie had donned her usual work uniform of jeans, a quarter-zip fleece—today's was red—and a down vest. Her ponytail swung back and forth as she and

Gordie walked down Main Street greeting locals and tourists alike.

A leash for Gordie wasn't necessary—he would rarely leave his mistress's side—but Cassie had found strangers to be much less wary and much more comfortable knowing he was tethered to her. He was a ridiculously friendly dog and wanted to say hello to everybody. The locals all knew and loved him, but there were a few tourists here and there who were not dog people (something Cassie would never understand), and they'd get a particular expression of anticipated fear when they saw his furry face with its mismatched eyes and no leash.

"Can I pet your dog?"

A child's voice pulled Cassie's attention downward to a girl of about six, holding her mother's hand and waiting politely for an answer before reaching toward Gordie.

"Gordie, sit," Cassie commanded, and her dog immediately did as he was told, though it was obvious from the excited tension in his body that it was all he could do to keep from bathing the little girl's face with kisses. Cassie squatted down and said to the girl, "You sure can, and thank you for asking first."

The sun glinted off perfect blonde ringlets as the girl tentatively reached one hand toward Gordie, the other holding tightly to her mother who smiled down at them.

"Is he blind?" the girl asked quietly, as if worried about insulting the dog. "In this eye?" She pointed to Gordie's one blue eye.

Cassie grinned. "No, but lots of people think he is. It's just that his mommy had brown eyes, and his daddy had blue eyes, so they each gave him one."

The girl seemed to absorb this as she stroked Gordie's soft head. Then she smiled widely and pronounced, "That's cool." After another moment, she thanked Cassie and placed a gentle kiss on Gordie's head before continuing on her way with her mother, waving as she went.

"Bye," Cassie called, then gave Gordie a gentle tug. "Good boy."

It was strange to arrive at The Lakeshore Inn and momentarily forget that Caroline Rosberg would not be at the counter. Cassie went from smiling to almost hesitant in a mere millisecond and had to stop outside the office door and collect herself before proceeding in.

Mary stood behind the counter, her hands folded neatly in front of her, forearms on the counter, gaze focused somewhere out the window and over the water. She seemed to be much more in control than she'd been the last two times Cassie had seen her, but of course, she was far from her old, cheerful self.

"Morning, Mary," Cassie said more quietly than she normally would. Mary jumped anyway, and pressed a hand to her chest. "Sorry," Cassie added, holding her hands up in a placating gesture. "I was trying not to scare you."

A smile crossed Mary's face then, and Cassie returned it. "Hi there, Cassandra. How are you this morning?" Her eyes fell toward the floor and she saw Gordie. "And there's my boy. Come here, handsome." Gordie looked up at Cassie, who unclipped his leash.

"Go ahead. She's going to spoil you, you know."

Mary bent down to put her arms around the dog, and not for the first time, Cassie was so grateful for Gordie. He knew how to make just about anybody feel better. She followed the woman and dog behind the counter and back into the kitchen.

"How are you?" Cassie asked as she watched Mary give Gordie one of the all-natural treats she left in the kitchen specifically for him.

"Oh, you know," Mary replied, her focus still on the dog. "It's hard. There's so much to do, and we're completely booked for the next couple of months, and..." With a deep sigh, she lifted her arms out and let them drop back to her sides. "I can't believe she's gone."

Cassie nodded. "I know. It's so weird to be here and know she's not." They each took a moment to gather themselves. Then Cassie said, "Well, I'm here to help. Mom's got the store under control, so we're at your service for a couple hours, me and Gordie. What do you need?"

"Oh, you dear girl." Mary stepped forward, took Cassie's face in her hands, and kissed her on the cheek.

The side door opened just then, startling both of them. Cassie recognized Caroline's daughter, Emerson, dressed in baggy, gray drawstring pants and a loose black T-shirt, as she stepped into the room.

"Sorry," Emerson said quietly. "I don't mean to interrupt." She cleared her throat and jerked a thumb over her shoulder. "There's, um, no coffee in the cottage."

"No, your mother was a tea drinker." Mary gestured to the full pot on the counter. "Help yourself. Mugs are in the cupboard above. Sugar's right there. Cream in the fridge."

"Thanks." Emerson busied herself fixing a cup, and Cassie studied her from behind. There had been so many people at the services, Cassie'd never gotten the chance to really *look* at Emerson. Her blonde hair was cut short and exposed a long, elegant neck. The cotton pants hugged what looked to be a very pleasing figure, slim hips, and long legs. She was tall—a good three or four inches taller than Cassie, which would put her around five-ten. And today she was wearing what Cassie recognized as Caroline's fuzzy slippers instead of the heels that had made her that much taller at her mother's services. Gordie positioned himself to Emerson's right, sat, and waited politely for her to notice him, which she did.

"Hey, dog," she whispered, gave him a pat on the head.

"Emerson, have you met Cassie Prescott?" Mary asked by way of introduction.

Emerson turned to regard Cassie with the most beautiful ice-blue eyes Cassie had ever seen. "Hi," she said and held out a hand.

Cassie took it and held on to its surprising warmth, not wanting to point out that they'd met at both the wake and the funeral services, and also attended the same high school, albeit three years apart. "I'm so sorry about your mom."

"Thank you." There was a beat of awkward silence, then Emerson let go of Cassie's hand. She gave an uncomfortable half-wave, murmuring, "Well. I've got to get back," and left the way she'd come, the mug of coffee in her hand. Mary and Cassie watched her go, and a moment passed before Mary turned to Cassie and rolled her eyes.

"I don't know what to make of that girl," she said, almost to herself.

"Why do you say that?" Cassie asked as she followed Mary back out to the counter.

Mary shook her head. "I sometimes feel like she's never been here before. The way she walks around all fish-out-of-water? You'd never know she grew up here. Not only that, she was a minor celebrity. She called Caroline of course, but the last time she was here was five years ago."

"Five years?" Cassie was stunned. "I didn't know it had been that long. I can't imagine not seeing my mom for five years."

"Well, Caroline visited her once or twice in California, but that was it. She missed Emmy so much." Mary's voice was soft.

"What will happen to the inn?" Cassie was almost afraid to ask, but it was something she'd been wondering for a couple days now.

"I'm not sure." Mary's gaze was fixed on the monitor as she tapped some keys on the computer. "I know Caroline had a will, but I'm also pretty sure she didn't think she'd be gone so soon. I don't know how up-to-date it is." She swallowed audibly. "I imagine it will be passed to Emerson. God, I hope she didn't leave it to Fredrik, that ass." She grimaced at the mention of Caroline's ex and Emerson's father as she tapped a few more keys. "Okay. Here we go." She shifted noticeably from quiet sadness to business. "Rooms three, five, and six are all checking out this morning, so they'll need to be cleaned. Two of them will have new guests by three."

As if on cue, a middle-aged couple entered the sitting room and set their suitcases near one of the leather couches.

"Ugh," the woman said, leaning heavily on the counter. "We don't want to leave. Don't make us."

Mary smiled. "You are welcome back any time, Mrs. Todd." As Mary typed on the computer and printed out the couple's final bill, Gordie sat next to Cassie's feet, his whole body thrumming with the desire to greet these people.

"Stay," Cassie commanded softly.

The woman heard and peeked over the counter. "Oh my god, he's beautiful. Is he an Aussie?"

Cassie nodded, then said to Gordie, "Okay. Go say hi."

Gordie zipped around the counter faster than a fleeing centipede, and the woman squatted to lavish attention on him while Mr. Todd paid the bill.

"Seriously, we love it here," he said to Mary. "We'll be back next year."

"Or sooner if I have anything to say about it." Both Cassie and Mary laughed, as neither of them could see Mrs. Todd, but her voice was clear as could be. Her husband shook his head good-naturedly.

Mary finished up the paperwork, and with a last goodbye to Gordie, the Todds grabbed their luggage and headed for the door.

"See you next year," Mrs. Todd promised.

Mary sighed as the door closed behind them. "I hope we're here next year."

Cassie spent the next three hours cleaning the vacated rooms, changing sheets, running the vacuum, and thinking about what Mary had said. How strange that it hadn't occurred to her that The Lakeshore Inn might be closed. Caroline only had one child, Emerson. Her parents were gone and there were no siblings. Of course she'd have left the inn to Emerson. It only made sense. But Emerson didn't live here. Emerson hadn't lived here in more than ten years. What were the chances of her staying in Lake Henry and keeping The Lakeshore Inn up and running?

"Pretty slim," Cassie whispered as she threw a load of sheets into the high capacity washing machine in the inn's laundry room. Her cell phone rang, interrupting her thoughts. Checking the screen, she saw that it was Jonathan.

"Good morning, gorgeous," he said by way of greeting.

"You sure know how to make a girl feel good," Cassie said. "We should date."

"Bitch, please. You could not handle this much sexy."

Cassie barked a laugh. "That's true. Also, you're way too high-maintenance for me. Girls are much easier."

"How are you doing, sweetie?" Jonathan's voice gentled. "Are you at the inn now?"

"Yeah. I didn't want Mary to have to do everything herself."

"You're a good friend, Cassandra. How's our favorite innkeeper doing? Hanging in there?"

"As well as can be expected, I guess." Cassie finished loading the sheets one-handed, set the washer, and pushed start. "But I think she's worried about what's going to happen to the inn. I never even thought about that. I mean, what happens now? It's not hers. It was Caroline's."

"So it probably passes to the Ice Princess. Shit."

"Or Fredrik."

"The Ice King? No way."

"If Caroline's will is old, it could very well leave everything to him."

"God, let's hope not. This town isn't big enough for his ego. The Ice Princess is the lesser of the two evils."

"I saw her today," Cassie told him. "I mean face-to-face. We shook hands."

"You did? Were hers blue and freezing cold?"

Cassie chuckled. "No. She was nice enough. Didn't say much. And I think she was in her pajamas." Cassie flashed back to the outfit, the blue of those eyes. "She's really attractive."

"Yeah, well, looks aren't everything, my dear."

"Wait. What? They're *not*? I'm sorry, who is this, and what have you done with my friend Jonathan?"

"Hardy har har. I'm just saying the woman is cold. She was practically royalty here once upon a time, and then she just up and left and never looked back. All those people who helped her, supported her? She just left them in her dust." Altering his voice to a deep, resonating bass, he added, "Her heart is two sizes too small."

Cassie couldn't help but laugh. "Okay, Dr. Seuss. I get it. We still on tonight?"

"Are you kidding? There is nothing I want more than to sit with you and watch grown men skate around on the ice, slam into one another, and hit each other with sticks. I am so there."

They said their goodbyes, Cassie still smiling and shaking her head as she ended the call and put her cell back in her pocket.

CHAPTER FOUR

EMERSON FLOPPED BACK ONTO the couch, kicked off her pumps, propped her feet on the small coffee table, and groaned in frustration. Bringing the wine glass to her nose, she took a moment to enjoy the bouquet of the smooth Cabernet before taking a sip. The wine rack in the corner held about fifteen bottles, and she'd ended up doing eeny-meeny-miny-moe to decide which to open.

Flavors of plum and black cherries coated her tongue, and the wine finished with a slight hint of vanilla. *Delicious*, she thought, and felt her entire body relax into the cushions. She finally allowed herself to look around the small cottage and really study her mother's living quarters.

It wasn't a large place, really no bigger than a sizable one-bedroom apartment would be, but her mother had made it very cozy and welcoming. The living room held a couch and a reclining rocker. Emerson could picture her mother in the rocker on a cold winter night, covered with an afghan and reading a mystery. A large stone fireplace took up one wall, and Emerson noticed it had been altered to accommodate a gas insert. A stack of nicely aged wood looked ready to go, but she realized it was just for show. She picked up the remote on the coffee table, pointed it at the fireplace, and clicked. The flames blazed to life. *Probably won't be long until this needs to be used regularly*, Emerson thought. In Los Angeles, she didn't have much occasion to sit by a roaring fire, and she was not happy about the appeal she suddenly felt for it. Along one wall was the kitchen, simple in its make-up, but functional. A breakfast bar separated it from the living room, three high-backed barstools serving as the only place to eat a meal in the cottage.

Another large swallow of wine allowed Emerson to shift her gaze to the pictures that decorated much of the room. Some on the walls, some propped on a table, all were of Emerson. There was one picture of her and her father, Fredrik. He was young, blond, and ridiculously handsome, a wide-eyed Emerson sitting on his lap, holding up his Olympic gold medal. In the rest of the photos, she was in ski attire, often holding up her own award or trophy. Slalom. Giant slalom. Alpine downhill. Regional. States. Emerson had won almost every major skiing competition she could enter as a teenager. She was just like her father, and at almost nineteen years old, she was poised to make the US Ski Team and compete in the Winter Olympics in Salt Lake City.

That was before she'd completely lost her mind and done something inexplicably and selfishly stupid.

Shaking the memories from her head, she took another slug of wine and shifted her focus to the current problem at hand: The Lakeshore Inn. It was hers now.

Except she didn't want it.

She couldn't live here in Lake Henry. She already had a home. Well, an apartment. In L.A. On the other side of the country. What was she supposed to do with a small inn on a small lake in a small town in upstate New York?

Her cell phone rang before she could complete the thought. A glance at the screen told her it was Claire. Emerson took a deep breath, let it out slowly, and hit Answer.

"Hey there."

"Oh, hi, honey." Claire's voice dripped with sympathy. "How are you? Doing okay?"

"I am. I'm just tired." Emerson sipped her wine.

"I bet. Did you meet with the lawyer today? How'd that go?"

"It was…ugh. I don't know." Emerson could picture Claire sitting at her big mahogany desk in her office, the surface littered with sheets of numbers and data. It was late afternoon on the west coast, and she'd be getting ready to wrap up her day as an accountant for a large pharmaceutical company.

"Yeah? How so?"

"Everything was left to me."

"Not surprising."

"True. But now I have to figure out what to do with it all. There's the inn, the cottage she lived in—where I'm currently staying—a commercial rental property in the village, her car, all her stuff." Emerson groaned. "It's a lot."

"What do you want to do with it all?"

"Sell it, I guess. I don't know. I mean, according to the lawyer, the rental property is set up with a rental company. My mom didn't have to do anything. She kept an account with money in it in case of repairs or something. The rent from the tenants gets deposited into that account, and she took money out if she needed it, though I don't think she made much on it. The lawyer said she hadn't raised the rent in ages, which is typical of my mom. But it's basically hands off, which is good."

"So, you could keep that running the same way, but do it from afar if you want." Emerson could hear Claire shuffling papers on her desk; her ability to multitask was amazing.

"I could, though I'd still have to deal with any big problems, which would be really hard to do from clear across the country.

The inn is a different story. Did I tell you about its original layout?"

"No, I don't think so." The shuffling stopped, and Emerson could picture Claire cocking her head to the side in curiosity, her chestnut brown hair probably pulled back in a complicated knot of some sort.

Emerson finished her wine and got up to refill her glass, talking as she went. "The original Lakeshore Inn was three buildings: the main building up on a hill on the other side of the street, overlooking the lake, a smaller building of eight waterfront rooms right on the lake, and a separate cottage, also on the water. It all belonged to my grandparents way back before I was born. When they died, it was passed on to my mom. I think that was eighteen or nineteen years ago. I was in high school. Anyway, my mom was not a great money manager back then, and it wasn't long before she was in the red in a pretty significant way. Luckily for her, she got an offer she couldn't refuse from a real estate developer from downstate. Initially, he wanted the whole business, all three buildings, but Mom couldn't bear the thought of losing the entire inn, so they struck a deal where he bought the main building overlooking the lake and Mom kept the waterfront building and separate cottage. And she got to keep the name The Lakeshore Inn. He changed the main building to The Lakeview Hotel."

"Wow. So different, those names," Claire said with sarcasm.

Emerson laughed and returned to her spot on the couch. "I know, right? But it ended up being a good deal, I think. Mom brought in Mary O'Connor, and they've been running the place together for years."

"Just the two of them?"

"I'm sure Mom hired a few others here and there to help out." Her brain flashed on Cassie Prescott, whom she'd seen through the cottage window dragging a vacuum cleaner from one room to another, her dark ponytail bobbing as she walked, her dog following on her heels. "It's a lot of work. And I'm sure there must be a gardener or landscaper of some kind. And somebody to plow in the winter. These are things I need to look into. I wish I knew more." A pang of guilt poked her in the stomach.

"What's your next step?" Claire asked. "Want me to come out there?"

"No," Emerson said quickly, then wondered if Claire had felt it. She liked Claire. She was fun and attractive and smart, and the sex was great, but Emerson preferred her in small doses. After spending more than several hours with her, Emerson always found herself looking frantically around for an escape route. "No, it's fine. I'm fine. I don't plan on being here much longer. I need to check in with work, and then I'll put my nose to the grindstone and figure out what to do here."

"All right. As long as you're sure. I can be there in a flash if you need me. Just say the word."

"Promise."

They chatted for a few more minutes about mundane things until Emerson could hear somebody else enter Claire's office and speak in hushed tones. They said their goodbyes so Claire could bustle off to a meeting.

Sipping her wine and sitting quietly, Emerson sank deeper into the couch, feeling more relaxed than she had in months.

Her knee took that moment of relaxation to make itself known, sending a shooting pain up through her thigh. She winced and rubbed at it with her fingers.

"I wish I could quit you," she said softly to the heels she'd dropped on the floor, then shot them a glare for good measure. She did her best to avoid the prescription pain killers her doctor had given her, but every so often, she caved. This was one such occasion. Too much standing at the wake, then the funeral service, then off to the lawyers, and the damn cobblestones didn't help. There really was no reason to wear the heels here, and she knew it. With a sigh, she got up, hobbled to the bedroom and her luggage, and took out the pill bottle.

Knowing the meds would most likely make her tired within the next thirty minutes, Emerson decided she should check in with her office while she was still coherent. She picked up her cell and dialed into her voicemail.

"*We're sorry. You have reached a number that has been disconnected or is no longer in service. Please check the number and try again.*" The recorded voice was robotically female.

"That's weird." Emerson tried again and got the same message.

Shifting her focus, she dialed the main number of McKinney Carr. Maybe her voicemail had gone screwy and Maggie, the receptionist, could connect her manually.

"*We're sorry. You have reached a number that has been disconnected or is no longer in service. Please check the number and try again.*"

"What the hell?"

She tried again from her mother's land line, only to get the same results. With her hand resting on the handset, she stood still and tried to think. Work friends weren't something she had many of, but she suddenly recalled the cryptic message from Brenda a day or two ago. Something about some "funky shit" going down in the office. She returned to the couch and her cell phone, scrolled through her recent calls list, and found Brenda's number.

"Emmy? Jesus, I guess you heard, huh?" Brenda's voice was clipped. No greeting. No small talk. Unusual for her.

"Heard what?" Emerson asked. "I just tried to call into my voicemail, but I got a recording. Same thing when I tried the main desk. What's the deal?"

"You *haven't* heard." Brenda took an audible deep breath and blew it out.

"I've been a little busy burying my mother and all," Emerson said, snippier than she'd intended.

"Oh, god. You're right. I'm so sorry. How could you know when you've been dealing with that? Okay. Look. The company? Shut down. Completely."

"Shut down? What? What does that mean?" Emerson was confused and didn't like the agitated churning that began in her stomach.

"It means the company was *shut down*. As in closed. Bankrupt. People were sent home in the middle of the day on Friday. Sales reps out in the field were called on their cells and told to stop what they were doing immediately and go home. The T-751 knee replacements? The company's bread and butter? Yeah, the rumors we've been hearing are true. That one lawsuit has multiplied. They're defective, Emmy. *Coming apart*. Losing pieces. It's a disaster. There are now sixteen lawsuits in process and probably hundreds more on the horizon. McKinney Carr is done."

"What the fuck?" It was all Emerson could think of to say. The T-751 was a fairly new model. It represented a whole new generation of joint replacement, and McKinney Carr had built their reputation on it. Hell, Emerson had put thousands of dollars into her own pocket by convincing some of the finest orthopedic surgeons in California to use it. "This is a fucking nightmare."

"I know. I can't even believe it. We are now unemployed, my friend. And better yet, we may have to testify down the road."

"What?"

"If the lawsuits go to trial, they might need the salespeople to testify that we knew nothing about the defects."

Emerson started to sweat. "I didn't. Did you?"

"Of course not. Nobody had any idea. Not any real idea. We all heard the talk, but that's all I thought it was. Talk. Nasty rumors started by our competitors."

"Me, too. Holy shit, Bren."

"I know."

They talked for a few more minutes, then hung up. Emerson sat in stunned silence on the couch, unable to comprehend the fact that she was out of work. No warning. No severance. No time to find another job. Being away from L.A. wasn't helping. McKinney Carr had twenty-three sales reps, and Emerson was certain that most of them spent the weekend calling and visiting the competition, hoping to be hired, while Emerson was three thousand miles away stumbling over cobblestones and staring at reminders of what might have been.

Maybe it wasn't as bad as it seemed.

The thought hit out of nowhere. It was possible. Brenda was a little quirky, it was true, but could she be mistaken about something so big?

Deciding some research was in order, Emerson punched some buttons on her phone to get to the Internet before noticing she had very little battery life left. "God damn it." She plugged her phone in and dug out her laptop instead. It booted up and immediately asked her for the password to her mother's WiFi. "God damn it," she repeated, a bit harsher this time. The small desk in the corner of the living room seemed a safe bet. Rifling through the piles of papers there, Emerson surmised it was where Caroline paid her bills and took care of paperwork before Emerson located a Post-It with an alphanumeric code. Taking a chance, she punched it in and was rewarded with success. She hopped online and the e-mail she had received from the HR Department at McKinney Carr confirmed what Brenda had said. It was simple—almost too simple—and basically said the company had shut down with no intention of reopening and that a representative would contact her in the near future. Her work number—which was automatically forwarded to her cell—had been disconnected and no messages would be forwarded. This was to save her from the barrage of customer phone calls she'd likely get, which Emerson thought seemed incredibly cold. The thought of her clients trying to get ahold of her and being unable to do so bothered her...not that she wanted to field their calls, as she had no idea what she'd say. When she tried to send a reply to the e-mail, she received a MAILER-DAEMON failure notice telling her the address she was sending to was invalid.

Shifting gears, she went to Google. One search of the T-751 artificial knee was all it took for dozens of articles to pop up detailing the problems with the model. Countless lawsuits were pending.

"Son of a bitch." Emerson rubbed her hands over her face in disbelief. How was this even possible? In this day and age, how was it possible for such an important piece of medical technology to go so horribly awry? Absently massaging her own knee, she thanked her lucky stars the T-751 hadn't been invented when she'd had hers reconstructed. She could almost imagine what the recipients of the McKinney Carr knee who had *not* had problems were thinking right now. Several of the articles mentioned the recommendation of having an additional surgery to replace the knee replacement and prevent possible future issues. That would be the last thing they'd want to do, given the lengthiness and excruciating pain of the physical therapy the first time around. Do it all over again?

"No, thanks." What a nightmare.

Emerson sat back and stared out the window at the growing darkness, the water clear and calm as glass as her mind reeled from the sheer scope of everything that had been thrown at her in the past week.

"What the hell do I do now?"

CHAPTER FIVE

EMERSON WAS DREAMING. That, she was sure of.

Bells.

Ringing.

Her brain struggled to make sense of the sounds until she gradually woke from a very sound sleep and realized her cell phone was ringing. A quick peek at it through one squinted eye told her it was barely 5 AM. The number was international, and she groaned, but then cleared her throat and hit the green button.

"Hi, Dad."

"Emmy! My sweet girl. How are you? Are you okay? I just heard. I'm so sorry." Fredrik Rosberg spoke quickly, his accent barely detectable. Emerson was constantly amazed by the quality of English they spoke in Sweden. In all of Scandinavia, really. His English was better than hers.

"Yeah. Thanks. I'm okay."

"Are you in Lake Henry?"

"Yes. Where it's 4:53 in the morning."

"Oh, for god's sake. I'm sorry, honey. I forget." He always forgot. It was a regular thing, and Emerson had learned if she ever wanted to speak to her father, she was most likely going to have to do it in the wee hours of the morning while she was bleary-eyed and foggy-headed.

"S'okay," she said, not bothering to stifle her yawn.

"I'm sorry I missed the funeral. I was in Oslo visiting with Ellen's family, and I couldn't have gotten a flight to get me there in time. She wants to get married in the spring. I figure, why not?"

His ability to shift from something as serious as her mother's death to the subject of his own love life so smoothly never ceased to amaze Emerson. It was a gift her father had. Playfully sarcastic tone firmly in place, she asked, "Fifth time's the charm, huh?"

Fredrik's laughter rumbled through the phone and vibrated in her ear. Emerson could picture him, his too-long, wavy blond hair falling across his forehead, his face almond brown almost year-round from time spent on the sunny ski slopes all over the world—painfully good-looking, even as sixty was moving in at breakneck speed. He was famous, at least to the world of championship skiing, with a gold and two bronze Olympic medals. Female companionship was not something he ever lacked; Emerson's mother was merely the first in a long line of women. He'd married and divorced four of them, including Caroline. Emerson knew Wife #2, Marlena, very well. She'd ended up being the big sister Emerson never had. They were in touch on Facebook, and talked on the phone fairly often. She lived in Colorado with her husband and baby, and was one of the few people Emerson felt *really* knew her. Wife #3, Anna, was only in her twenties and wanted to have children, but Fredrik was "way past fatherhood," as he told her. She was the only one of the four who served *him* with divorce papers rather than the other way around, and that earned her Emerson's grudging respect. Wife #4 was Shannon, a supermodel from the UK, and Emerson hadn't met her at all, mostly because the entire union lasted less than a year. Ellen was Norwegian, and had been on her father's arm for nearly six months now—a new record for him. Emerson met her over the summer when the couple had come to L.A. so Fredrik could narrate a documentary on the history of downhill skiing. Ellen seemed very nice, and they'd gotten along quite well. She seemed almost too down-to-earth for her dad, but Emerson had learned long ago that Fredrik was a big boy fully capable of making—and handling—his own mistakes. He was a ladies' man and a crappy father, but he was the only one she'd ever have, so she put up with his idiosyncrasies and took whatever time and attention he was willing to give. It wasn't much, but it was as good as it would get, and Emerson had made peace with that a while back.

"Seriously, my girl," he said now, his voice gentling. "How are you? Are you doing all right?"

Emerson nodded. "I'm okay. It's hard. It's hard to be here in Mom's house with her things, and it's hard to be back in this town."

"I know. Some bad memories there for you. When was the last time you visited?"

"Long time ago," she evaded, not wanting to admit to the truth.

"Do you miss the city?"

"Oh my god, it's so quiet here!" She laughed at that, trying to lighten the mood. "I forgot about that. I'm used to L.A. We don't have cicadas there. We have traffic. Always."

"That's one thing I really liked about Lake Henry. The quiet. I don't think I have relaxed quite as well anyplace else. You should give it a try, my girl. Just sit by the water and clear your mind. It's rejuvenating."

"I'll try that," Emerson said as she rolled her eyes. Meditation was so not for her.

"Okay, love. I have to run. I just wanted to check in with you and make sure you're doing all right."

"I am."

"I am really sorry about your mother. She was a wonderful woman."

She appreciated his words, especially since her parents' split —albeit ages ago—had been anything but pleasant. "She was. Thanks."

"You take care of yourself."

"I will."

"Good. I love you, my girl."

"Love you, too, Dad."

A strange sense of loneliness seemed to settle over her once she hung up, and she found herself suddenly missing the sound of her father's voice. Baffling. Not the kind of person who needed a lot of human contact, the melancholy feeling surprised her, but she wasn't sure what to do about it. She lay in her mother's soft bed, warm under the down comforter, and listened to the early morning, something she'd often done as a child. It was still dark out, but she could hear the various creatures near the water. Bullfrogs, birds, the occasional cicada, a snapping twig that indicated something larger…a squirrel or fox or maybe a deer. Straining her ears, she was momentarily taken back to her childhood when she'd lain in bed and tried to identify each gentle sound of nature she heard in the early morning quiet, as if each creature was moving on tiptoe, trying not to wake the still slumbering humans.

The reminiscent peace didn't last long as Emerson glanced from the window to her mother's dresser, and it occurred to her just how much there was to be done. On the footsteps of that thought came the reminder that she was now unemployed and had nothing that would make her speed up the cleaning and sorting process, which then led to a sad depression that seemed to push her down into the mattress with its weight. Her brain felt no clearer this morning than it had last night; she still had no idea what to do.

Emerson knew there would be no more sleeping today. Her body felt sluggish and gooey, and she suspected it was because she'd gotten very little physical activity since she'd arrived. She couldn't run the way she did when she was younger, not with her knee, but she could bike. She needed to. Rarely did she go two consecutive days without a ride, so it was no wonder she was feeling blobbish. When her father spoke of meditation clearing his head, Emerson equated that to biking. That was how she cleared hers. She hadn't been able to bring her bike with her on the plane, but she needed to do something.

Throwing the covers off, she announced to the room, "A brisk walk it is then."

Not having much in the way of exercise clothes in her suitcase, she donned a pair of tight-fitting workout pants over the ACE bandage she wrapped around her knee for extra support, then rifled through her mother's dresser drawer and found a soft gray long-sleeved T-shirt that was emblazoned with Adirondack Girls' Hockey on the front in white.

"Perfect." Thanking her lucky stars for whatever reason she'd decided to pack her sneakers, she laced them up, grabbed a jacket from the hook near the door, and headed out. Maybe she couldn't catch any sleep, but she could certainly load up on fresh mountain air.

If her memory served her, Lake Henry was just over three miles around. Emerson had done one lap at a somewhat brisk pace, but now slowed a bit and allowed herself to relax, to just take in the fresh air, the sounds of nature. She hated to admit that her father was right, but something about the quiet of the woods and clear reflection of the lightening sky in the lake put her mind at ease. She felt infinitely better than she had last night.

Walking had been a grand idea. Her legs were working, her knee was no longer stiff, and she felt at peace for the first time in...well, since she'd arrived. She'd passed a grand total of four people during her trek, two joggers, one biker, one walker, and they'd all smiled, nodded, and continued on their way.

Hearing the slap, slap of running shoes on the path behind her, she inched herself to the right to allow room for the runner to pass.

"Thanks," the runner said as she went by, giving Emerson a quick glance before continuing on her way, doing a double-take, and turning back. Cassie Prescott pulled her ear buds from her ears and said, "Hey, you," with a cheerful smile. She pulled up alongside Emerson and slowed her pace so she jogged almost in place next to her. Dressed in black running pants, a purple hooded pullover, and expensive-looking Nikes, she kept up the grin, and her dark ponytail bobbed at the back of her head as she fell into step. "Good morning. How are you?"

"Morning," Emerson said, instantly irritated at being interrupted. She wasn't a fan of tandem workouts. She preferred to exercise on her own, in silence rather than carrying on a breathless conversation, but she also had manners, so she answered. "I'm okay. You?"

"I'm great." Cassie's brown eyes sparkled as she looked at Emerson. "I love this time of the morning. It's so...brisk and fresh."

"And quiet," Emerson added, but Cassie kept smiling and didn't seem to catch on. *Okay. Mundane conversation then.* "You run every morning?"

"I try to. Pretty soon, it'll get too dark and cold, and I'll have to resort to the indoor track at the fitness center. Stupid Daylight Savings Time."

Emerson nodded.

"What about you?" Cassie asked. "You walk daily?"

"I usually ride my bike, but I didn't bring it with me."

"Oh, right. Bummer. How long are you staying?"

The question was innocent, but Emerson wasn't ready to talk about the loss of her job. Of that, she was certain. "I don't know yet."

"I ask because my friend owns the bike shop in town, and she has a huge selection of rentals. I'm sure she has one to get you by until you leave."

"I'm sure. Something with a bell and a basket isn't really my speed."

Cassie's eyes narrowed slightly, as if trying to decide whether Emerson was kidding. "Oh, I can assure you she has something much tougher than the little pink city bike you're probably used to."

Their gazes held for a beat until Emerson nodded. "I may look into that." They continued their trek in silence for a moment or two, and Emerson found herself quickening her pace a bit so Cassie didn't have to stop running completely. Soon they were both jogging, albeit at a very slow rate.

"You know," Cassie said. "I'm not sure if you remember, but there's a great trail up Jones Mountain. It's tough, but it's a hell of a workout. I've run it before, but people bike it as well. The view from up top is spectacular."

"I remember."

"You should give it a try while you're here. I don't do it often, but when I do, it's a great workout and quite a rush."

"I bet."

"We should bike it together some time."

"Sure." Cassie was obviously not the kind of girl to easily take the hint from Emerson's clipped answers, but she seemed to finally get it.

"It could be fun." Cassie started putting her ear buds back in. "Well, I don't want to infringe on your morning workout. I hate when people do that to me." She grinned again, and Emerson found herself almost grinning back. Did this girl ever not smile? As Cassie jogged backwards, she pointed at Emerson's torso. "And I own The Sports Outfitter on Main Street. Stop by if you want a couple of your own shirts to wear while you're here. I'll even give you a discount."

Squinting down at her shirt, Emerson said, "How do you know this isn't mine?"

"I gave it to your mom for Christmas last year. I help coach the girls' hockey team." With a final glance directly at Emerson's chest, Cassie winked, turned, and sped away.

Emerson waited until Cassie had rounded a bend and was out of sight before she stopped jogging completely and doubled over. Hands on her knees, she stayed that way for long moments, squeezing her eyes shut and massaging her knee. Running was stupid and she knew it. Pushing the bike pedals was work, but it wasn't jarring like running, which was hell on her knee. But for some weird reason, she didn't want to show any weakness to Cassie. Her lack of endurance surprised her, though. She was slightly winded. Already. How the hell did she end up this out of shape? She biked often. *I am obviously not pushing myself hard enough.* There was no way she'd survive a journey up Jones Mountain by herself, let alone with Cassie, somebody who ran without breaking a sweat. The poor girl would end up carrying her back down. Not that she had any intention of doing anything around here. With anybody. She needed a plan to get done what needed to be done and then get the hell out.

When her knee finally stopped screaming its dissatisfaction at her, she looked around and realized she wasn't far from the inn.

"Thank god," she muttered as she walked to the entrance gate, then followed the little brick sidewalk to the cottage. Once there, she glanced at the lake, which immediately pulled at her, and her need to get away evaporated. She felt the tug of the water, recognized it, and went with it, following a narrow path that led to a small private dock. The sun was just peeking over the horizon as Emerson sat down on the very end, sucked in a lungful of fresh air, and just relaxed.

The water was calm, smooth as a slab of marble. An occasional fish would jump, the splash seeming loud in the quiet of the morning, but other than that, there was nothing but the rest of nature. So shockingly different than the loud, dirty, obnoxious city she now called home, and for a moment, Emerson allowed herself to remember what it was like to be a child here in Lake Henry. To grow up here with the lake as her playground and Mount Hank as her backdrop.

In the distance, she could just make out the tip of the ski jump on Mount Hank, and then all of it came crashing back. The skis, the snow, the pain, the hospitals...

Emerson shook her head, willing the memories away, and for the first time since her arrival in Lake Henry, she wished her mother were there.

CHAPTER SIX

WALKING WAS NOT GOING to cut it.

Walking was nice for a little fresh air, some gazing at nature, to help digest a big dinner. But this morning's walk didn't help Emerson sweat off the stress. It hadn't cleared her head, not like riding would have. It wasn't nearly the same as biking. Biking gave her control. She could bike casually, easily. Or she could bike hard, get her heart pumping and her blood racing, the wind in her hair reminding her that nobody could touch her. The speed was her drug. It was what got her adrenaline flowing.

It was the closest she'd been able to get to skiing in over a decade.

The lack of biking was making her feel tense, stressed, and sluggish. She'd been walking as much as she could, but she'd left L.A. almost a week ago, and after that long not biking, she was beginning to feel it.

A tiny bell over the door tinkled her arrival as she walked into Wheels. It was the only bike shop she could find in the little downtown stretch of Lake Henry, so she had to assume it belonged to Cassie's friend.

The shop itself was petite inside, but every inch of space available was used. Bikes hung on the walls, were suspended from the ceiling, and filled a rack that lined the left wall. In front of the rack and forming the only two aisles of the store, shelves were crammed with every bit of biking paraphernalia you could think of: helmets, gloves, seats, tire tubes, air pumps, pedal clips, water bottles, chains. The inventory was surprisingly complete for such a small space.

Behind the counter, a bike was up on a stand, and Emerson could just make out the top of a blonde head. Through a doorway beyond, a couple more bikes, as well as various bike parts strewn on the floor, could be seen.

"What can I do for you?" came a friendly female voice from the vicinity of the blonde head.

Emerson walked up and put her forearms on the glass counter top, leaned over a bit. The blonde woman was squatting, cranking a ratchet, and had her back to the counter. The soft, rapid clicking of the tool reminded Emerson of her grandfather, a guy who could fix just about anything and gave it his best shot, even if he failed.

"Um," Emerson began. "Cassie Prescott suggested I come see you about renting a bike for a few days."

The blonde woman stood—which didn't change her height all that much, as she couldn't have been taller than 5'1"—and when she turned to face Emerson, her bright blue eyes flew open wide, causing Emerson to stand up in alarm and quickly glance over her own shoulder. Nobody was there.

"*Holy shit!* Emerson Rosberg. In *my* shop. I can't believe it!" The woman held out her hand, and Emerson warily took it. The blonde closed her other hand over Emerson's and shook it heartily. "I'm Mindy Sullivan. You were so amazing on the slopes. I watched every one of your races. I'm a huge fan." Suddenly blinking hard, her expression changed, and she lowered her voice. "Oh, my god. I'm so sorry about your mother. I'm such an idiot. Here I am going on and on about me when you're here under such shitty circumstances. I'm so sorry."

It took Emerson a couple seconds to get her bearings after so many words, and when she realized that Mindy had stopped talking and was waiting for a response, she cleared her throat and spoke. "Oh. Um, thanks. I appreciate that."

Mindy wiped her hands on a grimy rag and spoke like she and Emerson were old friends. "You haven't been back to Lake Henry in a while, huh? Is it weird? I mean, the situation notwithstanding."

Emerson felt oddly comfortable with Mindy. "Yeah, it is. The last time I was here was about five years ago, and even that was a short visit."

"Crappy memories?"

Emerson blinked at her in surprise and thought, *You're the first person to actually get that.* Aloud, she said, "You could say that. Yeah."

Elbows on the counter now, chin propped in her hands, Mindy said, "Your mom was a really awesome lady. I liked her. And she talked about you all the time. Said you were working for some medical company in Los Angeles and doing really well for yourself. She was very proud of you."

The words had a strange effect on Emerson, and she swallowed down a sudden lump of emotion. As if sensing a change of subject was needed, Mindy stood up straight and clapped her hands together. "You need a bike, you said?"

Emerson cleared her throat again and nodded. "Yes. That'd be great. I'm really missing mine."

"Well, come on back here and let's see if we can't get you all hooked up." Mindy waved Emerson around the counter and into the back room, which smelled of equal parts metal and WD-40.

Half an hour later, Emerson exited Wheels with a bicycle slightly nicer than her own back home, and a helmet to boot. Mindy had been extraordinarily helpful and had charged her next to nothing for the rental. Emerson had insisted on buying the helmet and pedal clips, deciding she could just donate them back when she was ready to leave. It was the least she could do to thank Mindy for her help and generosity.

Climbing onto the bike—and loving how perfect it felt, thanks to Mindy's adjustments during the fitting—Emerson coasted gently down Main Street until she hit the path that circled the lake. Picking up speed a bit, she began a moderate pace, already feeling a thousand times better than she had just an hour ago.

The first lap went by quickly, and Emerson settled into a steady rhythm, letting her mind drift, focus, drift some more. Biking was her favorite. Nothing else helped her organize her thoughts, work through her anger until it dissipated, and maybe come up with a solution to a work problem. When she was young, she ran religiously, but running on a fake knee was a big no-no. Emerson was always amused by the irony; how bad must running be for your actual knees (made of cartilage and bone) that it is forbidden for you to run on your fake knees (made of metal and high-impact plastic) because you could break them?

That thought drifted away, and her mind settled on the work that lay ahead. She needed to decide what to do about the inn. She had to figure out what to do about the rental property. She had started going through her mother's things, but it was harder than she'd expected. She'd been in Lake Henry for nearly a week, had met with the lawyer (and would meet with him again on Friday), had gone through scads of papers, and felt like she'd made very little progress. She'd be less confused—less torn, at least—if she hadn't found herself unexpectedly unemployed, but the formal phone call had come yesterday, as promised. It was a "representative of the company," which Emerson knew to mean "lawyer." She was given a brief—and useless, in Emerson's opinion—explanation of what had happened, told her belongings from her cubicle would be boxed up and shipped to her home address, and reminded of the confidentiality clause in her contract with McKinney Carr. She was not to speak to any of her now-former clients, nor was she to speak to anyone from the press, under penalty of legal action. Her work number and work e-mail had been disconnected, which she already knew, and her final paycheck had been deposited into her bank account the day before. That was it. End of conversation. No time for questions. Done. Six years of her life, just finished.

Her savings account had some money, but not much. The cost of living in L.A. was ridiculous, with her rent alone coming in at nearly two grand a month for her small one-bedroom apartment. She wouldn't be able to pay that for more than a couple more months without finding other employment, and the thought of job hunting on top of everything else she was dealing with made her want to hide under the covers and not come out.

Another thing costing her money was the damn rental car sitting in the parking lot. She needed to return it, but she also needed somebody to come with her and drive her back to Lake Henry. *What a pain in the ass.*

Shaking away the stressful thoughts, she focused on the trees flying by as she rode, the leaves boasting fiery reds, brilliant oranges, and sunny yellows. There was no denying the beauty of Lake Henry, especially in the fall, which used to be her favorite season when she lived here. It meant impending winter, and winter meant ski season. The Adirondacks got colder sooner than the rest of the state, and most years, she could get a head start on her runs. Fall meant school, but it also meant practice, and on the slopes was where teenaged Emerson could be found eighty percent of the time from October through April. There was nothing quite as breathtaking as flying downhill on manmade powder seeing those bursts of color fly by because the leaves hadn't all fallen from the trees yet.

Emerson inhaled deeply, taking in the scent of her childhood—the earth, the leaves, the water—and remembered what it was like to live here. Just as quickly as the sense memory hit, so did flashes of flying snow, of snapping skis, of blinding pain. She squeezed her eyes shut for a moment, willing away the recollection of everything this godforsaken town had taken from her.

"Enough," she said aloud, and steered the bike off the trail back into town, her throat suddenly as dry as tissue paper and feeling just as brittle. She needed to stop, to breathe, to get something to drink, and to focus on what the hell she needed to do to get out of here and back to L.A. As soon as she possibly could.

Cassie was a huge supporter of small, local business. Obviously, as she was the owner of a small, local business herself, and that's how she helped keep the town thriving and her local friends working. Lucky for her, the only local coffee shop in Lake Henry had closed its doors for good over a year ago. No so lucky for the owner, Cassie understood, but at least she didn't feel layers of guilt upon her as she stood in line at Starbucks. And they really did have the best coffee on the planet.

Jonathan had gone a little heavy on the cologne today. She was normally a big fan of most of his scents, but this one was a bit cloying, even well into the afternoon, and she tried to be subtle about keeping a few feet between them. As she maneuvered slightly away from him in line and turned to look out the front of the shop, she saw Emerson pull up on a bike.

"What are you grinning at?" Jonathan asked, following her gaze. Then, "Oh, goodie. The Ice Princess is here."

Cassie shot him a look. "Stop calling her that."

Before he could defend himself, the cashier asked for their orders. Cassie ordered a simple Blonde Roast with room for cream.

"I'll have a grande caffe espresso frappuccino, please," Jonathan said sweetly. "But could you make that with soy milk? And hold the whipped cream. But add extra of that chocolate drizzly stuff."

Cassie shook her head and rolled her eyes. "You are so complex."

"And don't you forget it."

They paid, Cassie took her coffee, and they moved down the counter to wait for Jonathan's order. Cassie saw Emerson enter the shop, bike helmet in hand, and gave her a quick wave. Emerson waved back, then took her place in line.

"I'm going to go say 'Hi,'" Cassie told Jonathan.

"You just did say 'Hi.'"

"I'm going to go talk to her," Cassie said with a sigh. "I'll be right back."

Emerson's cheeks were flushed a healthy pink, and her blonde hair stuck out in the back from where she'd removed her helmet. "Hi there," Cassie said as she approached.

"Hi."

"You got a bike."

"I did."

"I'm glad." They moved up in line together, taking one step at the same time. When Emerson said nothing more, Cassie dove in to break the awkward silence. "So, things going okay?"

With one nod of her head, Emerson replied, "Yeah. Fine."

Jesus. Talking to her is like pulling teeth. "Are you bored out of your skull yet?"

Emerson turned to look at her then, her ice-blue eyes almost startling Cassie. Then, much to Cassie's surprise, one corner of Emerson's mouth lifted slightly. "God, yes."

Cassie hoped her sudden laughter didn't sound as relieved as it felt. "I bet. You should come over to the rec center tonight. There's a hockey game." Emerson's grimace made Cassie open her eyes wide in mock indignation. "Don't tell me you don't like hockey."

"Okay."

"Oh, no. No, no. I cannot have this." Cassie shook her head. She was rewarded with what sounded almost like a chuckle from Emerson.

"You can't have it? Why not?"

"Because hockey is the most awesome sport on the planet."

"Really."

"I kid you not. Tell you what. You come to the game tonight and sit with me. I'll answer any questions you have, I'll teach you the rules, and if you don't love it by the end of the game, I will owe you a drink. Sound fair?"

Emerson studied her face intently, and Cassie could feel herself warming from the inside, even as she stared back. Finally, Emerson gave another nod. "I'll think about it."

Before they could continue the conversation, Jonathan approached them. "I've got to get back to the store," he said.

"Okay." Cassie intended to introduce him to Emerson, but he was making his way to the front door before she could even begin. With an apologetic expression on her face, Cassie squeezed Emerson's upper arm as she took a step in Jonathan's direction. "I'll be there by 6:45. Game starts at seven." With a quick wave, she was out the door.

Outside, she caught up with Jonathan, who was half a block down the street. "Hey," she said when she came alongside him. "What the hell was that? Besides rude?"

He gave her a sideways look. "I don't like her."

"Why? You don't know her."

"Neither do you, but that hasn't seemed to stop your schoolgirl crush."

"Seriously?" She arched an eyebrow at him. Luckily, she knew him well, and therefore was clear on when he was in a snit and there would be no reasoning with him. She mentally shrugged off the entire subject. "I'm just being friendly. For Christ's sake, the woman just lost her mom. Cut her some slack." After a few more steps in silence, she changed topics for him. "What's on the agenda the rest of the day?"

"You know, it's been busy today. I think I'm going to look into that new glass display counter I've been talking about for ages. Patrick will blow a gasket when he sees how much it costs, but—"

"You can blow something else and get your way?" Cassie finished with a wink.

"Exactly."

Patrick Farnsworth was Jonathan's sugar daddy. Not that anybody called him that besides Cassie. And even then it was only in her mind. He was very wealthy, having come from old money. He was also nearly thirty years older than Jonathan, which would have seemed a little creepy to Cassie if the two men weren't so ridiculously happy. Patrick owned Boutique and let Jonathan do whatever he wanted with it. In turn, Jonathan attended fundraisers and banquets on Patrick's arm, playing dutiful—and devastatingly handsome—husband. They shared a sprawling ranch set up high on one of the smaller mountains just outside of the village, with a stunning view of Lake Henry, and their dinner parties and holiday gatherings were legendary. It was a good life, but there was one thing Jonathan wanted that Patrick hadn't given him; a marriage proposal. Every now and then, Cassie would mention a same-sex couple that was having a wedding, or she'd point out a dress she liked for someday down the road when she got married, and she'd catch her friend with a far-off, wistful look on his face.

Before her thoughts could continue, they were in front of their respective stores.

"You going to watch the kids play tonight?" Jonathan asked.

"Yeah. Trevor's starting again." Cassie's fourteen-year-old nephew was the youngest player on Lake Henry's varsity hockey team, and she was anxious to see how he did. She was not anxious to tell Jonathan that she'd invited Emerson, so she left that part out.

"Wish him luck for me. Patrick and I are going furniture shopping tonight."

"What for?" Cassie made a face of disbelief. "You just got new furniture."

"That was for the living room, sweetie. This is for the rec room downstairs."

Patrick and Jonathan's finished basement rec room was nicer than most upscale bars and restaurants she'd ever been to. A wet bar made of teak and polished to within an inch of its life, brass bar rail, expensive track lighting, leather stools and couches, a pool table, dartboard, enormous television; it had everything. Cassie had said many times that she could easily live in Jonathan's basement.

"Unbelievable." Cassie just shook her head and chuckled. "Have fun."

"I intend to."

"It's okay, Trevor!" Cassie called out in support of her nephew as he skated off the ice. He was quick and wily, his still-scrawny body allowing him to weave between and around opponents. But when they got him, they got him good. Being body checked by a guy twice his size had to hurt, but he looked determined and ticked off as he left the ice. The first period was almost over and Cassie glanced at the clock. 7:28. Apparently, Emerson had decided against coming. Cassie was surprised by the strength of her disappointment. She'd felt the chill. She wasn't stupid. She'd recognized Emerson's lack of welcome openness. Being friends wasn't something she necessarily wanted, and she made it obvious. But Cassie refused to accept that message and leave her alone. There was something about Emerson that just...drew her.

She blew out a frustrated puff of air just as an older guy she knew waved to her from a couple rows down. She waved back, smiled just as somebody plopped into the seat next to her.

"Hey, you."

Cassie turned to meet smiling hazel eyes that were as familiar to her as her own. "You're back," she said with excitement and threw her arms around the man, hugging him tightly. When she let go, she asked, "How'd it go?"

"Fantastic. They hired me."

Cassie squealed with joy and hugged him again.

Michael Prescott would always look younger than he was. With his slight build, smooth skin, and kindhearted grin, he'd be getting proofed at bars well into his forties. Cassie had known him since the fifth grade. They'd learned to ice skate together. They'd spent summers working the canoe and kayak rental shop when they were teenagers, then waiting tables at various restaurants during college. After college, they'd spent four years as husband and wife. Michael was the best man Cassie had ever known aside from her father, and those were some big shoes to fill. Even after she'd come to realize exactly why she couldn't relax into their marriage, why something felt wrong, even after she sat him down, told him, and tearfully asked for a divorce, he didn't hate her. He'd been hurt. Devastated, even. But he never stopped loving her. Their hearts were tied together forever. Even two years later with him remarried, he was still one of her dearest friends.

"You'll work from here?" she asked him.

"Yep. I'll have to travel to Manhattan a couple times a year, but I think I can handle that."

"This is such great news, Michael." He was a computer genius and specialized in internet security for large corporations. "I'm so proud of you."

He bumped her with his shoulder, then changed the subject. "Trevor playing?"

"He was, but he got clobbered by a couple of forwards more than once. That boy needs to grow. Soon."

Michael chuckled. "He will. It'll happen overnight. Remember me?"

"Oh my god, that's right." Cassie reflected back on the summer after their sophomore year in high school. Cassie had gone away for much of the time to visit family in Canada. She was gone for the last month and a half of the summer. When she returned, Michael's voice had deepened, he seemed to have grown a couple inches in height, and she was certain his shoulders were broader than before. It was bizarre.

"It'll happen," he said again.

They chatted absently between cheering. A few moments later, he squeezed her shoulder. "There's Tina. Gotta run." He kissed her cheek.

"Tell her I said 'hi.'"

"Will do."

"I'm proud of you," she said again, and he waved over his shoulder as he made his way around to the other side of the arena. It was much too large for a simple high school hockey game, so the majority of the seats were empty. But Lake Henry was also home to several winter sports championships and tournaments, so the rink was big, the ski slopes were plentiful, and there was a bobsled run just three miles out of town.

As she watched Michael leave to meet his wife, the owner of one of the bars caught her eye and waved at her. "Hey, Carl!" She waved back as somebody took the seat next to her for the second time.

"Do you know everybody in this town?"

Surprise washed over Cassie as she looked into the startling blue eyes of Emerson Rosberg. It took her a moment to collect herself, but she did and replied, "Pretty much."

"Seems like it." Emerson gazed out onto the empty rink. "Is it halftime?"

Cassie grinned. "Um, no. Hockey doesn't have halftime."

"No halftime? What kind of sport is this?"

"Hockey has intermissions. This is first intermission."

"Did I miss anything good? Is that even possible?"

"I will pretend you didn't just mock the great sport of hockey and simply say that, sadly, it's been an uneventful first period." Cassie studied Emerson. She wore jeans and the same running shoes she'd had on this morning, a long-sleeved white blouse open at the throat, and a navy blue jacket that Cassie thought might have been Caroline's, as the sleeves were a bit short on her long arms. Her short, blonde hair shone in the arena lighting, and dark mascara accentuated her eyes. Slightly flushed cheeks topped it all off. She was beautiful. Stunningly so. Cassie thought so immediately, and she had to consciously pull her eyes away from the teasing peek of collarbone inside the shirt. *And sexy. Don't forget sexy.*

Catching her gaze, Emerson said, "You didn't think I was coming, did you?"

"You weren't, were you?"

"No." They both laughed. "I have a lot to do. I've been working on it and…I just needed a change of scenery."

"This is a pretty big change," Cassie remarked as the timer sounded and the kids skated back onto the ice.

"So, round black thing into the goal, yes?"

Cassie laughed. "The puck. Yes."

"Got it."

They watched for several minutes as the boys skated around the rink, passing to each other, taking shots on goal, and slamming one another into the boards.

Finally, Emerson commented, "This is kind of rough."

"Not for the faint of heart, that's for sure."

"You know these kids?"

"Some of them. And my nephew plays, but he's riding the bench right now."

"Bummer."

"It's okay. He's young. He's learning."

One player crushed another into the Plexiglas close to their seats and Emerson winced. "Okay, that can't be legal."

"Actually, that was a clean hit," Cassie told her. "He had the puck. You can't just hit a guy who doesn't, though."

Emerson suddenly sat up straighter and looked at Cassie. "Didn't you say you coach *girls'* hockey?"

"I did. Assistant coach."

"Are they this brutal with each other?"

"They're worse." At Emerson's shocked expression, she laughed. "Believe me. It's true. Girls are much meaner. These boys generally want to hit each other. The girls? They want to *kill* each other."

Emerson gave it some thought, nodded. "Yeah, I can see that."

They sat in comfortable silence for a while, Emerson asking an occasional questions, Cassie explaining as best she could, and soon the buzzer sounded the beginning of second intermission.

"So, tell me about the bike," Cassie said, turning slightly and giving Emerson her full attention.

"I went to Wheels. I hope that's the place you were talking about because it's the only bike shop I could find, and Mindy knew you."

Cassie smiled. "That's the place. Mindy's awesome."

"She was. She fit me for a bike, let me rent it on a day-to-day basis. I hopped on and rode for more than ten miles. It felt great."

"I'm so glad." And she was. Something about Emerson's demeanor was a bit different, and she said so. "You seem much more relaxed. Not that I know you well," Cassie rushed to add, laying a hand on Emerson's thigh. Realizing it, she snatched it way as if she'd been burned and rushed to keep talking. "But, you just seem…I don't know. Easier."

Emerson looked at her for a long time, until Cassie began to worry that she'd gone too far, was too touchy, had gotten too personal. "Biking helped a lot."

"Are you making any progress on your mom's stuff?"

Emerson rolled her lips in, grimaced. "Do you think we can talk about something else?"

Cassie blinked. "Oh. Sure. Of course." Interrupting her apology, a girl's voice called out.

"Cassie!"

Before she could say a word, ten-year-old Grace Turner flew at Cassie and wrapped her arms around her. Cassie swallowed down her shock and hugged the girl back. "Hey there, Gracie."

"I saw you from way over there," Grace said, helping herself to a seat on Cassie's lap, despite being a bit too big to do so, as she pointed at a faraway entrance. Her face was wide with a smile, showing overlapping teeth that were going to cost her parents several thousand in braces soon.

She no sooner thought of Grace's parents then her mother, Vanessa, appeared, looking just as uncomfortable as she usually did lately, and even more so when her eyes stopped on Emerson. "Hi," she said and forced a smile that came and went in a blink.

"Hey." There was an awkward beat, then Cassie continued, asking about Vanessa's nephew. "Here to watch Kyle?"

Vanessa nodded.

"He looks good so far."

Clearing her throat, Emerson stood up and held out a hand to Vanessa. "Hi there. I'm Emerson Rosberg."

"I know who you are," Vanessa said, before quickly catching herself, forcing another smile and taking Emerson's hand. "Nice to meet you."

"God." Cassie shook her head. "I'm so sorry. Where are my manners? Emerson, this is my...friend, Vanessa Turner. And this," she tickled Grace's ribcage and was rewarded with giggles, "is Grace-face."

Emerson gave a nod and a smile.

The crowd cheered suddenly, and the four of them looked toward the rink to see what had transpired. A near-goal, apparently. After a moment, Vanessa held her hand out to her daughter. Cassie stared at it, at the pale skin, the neatly manicured nails, the wedding ring. She swallowed hard.

"Come on, Grace. Daddy's waiting for us."

"Aww. I want to sit with Cassie." Grace wiggled her bony butt on Cassie's lap as if digging in.

Cassie bounced her knees a couple times and said quietly to Grace, "Be a good girl, and do what Mommy says. Okay?"

Grace sighed dramatically and took her time sliding to the ground. "Fine." She held out her hand, and Vanessa grasped it.

"It was nice to meet you, Emerson," Vanessa said.

"Same here," Emerson replied as they watched the two walk away. After a moment, Emerson said, "Wow. That wasn't awkward at all."

Cassie sighed, shook her head with a grimace.

"What was that about?"

Cassie looked down at her hands in her lap and tried not to let the nausea take over. She inhaled slowly, swallowed, let it out. When she looked up at Emerson, she hoped the wetness in her eyes wasn't glaringly obvious as she tossed Emerson's words back at her. "Do you think we can talk about something else?"

Emerson held her gaze, and her expression softened. "Sure."

CHAPTER SEVEN

VANESSA TURNER WAS OVERWHELMED. Overwhelmed and irritated and fed up. And nervous. A little nervous.

"Stop pushing me, Jeremy." Vanessa's daughter was learning to stand up to her big brother when he got all alpha male on her, not that it did any good. Jeremy still bumped Grace out of the way and went into The Sports Outfitter ahead of her, muttering an unflattering name at her under his breath.

"Hey." Vanessa swatted the back of his head, not hard, just enough to get his attention. "Don't talk to your sister like that or we will turn around and go home, and you can keep wearing sneakers that don't fit. Understand?"

"Whatever." He took a left in the store and headed towards the shoe section.

That was the most dialogue she had with him on an average day, and she sighed now in frustration. Jeremy was thirteen. He'd be fourteen in a couple months. He was already the epitome of a teenager: sullen, brooding, bored with everything except his iPhone (which she could kill Brian for getting him), and his video games. He did all right in school, thank god, but there were another four or five years of this to come. This was only the beginning. Vanessa didn't know how she would survive.

The store was busy. That was good. More people meant less focus on her. Maybe they could get the kids sneakers and get out before—

"Cassie!" Gracie ran from Vanessa straight down an aisle, slickly dodging several customers in her path, and threw her little arms around Cassie's hips.

Okay. Jumping in with both feet, I guess. Vanessa slowly followed the same path her daughter had taken.

"Hey there, Grace-face. Two times in one week I get to see you?" Cassie squatted down so she was eye level with Gracie, something Vanessa always found endearing. "What's new?"

"Hopefully, some sneakers," Grace said looking around. "Where's Gordie?"

"He's downstairs helping my mom."

Gracie turned her big blue eyes in Vanessa's direction. "Can I go down and see him, Mom? Can I? Please?"

Vanessa had a hard time denying her daughter anything (which was going to be a problem down the road, or so her sister kept telling her), especially when she remembered to say please. "You are not to bother Mrs. Parker." As Gracie skittered away, Vanessa added, "I mean it!"

And then they were alone.

Not alone, obviously, as the store was full of people. But it felt like they were alone. Cassie's big brown eyes caught hers, then darted away. "How are you?" she asked.

Vanessa cleared her throat. "I'm okay. I'm good. How about you? How are you?"

Cassie nodded, her voice low. "I'm good."

"You look great." It was true. Cassie rarely dressed up, but she didn't have to. Her beauty was natural. Athletic. She wore olive green cargo pants and a black quarter-zip pullover. Black always made her look so attractively mysterious, made her dark eyes even darker.

"You, too."

The awkwardness stretched.

"Good game the other night," she said.

"It was."

Vanessa looked around for something else to say. "Busy today. That's good." She swallowed hard, the same word flashing through her head over and over: *Lame. Lame. Lame.* Why did conversation have to suddenly be so hard? She and Cassie could talk about anything and everything. *Had* talked about anything and everything.

"Yeah. It's busy season."

Cassie looked down at her hands, then up at the store. Vanessa looked down at Cassie's hands, and her gaze stayed there as memories flooded her brain, memories of those same hands holding her face, tangled in her hair, kneading her breasts, those fingers sliding through her wetness and right into her body, her muscles contracting, trying to hold them there forever…

When she looked up again, Cassie was watching her, the expression on her face a mix of anger, hurt, and longing. There were so many things Vanessa wanted to say at that moment. *I'm sorry. Forgive me. I love you.* And she wondered about Emerson Rosberg. Were they seeing each other now? She wanted so badly to know, to ask. Instead, she remained silent.

"Excuse me." A woman of about fifty approached Cassie with a question, and Vanessa bowed out politely to let Cassie work, simultaneously annoyed with the woman for interrupting and relieved to be released from the painful awkwardness.

Now if she could only ditch her kids so she could go out to the car and sob her eyes out, her day would be complete. As it was, she'd managed to completely avoid seeing Cassie for nearly three weeks, yet she'd still cried at least once every single day.

And then she'd seen her at the rink Tuesday. Her and the Rosberg woman, smiling, their heads close together. It had been inevitable that she'd run into Cassie eventually. It was a small town. But seeing her with somebody else...

Her stomach churned.

Vanessa wandered to the shoe section where Jeremy was absorbed in texting on his phone rather than looking at sneakers, and she just did not have the energy to fight him. She felt like a deflated balloon, and she was on the verge of tears. Detouring away from Jeremy, she wandered toward the women's clothing and tried to focus on the racks for a few moments hoping to collect herself.

Brian was worried about her. They'd been married for fourteen years; he knew her, and he knew when something was wrong. She'd lost weight. She wasn't eating. Her sleep was restless. She seemed far away and sad all the time. These were things he'd noticed, things he'd brought up. He wondered what he could do to help. Worse, he worried that he had done something, that she was upset with him, that he had somehow caused this depression she seemed to be in, this funk. He brought her flowers. He made dinner for her and the kids when he was home before her. He'd made a conscious effort to pick his dirty laundry up off the floor around the hamper and actually put it *in* the hamper. He was trying so hard.

He had no idea.

The guilt was crushing her.

It was a good thing, then, that Cassie had ended things with her. She'd had to, she said. She didn't want to. She'd *had* to. There was no choice any more. She said she couldn't go on sneaking around, pretending not to be who she really was. She wanted Vanessa to leave Brian so they could be together, and there were times Vanessa thought it might be the path to take. Cassie had left Mike. More than two years ago. It hadn't been easy. She'd been the talk of the town for a while, though nobody really knew the details. Mike was a great guy. He'd understood. He'd known Cassie since they were kids, they'd been married for four years, and he understood. She was gay. Simple. It wasn't about him. It was about her. He'd gotten through it. He'd remarried recently. He and Cassie were still good friends.

Cassie had been so patient. She'd waited. And waited. And waited. But there was a difference she couldn't seem to accept no matter how many times Vanessa tried to explain it.

Vanessa loved Brian.

She loved Cassie, and she loved Brian, too. The same way. And she didn't want to leave him.

So Cassie had left her.

Exactly three weeks and two days ago, Cassie had put an end to their relationship, said she was tired of waiting, that she wanted to be with Vanessa, and if that wasn't going to happen, she needed to move on. Vanessa felt like a piece of her had been ripped away.

The tears were not going to be held back any longer. Vanessa grabbed two shirts off the rack without even looking at them and hurried into an empty fitting room where she clamped one hand over her mouth and used the other to brace herself against the wall. She'd become alarmingly skilled at silent crying, and she did that now, letting out as much of the hurt as she could. There was no way she wanted Cassie to see her like this. Cassie did what she had to do for herself. Vanessa knew this. She even understood it. That wasn't to say it didn't gut her completely.

It took her a few moments to pull herself together, and she hoped Gracie was still downstairs with Cassie's mom, absorbed in doting all over Cassie's dog. Just that morning, Vanessa's daughter had commented how Cassie didn't come over any more, and said she missed her. "I miss her, too," had been Vanessa's response, and truer words had never been spoken.

Brian was in sales, which meant he travelled a lot, so it was only natural that Vanessa would call a friend to come over while he was gone, somebody to keep her company. In fact, he preferred that she did just that. The thought of her stuck with the kids for days on end with no adult company bothered him. "Have Cassie over for dinner," he'd tell her over and over. So she did. They'd also had "girls' weekend" on five separate occasions. Vanessa told Brian it was only fair, since he did so much traveling, that she had the opportunity to get away as well. Brian, of course, was all for it. "Go. Have fun. I've got the kids. Enjoy yourselves." And they had. Usually, a cabin or a hotel room was involved. Their schedule was simple: make love, sleep, make love, eat, make love. Those were the only times she and Cassie had been able to actually spend the night together, to go to bed together and wake up with each other, and it was blissful. The ends of those weekends were hard for both of them, but they seemed harder on Cassie. Vanessa went home to her husband and children, whom she'd missed terribly. Cassie went home without Vanessa. Their last weekend together was the straw that broke the camel's back, or so Cassie had told her.

I can't stand it, V. I can't stand having you all to myself and then having to give you back. It's tearing me apart. I can't stand it. I hate sharing you.

Vanessa could still hear Cassie's anguished voice in her head. She would never go so far as to verbally give Vanessa an ultimatum, but that's essentially what it had been. She imagined in Cassie's mind, it was "Brian or me." In Vanessa's mind, she heard, "Your entire family, your home, and your whole identity and existence, or me."

It wasn't a choice she wanted to make. It wasn't a choice she *could* make, so Cassie had made it for her.

Rifling through her purse, she found a tissue, blew her nose, and blotted under her eyes. Thank god she'd started using waterproof mascara or she'd have spent the past three weeks looking like a raccoon. In with a deep, cleansing breath, out with all the negative energy. She did this three times, shook her hands vigorously, and opened the door to the fitting room. Time to find her children. There were shoes to purchase.

The parking lot for The Sports Outfitter was behind the store, between its building and the water. Cassie stood near the display of kayak paddles and surreptitiously peered out the back window as Vanessa loaded her bags into her minivan, and her kids climbed in the back.

Vanessa had been crying in the fitting room. Cassie saw her go in, suspected the emotional break, and could tell the second she'd seen her come out. Her makeup was perfect, her auburn hair twisted neatly into a French braid down the back of her head, but her eyes were slightly rimmed with red and her cheeks were unnaturally rosy. Cassie knew that face well enough to know when there had been distress, and it squeezed her heart not to cross a couple aisles, wrap Vanessa in her arms and hold her, tell her it was all going to be okay.

You will never have all of her.

Cassie knew this. She had to continually say it to herself, sometimes out loud. It was the only way to keep from plunging right back into the mess they'd shared for more than two years. She loved Vanessa. She absolutely did. She had loved her since their very first kiss. There was no doubt in her mind. But that was fading. Little by precious little, it was fading. Seeing her was hard. Knowing how upset she was and not going to her? Even harder. Cassie had made the right decision. For both of them. She understood that, but it still hurt.

"You will never have all of her." Cassie whispered it aloud this time as Vanessa's car pulled away and out of sight. As if sensing her sadness—or maybe sharing it, as he must miss the kids—Gordie sat down next to Cassie. She laid a hand on his head.

She gave herself ten more seconds, mentally counted them down in her head, then shook the emotions off and turned back to the store. There was business to attend to. Across the room, behind the cash register, Cassie's mother caught her eye, smiled. Cassie smiled back. Her mother mouthed, "Okay?" Cassie nodded and gave a thumbs up. Back to work.

Later that evening, Cassie sat at the bar in The Slope nursing a gin and tonic. Jonathan sat next to her, sipping his martini.

"Why do you pretend to like those?" she asked him as he made a face after a sip.

"I do like them."

Cassie grinned and shook her head. "You so do not."

Jonathan grimaced, accepting that Cassie was on to him. "They make you look all handsome and sophisticated. Like James Bond."

"You are a piece of work, Mr. Brickman." Cassie sipped her own drink.

"Enough about me," Jonathan said, adjusting his rear end more comfortably on the stool. "Let's talk about you. She was in the store today, wasn't she? I saw her in the back parking lot."

"She was. And I don't want to talk about it. You're supposed to cheer me up, not bring me down."

"Did you talk to her?"

Cassie sighed. "Jonathan."

"Come on, Cassandra," he said in a near whine. "How many times do I have to tell you I live vicariously through you? I'm a partnered man who has sex every Tuesday, Friday, Saturday, and every other Sunday. Boring! I need some excitement."

Squinting at him, Cassie said, "You do understand that having sex three to four times a week after five years of marriage is pretty awesome, right?"

"Pfft." Jonathan waved away her comments with a fluttering hand. "Stop it. Dish."

"Yes, I talked to her."

"How was it?"

"Awkward. Uncomfortable. Awful."

"Did she cry? I hope she cried."

Cassie straightened, irritation slipping in. "See? This is why I don't like to talk to you about her."

"I'm only feeling indignation for my friend." Jonathan sobered, and his expression said he was mildly insulted by Cassie's words. "She broke your heart, Cassie."

"No, that's where you're wrong. I broke hers." Cassie took a large gulp from her drink, signaled the bartender for another.

"She was never going to leave her husband."

"I know that."

"Fucking straight girls."

Cassie made a noise of noncommittal. She didn't believe Vanessa was straight, but she didn't want to get into yet another debate over bisexuality with Jonathan. He'd call Vanessa a fence-sitter, say she needed to "pick a damn side already." He didn't believe there might be more options than just two, just gay or straight. The issue wasn't about Vanessa not loving Cassie. Not at all. Vanessa loved her deeply. But Vanessa also loved her husband deeply. If they'd only met first... Cassie had mentioned the idea of Vanessa being bisexual on more than one occasion, but she always changed the subject, didn't want to get into it, joked her way out of a serious conversation. Eventually, Cassie had to accept that Vanessa would deal with it when she was ready, and she'd stopped bringing it up.

"Tell me she at least dropped some money in your store."

"Almost three hundred bucks."

"To silver linings, baby." Jonathan held up his glass and Cassie touched hers to it. "To silver linings."

CHAPTER EIGHT

TODAY WAS THE DAY she was going to get her shit together and get stuff done.

Damn it.

Emerson shook her head as she poured herself a cup of coffee from the small kitchen in the main house of the inn, then escaped back to the cottage before Mary saw her. She was avoiding the poor woman like she had a contagious disease, but Emerson knew Mary would ask about her plans, what she was going to do with the inn, and Emerson just wasn't ready to talk about it.

Truth was, she still had no idea.

That was the worst part of it: the indecisiveness. Emerson was a good businesswoman. She made important decisions regarding her clients, their needs, and their budgets every day. So why couldn't she just figure out what to do here?

She was going to sell. She had to. It was the only course of action. That was the fact of the matter. She had to sell her mother's stuff and move on. Get back to L.A. Find a job. There was really no other option. She couldn't stay here in limbo forever. She had to get home. She had an apartment. A life.

Rifling through her mother's desk, she found a pad of paper and began to make a list. Things that needed to be taken care of ASAP.

Call Rick. Her next door neighbor had a key to her apartment. He'd water her plants, get her mail, stuff like that.

Rental car. Jesus, what a pain. She really needed to get that back to the rental place; she'd already racked up a week's worth of charges and hadn't driven it anywhere. But it was nearly a three-hour drive back to Albany, which would make it six hours round trip, and she couldn't do it alone. Who the hell was she going to ask to give up six hours of their day and go with her? Maybe Mary could help her. She sighed heavily.

Pack Mom's things. This had turned out to be harder than Emerson expected. She'd dabbled a bit with the clothes, picked out a few things she might wear herself (though her mother was four inches shorter than Emerson's 5'10"), and had largely let herself be distracted by other things. A glance around the small living space of the cottage revealed to Emerson that it looked hardly any different than when she'd arrived. An entire week ago.

"Jesus Christ," she muttered.

PACK MOM'S THINGS, she wrote again, then traced over the letters with the pen, then underlined it. Twice.

Call Klein. Brad Klein was Caroline's lawyer. He was fortyish, had grown up in Lake Henry, and—Emerson guessed —handled the wills of just about every local. He was handsome and friendly and seemed competent enough. During their last meeting, he'd mentioned that he knew of somebody interested in buying the inn, and to let him know if she wanted a name and number. It was probably time to do that, at least to find out some details.

Her cell phone rang, interrupting her list-making. She looked at the screen and her entire demeanor softened as she recognized Marlena's number.

"Hello, evil stepmother," she said with a teasing lilt.

"Hi there, pain in my ass." Marlena's voice held a smile as she recited her line in their usual greeting to each other. Emerson could hear it, and she instantly felt relieved. Before Emerson could say more, Marlena went on. "Oh, sweetie, I am so sorry. I just heard about your mother this morning. Are you okay?"

"I am." Just hearing Marlena, the gentle calm, the love, made Emerson's eyes well up. "I'm in Lake Henry now, trying to take care of her stuff."

"By yourself?"

Emerson scoffed. "Who's going to help me? Dad?"

Marlena chuckled. "Yeah, I guess I forgot who he is for a second. How are you doing? Are you okay?"

"You asked me that already," Emerson said, grinning.

"I know. But I'm worried. Do you want me to fly there and help you? I can do that."

The offer warmed Emerson's heart, and for a moment, she couldn't speak. It was just like Marlena to be the one to step up. Swallowing down the emotion, Emerson said, "No. But thank you so much. Just the offer means a lot. And how early do you get up? What time is it there?"

"Don't you worry about that. I just wanted to talk to you, make sure you were doing all right. Is it weird being there?"

"Kind of. There's so much to deal with, and for some reason I can't explain, I'm having trouble getting started. I've been here a week and I feel like I've made no progress. I need to pack up her stuff. I need to talk to the lawyer about selling the inn. She's got a car and a rental property. There's just...so much, and I feel like I've gotten nothing done. What the hell is wrong with me?" When she finished, she made a sound of frustration and felt strangely better having just said it all aloud.

"Sweetie, this was a big blow. I know you weren't close to your mom, but she was still your mom and you loved her. Dealing with a loss like that isn't easy or simple. You can't just box it up and expect to go into work mode. If your head or your heart or whatever is telling you to take your time, then that's what you do." Marlena spoke gently, but firmly. It was one of the things Emerson loved most about her; she pulled no punches. She told it like it was, and she did it tenderly, while still making her point. "Are you at least enjoying the fresh air? It's got to be a lot easier to breathe there than in Los Angeles."

"It so is. I don't like to think about it because it reminds me just how much crap is in the air in L.A. Ugh. Actually, I've been doing a little biking, and that helps a lot. Cassie hooked me up with a bike shop, and I took a ride yesterday for the first time since I got here. It felt amazing."

"That's great. Now, who's Cassie? Is she the one who works with your mom?"

"No, that's Mary. Cassie is a little younger than me. She knew my mom really well, comes over here to help clean the rooms. She's been great. She's nice."

"She must be, since you rarely say that about anybody." Emerson could hear Marlena's grin. "Is she cute?"

"Stop it," Emerson scolded, but laughed anyway. "It's not like that."

"I didn't ask what it was like. I asked if she was cute."

"Yes. She's very cute. If you like bubbly and bouncy and obnoxiously cheerful all the time."

They talked a little longer. Emerson asked about Marlena's family and promised to visit soon, a vow she made often but rarely followed through on. Just talking about mundane things with her, though, had made Emerson feel so much better, lighter. She set her phone down on the end table and just sat for a few moments, looking out the window.

It had rained overnight, and the air was chilly. Emerson clicked on the gas fireplace, and in a few short minutes, she felt the warmth as she picked up her now lukewarm coffee mug, crossed the room to stand in front of the big picture window, and looked out at the calm of Lake Henry. Smooth as glass. It was a cliché, but it worked; that's exactly how the surface looked today. The flat evenness made her think of the ice rink last night. It had been fun. She had to admit that, and a small smile brought up the corners of her mouth as she sipped from her mug. Did she now love hockey? No. Definitely not. It was still way too long between goals, like soccer, and it was still as boring to her as watching grass grow. But Cassie loved it, and she was very sweet about explaining the rules and answering Emerson's questions, even the silly ones, so it ended up being a pretty pleasant experience. It was the first night in the past week that she'd actually enjoyed herself and momentarily forgot why she was here and how badly she wanted to leave.

According to Cassie, she'd been three years behind Emerson in school, but Emerson had no recollection of her at all. Granted, her school years had been taken up by all things skiing, reading anything she could about the sport, and traveling to ski tournaments, so her memories of the kids she went to school with were minimal. She really didn't have a ton of friends during those years, which never made her sad until now. She vividly remembered a conversation with her father when she was sixteen. She wasn't at all a social kid, but there was a party she'd been invited to.

"I want to go, Dad. Please."

"There is no time for a party. You have work to do. Your times yesterday were weak."

"I know, but everybody's going to be there. Just this once, can't I go? Sandy Fisher invited me." Sandy Fisher was one of the most popular girls in school, and being included in her circle made Emerson feel warm and accepted.

"Can Sandy Fisher get you to Regionals?" Fredrik asked pointedly.

Emerson didn't answer because she knew where this was going. She looked down at her feet instead as her father went on.

"Do you want to be popular with your classmates or do you want to be a champion?" Her father grabbed her chin, forced her to look him in the eye. *"Because you can't have both."*

Funny how she had precious few memories of anything not ski-related in her teen years, but that exchange had stuck with her so solidly.

An idea struck, and she set down her mug as she headed to her mother's bedroom. A quick search of the closet there, the closet near the front door, and a few cupboards yielded nothing, however, and Emerson wondered why she thought her mom would have a yearbook. In her quest, she did find a stack of four photo albums. She pulled them from the storage area under the TV and carried them to the couch where she plopped down and crossed her feet at the ankle on the coffee table.

They were heavy, and they smelled of old paper and cardboard. Who had photo albums anymore? Pictures were kept on computers now, and it only took a minute for Emerson to decide that was sad. Turning the pages and seeing three, four, five photos at a time was a wonderful way to stroll down memory lane. There were no folders to sift through. No order to the photos. They just were. Emerson ran her fingertips over the faces of her parents, so young, smiling their happiness to the camera. It was an old Polaroid print, the kind that was ejected from the camera and had to be shaken to help the development. The wide white band at the bottom was labeled in black marker. *Caroline and Freddie, 1982.* A year before she was born. Her mother's brown hair was big, and Emerson chuckled at the 80s style. Her father was actually sporting an almost-mullet, his sandy bangs half in his eyes. Their smiles were huge, and Emerson found herself almost relieved to know they'd had at least that moment of happiness. Emerson was born the following year, and Fredrik hadn't lasted much longer in one place. They'd stayed married for nearly four years before his gallivanting (her mother's generic term for his affairs) had forced Caroline to file for divorce.

She gave herself another moment to look at their happy faces, then turned the page. Dozens of baby pictures of Emerson followed. Emerson's first steps. Emerson's first dress. Her first teeth. Her first haircut. Her first day of school. Her first pair of skis. That was back when Fredrik still visited on a somewhat regular basis. The picture of nine-year-old Emerson and her father almost brought tears to her eyes. She was the spitting image of him: blond hair and blue eyes exactly the same, though the shape of her mouth was definitely Caroline's. He had his arm around his daughter, she was holding a trophy for a youth downhill race she'd won, and he looked *so damn proud*. Several more pictures followed, all of Emerson and her father, all of him filled with pride and smiling widely. They went on until she was eighteen.

Then they just stopped.

"You really were that predictable, weren't you, Dad?" She said it aloud, and her voice seemed brash in the quiet. "When my career evaporated, so did you."

With a hard swallow, she shook her head and moved on to the next album, which was mostly pictures of her on the slopes. She flipped pages casually, deciding there wasn't really any rhyme or reason to the way her mother had filed them. She came across a few photos of her with a group of smaller kids and a flash of memory hit.

"Oh, ski class," she said with a grin. At twelve years old, Emerson had been good enough to help teach some of the beginner ski classes. She remembered Craig Radford, the ski instructor back then, asking her if she'd mind helping with the younger kids.

They look up to you, Emmy," he'd said, *his eyes sincere.*

She'd agreed without hesitation, and had helped him for two seasons before she no longer had the free time.

Bending forward, she squinted at the photos, all of her towering over a handful of smaller kids, everybody smiling widely. She ran a fingertip over the little heads in each of the four pictures. Vague recollections of a couple of the kids scratched at her memory, but most drew blanks.

Except for one.

Her finger stopped on a young girl who wasn't looking at the camera, but up at Emerson with what could only be classified as admiration all over her face. She wore a red knit cap, matching red gloves, and a navy blue ski jacket. Her big brown eyes were unmistakable.

"You're doing great, Cassie. You just have to lean in a little more, and you'll have it down."

"I'm having so much fun. This is so much fun!"

Emerson grinned. "Good. It should be fun. As soon as it's not, you should stop and find something else to do."

"I never want to do anything else. Thank you so much for teaching me." Surprising them both, Cassie pushed up with her poles and kissed Emerson on the cheek. "I love you, Emmy!"

Twelve-year-old Emerson laughed out loud and brought her gloved hand to her cheek as little nine-year-old Cassie Parker pushed off with her poles and headed down the hill.

"Parker!" Emerson exclaimed now, a light bulb going off. No wonder she hadn't been able to remember Cassie from school, even though she insisted they were there at the same time. She'd had a different name then. *Huh. She must be married now*, Emerson thought.

The disappointment that tickled at her was unexpected.

Emerson stepped out of the shower, dried herself on a thick, soft towel, then dropped it on the floor and reached for the nearly empty coffee cup on the vanity. The bang against the side of the house was so startling, her entire naked body jerked enough to slosh coffee over her wrist.

"What the hell?" she muttered, scrambling for the towel. She wrapped it around herself and marched out into the living room. Out the window, she could see a ladder leaning against the house, and somebody's legs from the knees down. They were clad in navy blue work pants, heavy work boots on the enormous feet.

Irritated at the fright, Emerson angrily stepped into sweats and a T-shirt, and stomped outside barefoot, her hair still wet.

She rounded the corner of the house, following the brick pathway, until she came upon the ladder and looked up.

The man cleaning the gutter was familiar, but seemed to have aged twenty years since the last time Emerson had seen him. Jack Grafton—or Mr. Gruffton, as Emerson had always referred to him—had worked at the inn since her grandparents owned it. He had to be eighty years old. He glanced down at her, grunted what she could only assume was a greeting, and continued working.

"Hi, Mr. Grafton," she said, suddenly feeling ridiculous that she was outside and wet with no sleeves on. Goosebumps broke out across her arms, and she crossed them over one another. Winter was definitely on its way.

He grunted again, then dropped a handful of leaves, dirt, and crap from the gutter, narrowly missing her.

"You scared me. I didn't know you were working here this morning." She tried to sound firm, but was pretty sure she failed.

"I work here every morning," he replied without looking.

Emerson pressed her lips together, cleared her throat. "No. I know that. I meant here. On the cottage."

"Caroline asked me to check the gutters. They've been clogging. So I'm checking the gutters." Again, he didn't look at her, didn't stop his work.

Emerson scratched at her eyebrow. "Okay then." She backed away, shaking her head. As an afterthought, she added, "Um, be careful up there."

He grunted again.

"Nice talking to you," Emerson muttered under her breath as she headed back into the warmth of the cottage, returned to the bedroom, and closed the blinds and the door.

A little while later, Emerson entered the lobby area of the main house. Mary was at the computer, concentrating hard on whatever she was reading. She glanced up, smiled.

"Good morning, Emmy."

Emerson bristled at the nickname that very few people called her, but managed to smile back. "Morning." Before she could say any more, the door opened and Gordie came bounding in, followed by his owner. He made a beeline for Mary, whose voice raised in pitch by three octaves.

"There's my handsome boy," she cooed. "Guess what I have for you. Guess. Go on." He trailed her back into the kitchen as Emerson watched them go, shaking her head.

"Yeah, he has that effect on the ladies," Cassie said with a grin. She leaned a forearm against the counter. "Hi."

"Hey."

Their gazes held, and it occurred to Emerson that nobody else had such intense, direct eye contact as Cassie. Holding her gaze was fun. Sizzling. Kind of sexy. Cassie wore her usual wind pants and fleece pullover. Today's was bright blue, a color that looked great on her. Her dark hair was pulled back into a ponytail and she had light gloves on that she pulled off finger by finger as Emerson watched.

"Chilly this morning," Cassie commented.

"I know. I went out to yell at Mr. Gruffton for scaring the crap out of me."

"Mr. Gruffton?" Cassie snorted.

"That's what I always called him when I was a kid."

"It fits."

"Right?" Emerson asked, her eyes wide.

Mary and Gordie returned. "What's right?" Mary asked.

"That Jack's name should be Gruffton instead of Grafton," Cassie filled her in.

Mary chuckled, then waved the girls off, trying not to smile. "Now, now. Be nice."

"He put the ladder against the house and started cleaning the gutters while I was running around naked," Emerson told her. "He nearly gave me a heart attack."

"I doubt he would've noticed, honey," Mary said with a dismissive wave as Cassie raised an eyebrow, but said nothing.

"Well. Still." Emerson cleared her throat.

"He's having a hard time," Mary said then, her voice softening. "Your mom was like a daughter to him. He's known her since she was a child. He's grieving." She put a warm hand on Emerson's arm and squeezed. "Cut him a little slack."

Emerson nodded, feeling guilt settle over her.

"Caroline asked him several weeks ago if he could check her gutters," Mary said, turning wet eyes back to the computer screen as she absently petted Gordie's head. "So…" She lifted one shoulder in a half-shrug.

A beat of quiet passed.

Cassie tapped the counter. "So. What needs to be done today?"

"Hey, before you get into that, I need a favor," Emerson said, her focus on Mary. With a grimace, she explained the situation with her rental car. "With Mom's car already here, I don't need the rental and it's costing me a small fortune."

"How long are you staying?" Mary asked. "I thought you'd be heading out soon."

Emerson hesitated, looked from Mary to Cassie and back. "I'm not sure yet."

"Well, we're fully booked this weekend. I'm not sure about getting away for that long…"

"I can do it," Cassie said. Both women looked at her. "What? I've got enough people on at the store tomorrow. They won't miss me. Gordie and I like drives."

"What do you mean you like drives?" Mary said, confused. "You don't even have a car."

"You don't?" Emerson asked, surprised.

With a shrug, Cassie explained, "I don't really need one. I walk or bike everywhere I need to be around here. If I've got to drive someplace, I borrow one of my parents' cars. It's no big deal."

Emerson studied her. "Are you sure you don't mind? It's going to blow your whole day."

Cassie smiled warmly. "I don't mind."

"You can drive my mom's car."

"I have before. Not a problem."

On a sigh of relief, Emerson asked, "What's a good time?"

"You tell me. Gordie and I can go whenever."

"Is noon too late?"

Cassie shook her head. "Actually, that would be perfect. Gives me time to get things settled at the store, make sure everything is covered. We'll meet you here?"

"Perfect." Emerson's expression became serious. "Thank you so much."

"Of course. That's what friends are for."

CHAPTER NINE

"HELLO, MR. CROSS. MY name is Emerson Rosberg. My mother was Caroline Rosberg. I'm sure you remember her; she sold you part of the Lakeshore Inn several years ago. I got your number from her attorney, Brad Klein. He mentioned you were interested in possibly purchasing the rest of the inn as well as the rental property in the village of Lake Henry. I was wondering if we could have a conversation about it. Maybe next week? You can call me on this number, which is my cell, or you can contact Mr. Klein and he'll get the message to me. I look forward to hearing from you. Thanks."

Relaxing in the Town Car was lovely. Arnold Cross would have it no other way. If he was going to be sitting on his ass for hours on end, he was going to do so in luxury and style. Not quite a limo—that was a little too obnoxious even for him—the car had tinted windows, satellite television and radio, a built in Wi-Fi hot spot, and a mini fridge. Add in the buttery soft leather seats and the privacy panel he could slide up or down with the flick of a switch, and it might as well have been a limo.

A glance out the window told him they were about forty-five minutes from his home in Saratoga Springs. The races were over for the season, though there were a couple harness races tomorrow. Nobody really cared about those, but he planned to go the track and watch anyway, and take care of a couple of business transactions while there. He was greatly anticipating the warmth and comfort of his own bed. They'd been on the road for nearly three hours after his meeting in Manhattan, but Emerson Rosberg's call had him too wound up to doze in the car, so he gazed out the window and watched the lights of Albany whiz by.

Considering the majority of his business dealings took place in Manhattan, he'd save himself more than half an hour of drive time if he lived in Albany. But just the thought of the hundreds of underhanded, slimy politicians living in this city made his skin crawl. He had no intention of mingling with them. Despite the power that could come with it, Cross surprisingly hated politics and steered clear. He preferred to watch it zip by the windows of his car as he passed through town. No, he would never live here.

His fear of flying was irrational. He knew this. He wasn't afraid of heights. It wasn't the crowds—he had more than enough money to fly first class or better yet, charter his own plane. No, that wasn't the problem. The issue was that no matter how hard he tried, he could not wrap his brain around the idea of a giant hunk of metal weighing God knows how many tons simply floating through the air. It made no rational sense to him, which was silly. He knew this, too. But it didn't matter. He could not bring himself to put his life in the hands of some pilot he didn't know from Adam. No, there were other means of travel. He had the money, so he hired Jeff, his personal driver of the past three years. He paid the man well, and in exchange, Jeff drove him wherever he wanted to go whenever he needed to be there.

Thoughts turned back to the phone message. Well, wasn't that interesting? He'd been trying to buy the rest of that godforsaken inn for five years now, and that damned Caroline Rosberg wouldn't even entertain the idea. He was happy to hear that her daughter had other plans.

Not that he was happy Caroline was dead. Of course not. He wasn't made of stone. And she was actually a nice woman. Tough. He liked that about her. When her parents had passed, they left some debt, which came as a surprise to Mrs. Rosberg. She didn't want to sell the inn, but the debt was too much for her to handle, and he'd given her a very fair offer. To his surprise, she'd counter-offered, agreeing to split the inn into two parts: waterfront and water view. Cross wanted it all, but he decided to take what he could, and so bought the water view property. Over the years, he'd given her several offers for the waterfront piece, but the response had always been a resounding "no." He kept trying. She kept saying no. And much as she drove him crazy by steadfastly refusing any offer he might put forth, he had to admire her moxie. Not many people refused Arnold Cross. No. Scratch that. Not many people refused Arnold Cross's *money*. That was a more accurate statement. Those who said money couldn't buy happiness obviously never had any.

Cross scrolled back into his memory banks to come up with what he knew about Emerson Rosberg. It wasn't much, but it was enough. He had never lived in Lake Henry, so he wasn't around during her heyday, but there had been enough stories for him to get the gist. The daughter of prominent international downhill Swedish ski champion Fredrik Rosberg, Emerson was being groomed to follow in daddy's footsteps. And she was good. She had the makings to go all the way to the Olympics and more. She was a natural. And her good looks didn't hurt. Once she was too old to ski competitively, a career in sports casting would have been easy. She was tall, blonde, stunning; she'd have been a lock. Once upon a time, Emerson Rosberg was the poster child for downhill skiing...this would have been what? Ten, twelve years ago? Lake Henry was the perfect place for somebody like her to grow up. With its variety of ski slopes and home to dozens of important races—plus its never-ending bid to host a winter Olympics—she got the best training, had the best places to practice her craft right in her own back yard.

Cross didn't know much about what happened. All he had were the stories people had told him and articles he'd read. Apparently, Emerson had taken a final run down a slope in terrible weather conditions. There was no race, no crowd, no coaches. She was on her own, had been practicing, took a run, and wiped out. Badly. Shredded the insides of her knee so severely that after several surgeries to repair it, it had to be completely replaced. That was it. That's all it took. One poor judgment call. Career over at barely nineteen years old.

She left town after that. Cross heard Los Angeles. Clear across the country to a city that never gets snow. Emerson Rosberg obviously wanted to get as far away from Lake Henry and downhill skiing as possible. She was back now, but Cross would lay odds that she didn't want to stay long, and that she was itching to get back to the city where everybody was beautiful and nobody was real.

A grin spread across his face as he took a bottled water from the mini fridge and cracked the cap open with a twist. If he was right about Ms. Rosberg, and she wanted to get the hell out of Lake Henry as soon as possible, negotiations should be a piece of cake. He'd call her lawyer first thing Monday morning and set up a meeting.

Never a man to sit idly by and do nothing (that wasn't how you made money), he popped open his laptop and began crunching numbers. With property values still rebounding and the work that would need to be done on both the inn as well as the rental, he would be in darn good shape to make a nice, tidy profit on this deal.

He couldn't keep the grin off his face.

CHAPTER TEN

"THAT WAS EASY," CASSIE commented as Emerson plopped into the passenger's seat. Carrie Underwood sang softly from the stereo, and the interior of the car smelled like vanilla and lavender, and Emerson tried to be subtle about breathing it in. Gordie stuck his head between the seats and proceeded to lick Emerson's face. She patted at him absently. "Okay, bubs," Cassie admonished him. "Lie down."

"Yeah, it wasn't bad," Emerson said. "Do you want me to drive?"

"Nah." Cassie waved her off as she put the car in gear and pulled out of the parking lot. "You just drove three hours."

Emerson squinted at her. "Um…so did you."

Cassie chuckled. "That's true. I don't mind driving. If I get tired, I'll tell you." With a glance at Emerson's skeptical expression, she held up a hand. "Promise."

They drove for several miles in silence before Gordie decided to venture more affection. He put his head almost on Emerson's shoulder, and she couldn't help but laugh at the move.

"Oh, you are smooth, aren't you, buddy?" she asked, scratching his head.

"He's definitely a ladies' man," Cassie said.

"How old is he?"

"Almost four."

"He goes everywhere with you?"

"Just about. He loves people. He gets lonely if I leave him alone too long. He mans the store with me. He goes to my parents' house with me."

"I was kind of surprised not to see him running with you."

Cassie nodded. "Yeah, we tried that for a while. He always wants to be with me, but he didn't really seem to be enjoying it. I always cringe when I see somebody running and they're practically dragging their dog along. I didn't want to be that person. So he stays home when I run and seems much happier for it."

"And where does his name come from?"

Cassie gave a mock gasp and pressed a hand to her chest in feigned insult. "You don't know?"

Emerson arched one eyebrow, which made Cassie laugh.

"Gordie Howe? Also known as Mr. Hockey?"

"Figures."

"Hey. He is arguably the greatest hockey player of all time."

"Better than Wayne Gretzky?" Emerson asked, doubtful.

"Arguably," Cassie repeated. "There is many a debate on the Internet."

"Well." Emerson gave Gordie her full face and got bathed in kisses in return. "I think the name kind of suits him."

"I agree with you." They grew quiet again and drove along, Emerson relaxing. Idle chatter and small talk were not her favorite things, and despite Cassie being pleasant company, she preferred the silence. She spared a glance at Cassie out of the corner of her eye. Whatever she wore, she always looked casually comfortable, but not sloppy. Today, she'd chosen a simple pair of black yoga pants and a royal blue long-sleeved shirt with a hood. A black down vest served as a barrier against the increasingly chilly weather. Her hair was down today, something Emerson didn't see often, but immediately liked, the dark brown of it sleek and shiny in the afternoon light. And she had a great profile. Emerson wondered at that thought, but it was true, what with her smooth skin, softly defined chin, gently sloping nose, full lips... Inhaling quietly, Emerson could smell the unique vanilla scent that seemed to follow Cassie wherever she went.

Settling into her seat more deeply, Emerson felt peaceful and surprisingly comfortable considering she was cooped up in a car with somebody she didn't know well. She chose not to analyze why this was.

Soon, Cassie spoke. "So, how long do you think you'll stay?"

Emerson pressed her lips together for a moment, then shrugged. "I'm not sure."

"You keep saying that," Cassie pointed out. "You must have a great boss."

"I did," Emerson said before she could catch herself.

"You did?" Cassie glanced at her. "What do you mean?"

Shit. Emerson exhaled, annoyed with herself, but figured it was silly to try to sidestep it now. "I lost my job."

"What?" Cassie's eyes went wide. "When? What happened?"

"I mean I am unemployed." She tried not to snap her answer, wasn't sure about her success. "I got the official call on Wednesday."

Cassie shook her head. "I don't understand."

"Apparently, the knee replacements my fellow salespeople and I have been selling are defective."

Cassie's eyebrows raised up to her hairline.

"I know," Emerson nodded, and it just came spilling out. What was it about Cassie that made words pour from her mouth like water? "There'd been a little bit of a rumor swirling around the company about a pending lawsuit, but we all thought it was just talk. Nobody told us anything solid, they told us not to worry about it, that the rumors were just that: rumors. So we went about business as usual." She shook her head as she thought of all the doctors she'd sold the knees to, all the patients who may have to go through surgery again. When she glanced over, Cassie was looking at Emerson's knee with a question in her eyes. "Oh. No. I don't have that brand."

"Thank god," Cassie and Emerson said at the same time, then grinned at each other.

"Listen, I haven't told anybody, wasn't planning on telling anybody, so I'd appreciate it if you'd keep this under wraps." Emerson grimaced.

"Oh, of course. Of course." Cassie crossed her heart. "Gordie and I can keep a secret. Promise." After a beat, she glanced at Emerson and asked, "Why weren't you going to tell anybody?"

"It's nobody's business, is it?" She knew her tone had been a bit harsh as soon as the pained expression shot across Cassie's smooth features.

Cassie gave a nod, kept her eyes on the road. And stayed quiet, which bothered Emerson. Weirdly. She didn't like that she'd obviously hurt Cassie's feelings. She also didn't like the fact that she didn't like it.

"Hey," Emerson said, hoping to lighten the mood. "I told you a secret. I think it's only fair you share one too."

Cassie glanced at her. "What?"

With a shrug, Emerson said, "Fair is fair."

A small smile tugged at the corner of Cassie's mouth, and Emerson felt instant relief. "I don't really have any secrets."

"Oh, come on. We all have secrets."

"What do you want to know?"

"Tell me about the hot hockey mom at the game Thursday night."

"Oh." The smile immediately slid away. Cassie was quiet so long, Emerson thought she might not answer at all. She reached over, laid a hand on Cassie's shoulder.

"Hey, listen, I'm just kidding. You don't have to—"

"No, no. It's okay," Cassie said, her eyes on the road. She took a deep breath, then let it out very slowly. "Vanessa. Where do I start with Vanessa?" She seemed to be sifting through her brain trying to find the right place to begin.

"How about why there was such a weird vibe between you two? Do you hate her? Is she always that bitchy?"

Cassie shook her head slowly. "No. No, she is most certainly not bitchy. And I don't hate her. I loved her."

"You loved her."

Cassie nodded. "Yeah."

Emerson watched her face, and then got it. "You, like, *loved* her?"

Cassie nodded again. "Yeah. I did. I did love her." She glanced at Emerson, seemingly to gauge her reaction.

Emerson rolled the information around. "Interesting."

"Interesting? What, that I play for your team?" At Emerson's surprised look, Cassie chuckled. "I was good friends with your mom, remember?"

"Ah. Right. Well, your name when we were in school was Parker, not Prescott. I figured you must be married."

Another slow nod and Cassie said, "I was. Vanessa and I both were when we fell in love."

It was Emerson's turn to crank up her eyebrows. "Seriously?"

Cassie sighed. "Yes. It was all so...bizarre." Again, she became quiet, and Emerson felt immediately uncomfortable as she wondered if she'd opened a box that Cassie would rather keep closed.

"Hey, look, Cassie. I don't mean to pry. I was just kidding about the whole secret sharing thing. It's clear this situation is hard for you, so you don't have to talk about it." Conversations this personal were not Emerson's thing, and she tried—unsuccessfully—to subtly backtrack away from the subject.

With a grateful smile, Cassie reached over and squeezed Emerson's forearm, then forged ahead. "It's okay, Em. Really. It's a sensitive subject that I should probably talk about more often. Maybe that'll help me get past it all." With a determined nod, she said, "Prescott is my married name. Michael and I got married right out of college." At Emerson's amazed expression, she chuckled. "Yeah. I know. Way too young. But...did you ever see the movie *Imagine Me and You?*"

Emerson shook her head. "I don't really watch a lot of movies."

Undeterred, Cassie went on. "Really? Well, that movie was me and Michael. We were best friends. We'd been best friends since we were kids. It seemed perfectly natural that we should get married. So we did. And we were happy. Things were fine for nearly four years."

"Until Vanessa came along."

"Until Vanessa came along. I swear to god, I fell for her instantly. She was married. I was married. But we couldn't help it. There was something, some connection, some missing piece, something neither of us was getting from our marriage. At

least, that's how *I* felt. I knew the very first time I kissed her
that I was gay. It was like everything just fell into place, which
sounds so incredibly corny and cliché, but it's true. I suddenly
got it. Light bulbs went off all over the place. The clue bus
finally drove by with a big sign on it." With a self-deprecating
laugh she added, "I can't believe it took me that long."

"Well, you live in a small town. You do what you're
supposed to do. You can't be gay in Lake Henry without
everybody knowing about it. You can't do *anything* in Lake
Henry without everybody knowing about it—" She waved her
hand in the air. "Case in point. So the last thing you're looking
to do is create controversy. Plus, you had Michael. You loved
him and he was good to you. So you probably didn't go
searching."

Cassie grinned, obviously impressed. "You are exactly right.
If Vanessa hadn't come along, I'd probably still be with my
husband."

"No, you wouldn't. Some other woman would have shown
up."

Cassie looked at her. "You think so?"

"I'm sure of it."

"Huh." Cassie nodded slowly as she maneuvered the car
along the winding road.

"So? What happened?"

"It didn't take me long to figure out exactly what was going
on with me. I sat Michael down and we talked. For hours and
hours. I told him everything."

"Fun times."

"It was brutal. He was devastated. But here's the thing
about Michael: he's an amazing man. He's kind and loving and
has such a good soul. He hated what we were going through, he

hated losing me, but he wanted me to be happy, and he understood that he wasn't the one who could make me. It crushed him, but he understood."

"Wow." It was all Emerson could think of to say.

"I know. I was incredibly lucky. He could have been angry. Worse, he could have been mean. He could have trashed me around town. He could have trashed Vanessa. He could have told her husband. He had more trouble with the fact that I was sleeping with a *married* woman than that I was sleeping with a woman. He told me so." Cassie shook her head, slumped a little, as if the memories alone were pushing on her shoulders. "I'm just really lucky that Michael's a good man, that he's not vindictive. I hurt him pretty badly."

"So, you left your marriage for Vanessa. I assume she didn't do the same."

Cassie's voice went very quiet. "No. She didn't." She kept her eyes on the road and Emerson could see the pain on her face.

"Bitch." Emerson grimaced.

The hurt that had creased Cassie's face was glaringly apparent to Emerson, and she decided to leave well enough alone. She had enough going on without adding Cassie's emotional baggage to her already full plate. She sort of wanted to know more, but not if it hurt this much, so she let it go. "Hey, let's get something to eat. It's the least I can do to say thanks for helping me out. Is there someplace we can grab dinner and eat it outside with Gordie?"

A glowing smile replaced the discomfort immediately. "I know just the place," Cassie said, hitting her turn signal.

Half an hour later, they sat on the bumper of the open hatchback in the small parking lot of Jefferson's Roadside Grill,

Gordie on the ground between their feet. The air was brisk and a little chilly, and Cassie breathed in deeply through her nose.

"Ah. Smell that? Smells like winter's coming."

"I can't smell anything," Emerson said, holding a hand in front of her full mouth, "except for this most divine cheeseburger on the entire planet."

"Told you," Cassie said with a grin, seemingly pleased with Emerson's satisfaction. "Best burgers in the Adirondacks. Wait until you taste the fries."

They sat in very companionable silence, thigh to thigh, as they chewed and watched the stars slowly begin to glow as the sky darkened.

"Days are getting shorter," Cassie remarked softly.

Emerson gave a nod.

"Bet you don't get to see stars like this in L.A."

"Not this kind of star," Emerson said. "But I see lots of the other kind."

"Really? Who? Tell me who you've seen." Cassie turned so one leg was up in the hatchback and she was facing Emerson. She looked like a little kid, all giddy and expectant, her eyes sparkling, and Emerson laughed aloud.

"Well, let's see. I saw Luke Wilson in a grocery store once. Ryan Gosling stopped next to me at a stop light and waved. Jennifer Garner and Angie Harmon go to my gym."

Cassie's eyes were bright, even in the waning light. "No way! That's so cool."

Emerson gave a half-shrug. "I guess. You get used to it."

Cassie sipped her soda. "Do you like California?"

"I do," Emerson said quickly. "Can't beat the weather."

"I don't know." Cassie made an encompassing gesture with her arm, indicating the rainbow of trees that lined the edge of the lot. "Look at all this. It's beautiful. I think I'd miss the change of seasons."

"Everybody says that. But when it's ten below with five feet of snow here, it's seventy-five and sunny there. I'll take sunny."

Cassie tipped her cup so her straw aimed at Emerson. "I see your point." After a beat, she asked, "Do you have somebody there? Your mom could never really tell when you were dating or not dating."

Emerson thought of Claire, of how differently they would each describe their relationship. "I date," she said with a half-shrug.

Cassie studied her for a moment, and Emerson was prepared to shut the conversation down. Her love life was *her* business, nobody else's. Instead, Cassie surprised her. "Don't you miss Lake Henry even a little?" she asked softly.

Emerson swallowed, startled by the change in tone, and popped a fry into her mouth. She rocked her head one way, then the other, as if weighing the options. "Once in a while, I suppose. A little."

Cassie seemed to wait for more, but Emerson offered nothing further. Instead, Emerson crumpled her burger wrapper, turned to Cassie, and asked, "Ready?"

Emerson took the wheel this time, despite feeling tired. She knew it was from the constant conversation. She was quiet by nature, liked to be alone, didn't need endless chatter. Cassie, apparently, was the opposite because they had driven no more than a mile before she asked, "What do you think you'll do with your mom's stuff? Any idea?"

"Her stuff?" Emerson asked.

"Yeah. You know. The inn."

Pressing her lips together, Emerson thought about everything, from her indecision to her confusion to her phone call to Arnold Cross. Then she simply said, "I don't know yet."

"Are you going to sell it?"

"I don't know yet."

"You should talk to Mary." Cassie's gaze was out the window as she spoke. "She could show you the ropes. Or probably run it herself. You may have to hire somebody to help a little, because let's face it, Mary's no spring chicken. But she loves the place as much as your mom did." Suddenly, her eyes widened and she turned to Emerson. "Wait. You don't have a job anymore." She poked Emerson in the shoulder. "*You* could stay here and run it. How awesome would that be?"

"Oh, no. Not awesome. Not awesome at all. I'm going back to L.A." Emerson shook her head. "The last thing I want is to be stuck back here in this godforsaken town."

"Hey," Cassie snapped, causing Emerson to flinch. "This is where your mom lived. This is where I live, and I happen to think there's no better place on earth." She turned to gaze out the window, and her voice softened a bit. "You don't have to agree, but maybe you could at least think for a second before you open your mouth."

As if on cue, they passed the *Welcome to Lake Henry* road sign. Emerson felt heat crawl up her neck at having been scolded like a child.

Cassie kept quiet after that.

Emerson immediately missed her banter.

CHAPTER ELEVEN

THE MOUTHWATERING AROMA OF pot roast hit Cassie's nostrils the second she entered her parents' house at 6:35 on Sunday. Cassie had worked at her store from when they opened at nine that morning until closing at six. She was exhausted, but happy to be where she was. Katie Parker stood in the kitchen, black apron tied around her waist, mashing potatoes by hand. As Gordie headed off to the living room in search of children to kiss, Cassie took off her jacket and draped it over a kitchen chair.

"Hi, Mom," she said and kissed Katie on the cheek.

"Hi, sweetie," Katie replied.

"Why don't you use the hand mixer to mash those?"

"Because I like them to be a little bit lumpy." She grunted with effort. "Why don't you hang your jacket in the closet?"

"Because the kitchen chair was boring and needed a splash of color." Cassie grinned at her mother's glare, then took the masher from her hand. "Here. Let me finish." Katie brushed her hands on her apron and made room for her daughter to take over.

"Hey, Superpunk." Cassie's older sister, Chris, entered the kitchen and gathered up silverware. She'd christened Cassie with the nickname on Halloween when Cassie was eight and had decided to dress up as a super hero of her own creation. Superpunk had been born that night. And it had stuck.

Despite their six year age difference, Cassie and Chris could almost pass for twins. Their dark hair was exactly the same shade, their eyes the same color and shape. Chris would swear under oath that she was ¾" taller, but Cassie was of the "round up" rule, so she insisted they were the same height.

"Kids here?" Cassie asked unnecessarily as sounds of giggling came from the other room. She finished up her smashing and tapped the masher against the edge of the pot.

"Just Izzy and Zack . Trevor is off at a friend's."

"On a school night? Liberal of you."

Chris smiled. "He's not staying over. Not on a Sunday night. And not with the C in math he's currently got. I only let him go because he was driving me crazy, and I was afraid I might kill him."

"A C isn't awful."

"It is if you want to stay on the hockey team."

"Ah." Cassie nodded. "I didn't think of that. You're right. And Bill?"

"Working another weird shift," Chris answered, referring to her husband's whacky schedule of late.

"How was the day?" Katie asked Cassie, and Cassie knew she meant the store.

"Not terrible. Not great, but it didn't suck. Should've been a bit busier for a Sunday at this time of year, but I'm not going to stress over it."

Katie shot her a look that said, *Yes, you will,* but kept quiet.

The dining room table was a place of joy in the Parker household, more so this evening because this much of the family hadn't been together in nearly two months. Between Cassie's retail hours, her father's parent-teacher meetings and paper grading, and Chris's real estate job, not to mention all the sports and activities of the grandkids, and Bill's working trick work, getting the entire family together for a meal was next to impossible. As Cassie set the giant bowl of mashed potatoes on the table, she glanced into the living room to see both Izzy and Zack—Chris's two youngest—rolling around on the floor and trying to hide their faces from Gordie's questing tongue. Izzy would giggle, "No, Gordie," but then reveal enough of her face for him to lick before she'd squeal with delight and roll away. Gordie's entire body vibrated with joy, as this was his favorite game of all time.

"Cassandra," Jim Parker said from the recliner when he laid eyes on his daughter. "How are you, honey?"

"I'm good, Dad. You?"

"Can't complain," was his stock answer. He pushed himself to his feet and navigated the obstacle course made up of two children and a dog that blocked his way to dinner. He was a tall, lean man with salt-and-pepper hair and clear blue eyes that both his daughters bemoaned not inheriting. "Come on, kids. Time to eat."

There was a pretty steady hum of conversation for a group of only six people, but the kids had lots to tell. Zack was almost nine and was very excited for the skiing season to begin. He had important plans for some of the larger slopes this year, now that he was "big." Izzy, at five years old, was all about her new dollhouse and was saving her chore money so she could buy a new couch for her living room because the one she currently had had "gone out of style."

"Huh. Wonder where she gets that from," Jim said, sending a sideways glance at Chris.

"Isn't her mother on, like, her third couch since moving into that house?" Cassie asked, eyes wide with mock innocence. Next to her, Katie chuckled quietly.

"You can all be quiet," Chris said without venom, but with a slight grin.

"What are we doing for Halloween?" Cassie asked the kids. "Have we made final decisions on costumes?"

"I'm going to be Elsa from *Frozen*!" Izzy pronounced, using her fork to poke at the air.

"You are? Well, that's a shocker," Cassie said, then under her breath, added, "not at all."

"I'm going to be a ninja," Zack said.

"Weren't you a ninja last year?"

"Yup."

When no explanation came, Cassie simply said, "Okay then."

Changing the subject, Jim asked, "Hey, Cassie, how'd the drive go yesterday? All right?"

"Easy," she said. "Uneventful. Less traffic than I expected."

"Where'd you go?" Chris asked.

"I followed Emerson Rosberg to Albany so she could return her rental car and still have a ride back here."

"Emerson Rosberg, huh?" Chris's eyes glinted. "Interesting."

Cassie furrowed her brow. "What? I did her a favor."

"Oh, no. I know. I was just remembering her from way back."

"In school?" At Chris's nod, Cassie asked, "Was she in your grade?"

"A few years behind me, I think." Then her shoulders shook with gentle laughter. "You had *such* a crush on her."

"What? I did not. Did I?"

"Oh, you did. From the time you were Zack's age until…I don't even know how long. Through junior high and into high school, at least."

Cassie scoffed.

"Mom?" Chris asked.

"It's true," Katie said matter-of-factly. "Sorry, honey."

"Seriously?" Cassie was shocked.

"Seriously. In fact, Mom and Dad wondered about your—," Chris lowered her voice and glanced at her kids. They were having a subtle light saber battle with their forks. "Preferences," she whispered.

"No!" Cassie looked from her mother to her father and back again. "Seriously?" she asked again.

"Yup."

"I don't remember that. I mean, I remember liking her, but…why didn't anybody ever say anything?"

Chris shrugged. "Michael came along. You guys were joined at the hip and I think everybody breathed a sigh of relief." She glanced at Cassie. "No offense."

"How about after Michael? Why didn't you tell me then?" Cassie looked to her mom.

"Honestly, honey, I didn't think of it. Junior high was quite a while ago. I'd forgotten."

"Huh." Cassie let that roll around while she chewed a piece of roast.

"What's she like?" Chris asked.

"Who? Emerson?" Cassie shrugged. "She's tall." The adults laughed and Cassie went on. "She's nice enough. Doesn't talk much, but she's nice enough."

"Doesn't talk much or couldn't get a word in edgewise?" Chris asked.

"Har har. Doesn't talk much, though I did get her to open up a little, get her talking."

"Talking or listening until her ears bled?"

"Stop it," Cassie whined and tossed her napkin at her sister.

"I'm surprised she's still here," Katie said. "Everything I got from Caroline said Emerson hates it here. That's why she rarely visited."

"It was pretty clear she's not a fan of Lake Henry," Cassie said, remembering Emerson's disdainful remark.

"Would you want to stay after what she went through?" Jim asked, shoveling a forkful of potatoes into his mouth.

"She just ran out on the people who supported her all those years," Katie argued, shaking her head. "Barely so much as a goodbye."

"What happened?" Zack piped in.

Chris took up the story. "This woman was a very good skier when she was just a kid."

"How good?"

"Super good. Like Olympics good."

"Wow," Zack said.

"Yeah, but she got hurt."

"Bad?"

"Really bad. She hurt her knee so much she couldn't ski anymore."

"Ever?" Zack's eyes grew wide, as if he couldn't imagine never being able to ski.

"I'm afraid so. It made her very sad, so she moved away."

Zack blinked at her for a beat. "That sucks," he finally pronounced. "I'd leave too."

Chris tilted her head at her son. "It does suck. That's true. But it would make me sad if you left. Wouldn't you miss me? I'd miss you."

"So would I," Cassie added.

"And me and Grandpa," Katie chimed in.

"Not me," Izzy said, and the table broke into laughter as Zack bumped shoulders with his little sister. The mood lightened considerably, and Cassie was glad.

"I got the impression she's just going to stick around here long enough to figure out what to do with her mom's stuff, her property, the inn. Sounds like there's a lot to deal with."

"I can imagine," Katie said, then sighed. "Poor Mary must be on pins and needles waiting to see what happens."

"Mom, Mary's older than the hills," Chris said. "Retiring wouldn't be a terrible thing for her."

Katie shot her a look. "She is not that old. And she loves that place. She's already lost without Caroline. I don't know how she even goes in there every day without breaking down."

"I don't think she likes Emerson," Cassie said.

"That's not surprising. She saw every day how much Caroline missed her daughter. And now Mary's future is in this girl's hands? I'd be annoyed with her too."

"I guess." Cassie chewed and swallowed, then added, "I've been trying to go by every couple of days and see how she's doing, help out a bit." Cassie knew her mother was right. Mary was putting up a good front for the sake of the customers, but her red-rimmed eyes and the dark circles beneath them were pretty clear signs of how she'd been feeling. "I've got three people scheduled at the store tomorrow. I can probably snag an hour or two. Gordie and I will go check on her."

"Do you think Emerson will sell the inn?" Jim asked. "I hear Arnold Cross has been nosing around after it again."

Katie made a sound of distaste. "That man is shady. Let's hope he doesn't get his paws on that property. Lake Henry doesn't need to be developed. It needs to be left alone." Turning to Cassie, she repeated Jim's question. "Do you think she'll sell it?

Cassie sighed. "I really don't know. She didn't say. I can tell you she has no desire to stay in Lake Henry, so if she doesn't sell it, she'll have to find somebody to run it for her."

"Mary runs it now. Why not just leave it alone?" Chris asked.

Cassie lifted one shoulder. "I don't know what to tell you. She didn't offer up that much information. I honestly don't think she's made a decision yet."

Emerson wasn't sure why she'd felt it necessary to wear a suit. It was the one she'd worn as she flew from California to New York, a snappy gray number with brushed nickel buttons on the jacket and a sleekly smooth pair of pants that outlined her hips nicely. She wore a deep purple blouse underneath the jacket and her black pumps. At least this time she was able to drive rather than attempting to navigate the cobblestones in heels.

Brad Klein's office was just outside the village center, but still near the lake, and he had a parking lot with five spaces—gold in this town. She pulled her mother's Subaru into one of two empty spots remaining, finger-combed her hair, and checked her face in the rearview mirror. She'd never worn much makeup, but Claire had taught her to use mascara and lip gloss to her advantage. Now she never went to a meeting without them. Deep breath in, slow breath out, and she was ready.

The butterflies in her stomach were inexplicable. Why was she nervous? What was there to be nervous about? She was meeting with a businessman about a possible business deal. She did this kind of thing every day. Her leather attaché was on the passenger seat, and she reached for its soft handle. Another thing she really didn't need, but she felt more confident with it in her hand, so it came along.

The interior of Klein's office was modest, but neat and classy. Soft instrumental music surrounded her, a gentle sound for which she could find no source. A thick slate gray carpet covered the entire floor, and a bowl of potpourri in a subtle cinnamon scent sat on an end table in a corner, lending a warm, cozy feel to the reception area. Klein's secretary was pretty and blonde, maybe forty-five, and offered a friendly smile as Emerson entered.

"Ms. Rosberg?" At Emerson's nod, she continued. "They're expecting you. In the conference room. First door on the left."

"Thanks." Emerson lifted her chin, walked the short distance to the indicated door, straightened up to her full height, and entered.

"Ah, there she is." Klein stood, his hand outstretched toward Emerson. His handshake was firm, but not too firm, and she appreciated that he didn't crush her hand to show his dominance like so many men she'd dealt with in the business world. He was dressed in a black suit with a lavender tie, and Emerson mentally grinned at how well they coordinated. "Ms. Rosberg, this is Arnold Cross. Mr. Cross, meet Emerson Rosberg."

Emerson turned to face the man interested in purchasing her mother's property. He was standing, but it was hard to tell. He couldn't be more than five foot three, and Emerson towered over him by more than half a foot. He was more round than any other shape. His hand was small and warm, his fingers like puffy sausages. He had a donut of salt-and-pepper hair ringing his head, some independent strands sticking out in odd directions, doing their own thing. But his suit was perfectly tailored, and his aftershave was pleasant enough.

"Please," he said. "Call me Arnie." His voice was deeper than Emerson expected. He gestured toward the big cherry table. "Shall we sit?"

The room was simple and comfortable, with a gorgeous view of the lake from three very large windows. The table's surface was buffed to a perfect shine; Emerson could clearly see her own reflection. Six chairs surrounded it, deep gray cushioning the seat of each one, setting off the lighter gray carpeting nicely. The walls were still a lighter gray, an abstract painting in blues and purples hanging over the credenza against one wall.

The three of them sat, Emerson and Cross on opposite sides with Klein at the head of the table, a folder in front of him. He got right down to business. "As we discussed on the phone, Mr. Cross has prepared a very fair offer for purchase of The Lakeshore Inn, which you now own, as well as the commercial property at 217 Main."

Emerson nodded.

"I'm not sure you know," Cross said, "but I purchased the rest of the inn from your mother a little more than five years ago, and I think that worked out well for both of us. With the purchase of the smaller waterfront property, I can bring the whole inn back together, restoring it to its former glory. The price I'm offering you is fair. It takes into consideration all the work that needs to be done. Roof. New windows. And it's way past time for new paint. Your mother loved the place, but let's face it; she was not much of a business owner. Too much help with too little revenue. I'm certain with a little renovation, we could get two more rooms out of that place."

It was a sales pitch, no two ways about it, and Emerson knew that, even as she tried not to bristle at his criticism of Caroline's business sense. Part of her was irritated to have something her mother held so dear reduced to a sale item, but the rest of her knew this was just business for Arnold Cross. He had no emotional ties, no sentimentality for the inn. It was a money maker, plain and simple, and aside from the "former glory" comment, he was not trying to make it look like anything other than that.

Five years ago, Lake Henry was barely a blip on Emerson's radar. She'd been gallivanting around California, spending the last of the money she'd gotten in the few endorsement deals she'd had as a teenager—the ones that went bye-bye right along with her knee. She partied. She traveled. She drank too much. If she called her mother once a month, that was lucky. She'd had no idea there were financial issues. Her mother had taken the inn over from her own parents when they'd passed away, and the debt that was left was hefty and surprising. Caroline had done her best, but nothing was working. She'd toyed with simply selling the commercial property. Although that was a reliable source of income, it wasn't enough to keep the entire inn afloat. After much debate, she'd finally decided the only way to get out from under the mountain of debt and start fresh was to sell off part of the inn. She sold the big house on the hill to Cross; it eventually became The Lakeview Hotel, but she couldn't bear to part with the waterfront building and cottage. Emerson had no clue about the sale until she came for her last visit and saw the new sign with the new name. She'd been stunned.

"I did know that about the big house," Emerson said now. "I know you helped my mom out of a jam. Something else I know, Mr. Cross: my mother despised you. But that doesn't mean you're not the right man for the job."

Cross took the jab in stride, seemed almost proud of it. Emerson had learned the history through phone calls with her mother. She knew Cross had paid a fair price, but he'd been pushy and overbearing at a time when Caroline was emotionally raw, heartbroken to have to give up the big house, and no sooner had the ink dried on the paperwork then Cross had construction workers and equipment brought in to make dozens of changes inside and out. That left a bad taste. Over the phone, Emerson could almost hear the grimace Caroline would make whenever Cross's name came up.

"Well." Klein stepped in, sliding a stack of papers out of the folder. "Mr. Cross had his attorney write up an offer for you." He pushed the stack in Emerson's direction. She slid them the rest of the way so they lined up in front of her, but she made no move to turn pages or read what was written.

"If it's all right, I'd like to take some time to look it all over."

"Of course. Of course." Cross smiled, though it didn't reach his eyes, and his teeth were so white they looked utterly out of place in his face. "Take your time. I just assumed you'd want to be getting back to—where is it? Los Angeles?"

Emerson nodded, understanding that Cross was a man who covered his bases, and so it wasn't surprising for him to have researched her. Still, she didn't like him knowing things like where she lived.

"Yes. I just thought you'd want to be getting home as soon as possible. It's getting cold here." Cross chuckled, an obviously fake chuckle, and Emerson forced a smile. "You're probably missing that west coast sunshine right about now."

With another nod, Emerson looked to Klein. "All set then?"

Klein stood, effectively ending the session. Handshakes all around and then he walked Cross out. Emerson sat at the table, looking out the window at the slightly choppy surface of the lake instead of at the stack of papers. She felt Klein return more than saw him. When she looked up, he was studying her with wise blue eyes.

"You okay?" he asked, a gentleness in his voice.

Emerson released a breath. "I'm fine. I'm trying to figure out why I don't like him."

"Cross?" Klein laughed. "Nobody likes him. The guy's rich, successful, and buying up Lake Henry property like there's no tomorrow. What's to like?"

"I'm sure his offer is fair."

"It is. I wouldn't let you even entertain it if it wasn't."

"I just...I need to think on it. Is that okay?"

Klein's expression softened along with his voice. "Hey, Emerson, I work for you, remember? You're the boss here. Take all the time you need."

She slipped the offer into her attaché, bid Klein her goodbyes, and headed out to the parking lot. The air was crisp, probably not even getting to fifty degrees today as the beginning of November loomed. Emerson's heels clicked as she crossed the pavement to her car, but after tossing her attaché onto the passenger seat, she did not get in. Instead, she was pulled by the water, the lake seeming to beckon to her. She followed a narrow paved path around the side of Klein's office building until it led her to the lakeshore. A large swinging bench sat empty as if waiting for her.

She wrapped her arms around herself against the chill and sat, swinging gently, staring out onto the water.

CHAPTER TWELVE

CASSIE GAZED OUT THE window of her office at the choppy surface of Lake Henry two stories below. The day had started out sunny, but clouds had moved in, and the sky had turned the color of a dull nickel. She could see a few boats out on the water, diehard water lovers who refused to pack up their boats or kayaks until the first snowflakes fell.

Her desk was strewn with paperwork that she should be plowing through, but instead she stared at it blankly. Like a child who's reached the end of the day's kindergarten class, she just couldn't seem to get her brain to focus, no matter how hard she tried. The plastic jack-o'-lantern her mother had plugged in and set on a filing cabinet smiled menacingly at her, but even the promise of Halloween and trick-or-treating later that evening couldn't give her the kick-start she needed. Three monitors on the desk behind her showed the views from the security cameras in the store. Everything seemed fine. A glance at the black cat wall clock with the swinging tail pendulum told her she'd given up on doing anything productive nearly half an hour ago and had been staring out the window ever since.

A sharp knock on the door startled her, and her body jerked. Catching her breath, she said, "Come in."

Jonathan entered with two steaming cups from Starbucks. He set one on her desk. "For you. Happy Halloween."

"Oh, you're a lifesaver," she said, quickly peeling the lid off. She inhaled deeply and took a sip, the warm sweetness of the caramel macchiato coating her tongue.

"Am I? What am I saving you from?" He took the chair in front of her desk without waiting for an invitation.

"My own lack of initiative. I've gotten exactly nothing done this morning."

"Well, while you sit there like a shoe, I'll pass along the latest gossip on this Halloween in Lake Henry." At Cassie's raised eyebrows, he said, "Guess who talked to the Burgermeister-Meisterburger about selling The Lakeshore Inn?"

"No!" Cassie's eyes went wide. "Already?"

"First thing this morning."

"Is your source reliable?"

Jonathan feigned insult. "How dare you?"

Cassie chuckled. "I know. I just…it seems so soon. I wonder if she's said anything to Mary." She thought about how hard it had been for Caroline to sell off the big house, and she grimaced. "Ugh. I don't like that guy." Then she smiled and shook her head at the nickname Jonathan had given Arnold Cross the first time he'd seen him. "The Burgermeister-Meisterburger."

"He looks just like him," Jonathan insisted, not for the first time, referring to the villain in one of the Christmas television specials from the seventies. "That hair? His size? Come on. You see it, too. Don't deny it."

Cassie laughed. "I don't deny it." They were quiet for a beat or two before Cassie added softly, "Poor Mary."

"I know." Jonathan looked around the floor. "Hey, where's Gordie?"

"Downstairs with Mom. My idle nothingness got too boring for him, and he ditched me."

"Can't say as I blame him. Hey, are you coming over tonight?" Jonathan and Patrick always threw a small gathering on Halloween for their friends, complete with fancy Halloween cocktails and munchies, the required games such as bobbing for apples, and a ridiculously elaborate haunted house.

"I may stop by later. I promised Zack and Izzy I'd go trick-or-treating with them."

Jonathan waved a dismissive hand. "Kids. They take all the fun out of this holiday."

"Dare I ask about your costumes this year?" Jonathan and Patrick always dressed up together in some matching theme. One year, they were The Lone Ranger and Tonto. Another year, Bonnie and Clyde (Jonathan was Bonnie). Last year they outdid themselves in the categories of shiny and glittery by dressing as Liberace and his candelabra.

"We're keeping it simple this year. Simple, yet sexy. In keeping with the latest trend of superhero popularity, we're going as Batman and Robin."

Cassie grinned. "Perfect. Who's who?"

"Patrick will be Batman, of course. The strong, silent one. Robin is much more fun. And cuter. You know I'll rock the spandex." He lowered his head and batted his eyelashes at Cassie. "Now if you would just dress up as Wonder Woman, we'd have almost an entire Justice League."

Cassie held up a hand, traffic cop style. "No way. Not happening. I've told you a million times, I don't dress up."

Jonathan scoffed. "You lesbians are no fun. I still say you and Vanessa would've made a fabulous Rizzoli and Isles last year."

"Yeah, well." She shrugged.

Jonathan reached across the desk and patted her hand as he stood. "It's okay, *cheri*. You come by tonight, and I'll give you a cocktail that'll wipe all your worries and cares right out of your head. It's called a jack-o'-weenie. I invented it myself."

"A jack-o'-weenie? Really? Why am I not surprised?"

"I know you have an aversion to anything remotely associated with the word weenie since you've realized you're a giant vagina worshipper, but trust me. You'll love it."

Without missing a beat, their eyes met and they both blurted, "That's what he said!"

Jonathan opened the door, laughing, and told her, "Get some work done, for god's sake. See you tonight." And he was gone.

Cassie shook her head, smiling. She had no idea how he did it, but Jonathan could change the energy in the room. She wished she had similar powers, but maybe it was enough that she had him. She sipped the caramel macchiato, gazed out the window for another minute or two, then turned to her paperwork and forced herself to focus.

Emerson was pumping hard. She was off the lake trail today, had followed the road slightly out of town, and was surprised how wide the shoulder was, how much space she had to ride.

After the meeting with Arnold Cross, she'd needed to clear her head. Something about the man had been cloying; she felt like he was still with her even after she'd left Klein's office. A walk to the water had helped relax her slightly, but she still felt uncertain, indecisive. She'd driven back to the cottage, changed into some suitable riding gear (if she was going to stay much longer, she might be wise to visit Cassie's shop and get some new clothes), and hopped on her rental bike without stopping to talk to Mary, Mr. Gruffton, or anybody. She just pedaled.

It was cold. Colder than she'd expected now that the sun had disappeared behind the gray cloud cover. She'd passed three different houses decorated for Halloween before it had even occurred to her that today was October 31. She hadn't purchased biking gloves from Mindy, so she was wearing a light pair of knit gloves she'd found in the cottage coat closet. They were helping a little, but not a lot, and her hands and face were tight from cold. She knew if she glanced in a mirror, her cheeks would be bright red. Still, the physical activity felt amazing, and the briskness of the air was doing its job on her brain. She was no longer overwhelmed by her situation. It was still there, but she felt like she had a better handle on things. At least for the moment.

Her thighs were starting to ache with the exertion, and she took a few turns, then headed back to the cottage, slowing when she approached the path around the lake. On her way through town, there was a large number of tourists crowding the sidewalk, so she hopped off the bike and walked it for a ways, noting the shops as she passed. Peering through the windows of Cassie's store, she could see that it was bustling. Once through the main thoroughfare, she got back on the bike and pedaled the rest of the short way to the inn.

As she walked down the sidewalk past the main building on her way to the cottage, the bike next to her, a shrill beeping caught her ear. She stopped, tilted her head. Was that a smoke alarm? She leaned the bike against the house and went in the back door.

The kitchen wasn't filled with smoke, but there was definitely something ·burning. Just as Emerson opened her mouth to ask what was going on, Mary swore loudly and dropped a blackened pan into the sink. Then she leaned her hands on the edge of the counter, dropped her head down between her shoulders, and burst into tears.

Emerson swallowed hard, torn between the easiest course of action (leaving quietly) and what she knew was the right thing to do (stay). Her debate lasted a good fifteen seconds before she pressed her lips together, shook her head, and stepped farther into the room.

"Everything okay?" she asked loudly over the beeping. Mary's whole body jerked, and she wiped quickly at her face. Wanting to give her time, Emerson pulled a chair from a corner, stood on it and yanked the battery out of the smoke alarm. The sudden silence was blissful. She climbed down and opened a couple windows, helping to air out the room while Mary collected herself. After a few moments, Emerson asked again, "Everything okay?"

Mary sighed deeply, shook her head. "These damn muffins. These damn blueberry muffins of your mother's. They're a signature here. Every guest expects the homemade blueberry muffins each morning. They're in the pamphlet, for crying out loud. Today, I finally decided I should try my hand at making them, and this is the third pan I've burned to a crisp." Her eyes welled and she looked at Emerson with such pleading that Emerson would have done almost anything to prevent any more crying.

"I can make them," she said before she even realized the words were out of her mouth.

"You can?"

"Are you kidding? Mom showed me how to make her special recipe when I was ten. She was actually teaching me a lesson." Emerson smiled at the memory. "Remember that big snowstorm? When was it? 1994? All the schools were closed for, like, three or four days. On the third day, I told Mom I was bored. Big mistake. We made muffins for hours." Mary's face broke into a smile and Emerson felt a surprising wave of relief. "It's true. I've been making them for years. They're my go-to when I have to bring something to a party. I can't cook to save my life, but nobody can compete with my blueberry muffins."

Mary held Emerson's gaze, sniffed once, then gave a nod. "Okay. I think all the ingredients you need are right here. Except for the blueberries." She gathered things up off the table, shaking her head with irritation as she dumped them into the sink. "How much have I wasted on buying fresh blueberries just so I can torch them to bits in the oven?" she muttered. "I'll go pick you up another couple pints."

"You can get frozen ones, too. They'll work just fine," Emerson added as Mary left the room. "And they're cheaper," she called out. A few seconds later, she heard a car start up.

"Okay, then." Emerson stood, clapped her hands once, then rubbed them together as she surveyed the detritus scattered about. Mary wasn't kidding about having tried more than once. There was flour all over the table, dirty dishes lined with leftover batter, three spatulas, and the microwave stood open, as did the oven. The open windows were helping immensely to clear the air, even though the temperature in the room had dropped significantly. Emerson closed them back up and began the task of washing all the dishes.

She couldn't work in a dirty kitchen. That was rule number one.

"Let's get to work." For the first time in a very long time, Emerson felt invigorated.

Emerson was just about finished when she heard Cassie's voice from the other side of the kitchen door.

"Oh my god, what is that heavenly smell?" Emerson heard some muffled conversation, assumed a couple guests were on their way out. Mary's voice sounded from behind the counter.

"That, my dear, is the lovely aroma of the famous Lakeshore Inn blueberry muffins." Her voice grew wistful. "It's been less than two weeks, but boy have I missed that scent." There was a pause, then a change of subject. "Where's my boy?" She called out, and Emerson could hear the scrambling of canine paws.

"Weren't they Caroline's secret recipe?" she heard Cassie ask. "I didn't know you could make them."

"I can't. Emerson made them."

That was her cue. Emerson came out from the kitchen doorway. She wore her mother's floral print navy blue apron, handprints of flour decorating it. She was pretty sure she must have had a smear of batter streaked across her left cheek, because Cassie stared at her. In her hands, she carried a plate of enormous muffins that looked too beautiful to be eaten, even if she said so herself.

"Wow," was all Cassie could say as her eyes darted from Emerson's face to the muffins steaming on the plate and back again.

"Go ahead," Emerson said, gesturing with her chin. "Try one. They're just out of the oven, so they're hot. Be careful."

Cassie didn't need a second invitation. She and Mary each grabbed a muffin, Cassie tossing hers from one hand to the other to cool it down. Gordie sat politely, his eyes zipping from one woman to the other trying to gauge who was most likely to share. When Cassie finally broke a piece off and tasted it, her eyes closed and humming sounds came unbidden from her throat. "Holy crap." Cassie held her fingers in front of her mouth as she spoke. "These are *sinful*."

Behind the counter, Mary's eyes had filled with tears as she chewed. She turned to Emerson and smiled, and there was a combination of gratitude and grief on her face. "They taste just like your mother's," she said softly. "Thank you."

Emerson's gaze darted from the plate to the floor to Cassie and back. With a quick nod, she said, "Good. You're welcome." After another beat of awkward discomfort, she retreated to the kitchen. Cassie followed her.

"That was amazing."

"What was?" Emerson glanced over her shoulder as she slid a muffin pan into the oven.

"Making Mary feel better the way you did." Cassie leaned her forearms on the table, braced herself there.

Emerson lifted one shoulder. "It was nothing."

"It was something."

They looked at each other for a beat, and Emerson looked away first.

"Hey," Cassie said suddenly. "There's a Halloween party tonight at my friend's house. Want to go?"

Emerson cocked her head and gave Cassie a look. "Um, no. Halloween parties are not my thing. In fact, parties aren't really my thing. But thank you."

"What about trick-or-treating?"

"What about trick-or-treating?"

"Is that your thing?" Their eyes held and Cassie chuckled. "It's just that I promised my niece and nephew I'd take them trick-or-treating, give their parents a break. Plus, my sister likes to stay home and answer the door. It would be more fun if I had company."

"What about the party?"

Cassie waved a hand. "I can skip it."

Emerson's first inclination was always to politely decline such invitations. She didn't enjoy crowds or parties or groups of people she didn't know. She preferred to be either alone or with a small handful of friends. But she'd been baking muffins for a while now with no interruptions from Mary or anybody, so it wasn't like she was craving down time. Plus, Cassie was looking at her with those big, brown eyes and that expectant grin Emerson was growing used to. It was just trick-or-treating. Just walking. How bad could it be?

"Okay."

Cassie flinched as if Emerson had startled her. "Okay?"

"Okay."

"Okay, you'll go trick-or-treating with me?"

"Yes. I'll go trick-or-treating with you." Emerson couldn't help but grin at Cassie's excitement.

"Seriously?"

"You're pushing it."

"Okay. Sorry. That's great. That's awesome. I'm so happy!"

Emerson shook her head. "You're way too easy."

"Yeah, don't let that get around," Cassie said with a wink. "We'll swing by and pick you up around seven-thirty. Okay? It'll be me, a ninja, and Elsa from *Frozen*. And Gordie, of course."

"Of course." Cassie headed for the door when Emerson spoke. "Cassie?"

"Yeah?"

"Just to be clear, I'm not dressing up. I don't do costumes."

Cassie's grinned widened. "I knew I liked you for something other than your good looks." With a wink, she was gone.

Emerson stood smiling for several moments after Cassie had gone.

Nodding with satisfaction, she looked around at the dozens of muffins she'd made for Mary to freeze. She'd have to teach her how to make them before she went back to L.A., but in the meantime, she'd be able to simply defrost a batch, warm them up, and have them ready to serve to the guests each morning. That should keep some of the stressed sadness at bay for Mary, at least for a little while.

Rolling her head from one side to the other, she realized her shoulders had grown tight from all the hunching over the table and counter. A quick glance at the clock told her she had barely two hours until Cassie was back to get her. Enough time to take the last batch out of the oven, clean up the kitchen, and soak in the tub for a half hour.

But first…

She sat down at the table, took a muffin from the plate, and sampled it. Cassie was right. It was sinfully good. One thought came to her then, crystal clear in her head.

Mom would be proud.

At 7:25, there was a sharp knock on the door of the cottage. When Emerson opened it, two young voices shouted,

"Trick or treat!" and held out bags. Gordie sat in between the kids, looking just as expectant, and Emerson couldn't help but laugh.

"This is all I have to offer," she said, holding out two blueberry muffins. Only the ninja's eyes were visible, but he squinted and looked at Elsa standing next to him. She shrugged, and they both turned to look over their shoulders at Cassie.

"You can have those," she told them.

"You sure she's not a crazy child killer?" the ninja asked.

Cassie hid her grin. "Pretty sure."

That was enough for the kids, who each snapped up a muffin and bit into them without any further reservation.

Cassie met Emerson's eyes over the kids' heads. "Hi."

"Hey." Cassie looked great, and Emerson had to admire her sporty, perfectly color-coordinated attire. The whole athletic thing worked amazingly well on her. She wore jeans, hikers with lively yellow trim, and a bright yellow jacket with black gloves. Her dark hair was pulled back into a ponytail and a matching yellow fleece headband protected her ears from the chilly air. She smelled like vanilla, as always. And as always, Emerson tried to be subtle about taking in her scent. "Nice outfit," she commented.

"Thanks. I own the store." Cassie shrugged, then smiled.

"These are good," Princess Elsa said, her mouth as full of muffin as it could possibly be.

Cassie shook her head. "This is my niece, Izzy." She tapped the ninja on the head, "And this is my nephew, Zack. Guys, this is my friend, Emerson."

They each gave half a wave, then turned away from the door. "Come on, Aunt Cassie. We've got to go." Zack was halfway up the walk before he finished what he was saying.

Emerson raised her eyebrows and smiled, grabbed her jacket off the hook by the door. "Come *on*, Aunt Cassie," she said in a low voice. Cassie bumped her with a shoulder.

The air was beyond crisp, and Emerson could see her breath as they walked, the kids up ahead of them, Gordie on a leash next to Cassie. Dusk had faded into darkness quickly, but the kids each had a small flashlight. She walked next to Cassie with her hands jammed into her pockets for warmth, amazed by the number of costumed children out and about, and by how many people waved or greeted Cassie by name. She knew everybody.

"Busy night," Emerson commented.

Cassie nodded. "Well, the road around the lake is really the best place for trick-or-treating. Everything else is so spread out, you'd have to drive. This tends to be where the kids congregate." She looked up at Emerson. "Don't you remember?"

"I don't know that I did many Halloweens here. I was doing a ton of traveling for skiing by the time I was twelve. I don't remember a whole lot before then."

"That's too bad," Cassie said. "It's a great place to raise kids."

"Do you want kids?" Emerson asked as they stopped at the next house to wait for the kids. "One day?"

Cassie pressed her lips together, made a thinking face. "Not really. I used to think I did, but as I've gotten older, I'm beginning to realize I kind of like my freedom. Besides, I have Gordie." She ruffled the dog's head as he sat next to her. "What about you?"

"Nah." The kids ran to them then to show Cassie their bounty.

"Ooh, mini Snickers," Cassie said. "Those are my favorites, you know." She reached into Izzy's bag, but Izzy closed it on her wrist, squealing, "No!" and Cassie laughed. They moved on to the next house, and the kids ran up the driveway. Cassie looked back at Emerson, waiting, as if they hadn't been interrupted.

"I've never even really thought about it," Emerson said. "I didn't have dolls when I was little. I never wanted to play house or mommy or any of that. I wanted to make forts in the woods." She chuckled.

"Me, too," Cassie said.

"Plus, I'm not cut out to be a parent. I like quiet. I like my things just so. I think a kid would send me over the edge into insanity."

Gordie growled low in his throat as a tall kid dressed as a zombie ambled by, dragging one leg, his makeup making him look anemic and bloodthirsty. "It's okay," Cassie said under her breath. Then to Emerson, "That's a *good* costume."

"I'll say. Right out of *The Walking Dead*."

"You watch that?"

"Of course," Emerson said, and made a face as if that were the single stupidest question in the entire world.

Cassie laughed. "Me, too." And they spent the next twenty minutes chatting back and forth about the TV show.

"Hey, we're halfway around already," Emerson said, surprised.

"It's a gorgeous night," Cassie said, throwing her arms out to the sides. "Clear. Warm." She glanced at Emerson, whose hands were still in her pockets, and whose chin was tucked into the collar of her jacket. "Okay, not freezing."

Emerson had to admit the cold had become more bearable than earlier, though her knee disagreed. "I might have just gone numb," she told Cassie jokingly.

"You've been in California too long. Lost your tolerance for the cold."

"Could be. Though I refuse to complain about eighty degrees and sunshine."

"You really don't miss the change of seasons?"

Emerson gazed upward, really thinking about the question. Something about Cassie's tone made her want to be truthful, not make a joke or be sarcastic. Cassie seemed to have that effect on her. "Sometimes. More so when I first moved there."

"How come you did that? Moved, I mean." Cassie's voice was soft, nonthreatening, and again, Emerson felt the need to be honest.

"It's not something I talk about much," she began, and shrugged. She stared off down the street.

"Was it because of the accident? With your knee?"

With a subtle nod, Emerson went on. "I had to get out of here. I just felt all these...eyes on me. Wherever I went, I felt judgment. And I was pissed. There was no way I could be that girl that blew it, you know?" Her pale eyebrows met above her nose as she lowered her tone to mimic Fredrik's. "I was raised to be a champion. And I blew it. Suddenly, I was a loser. And all those people knew it." She shrugged again and cleared her throat. "I couldn't take it. I had to get the hell away as fast as I could."

"You said a bad word," Izzy scolded, seemingly coming out of nowhere, her costume falling off one shoulder.

133

"I did," Emerson said. "I apologize. Don't say it. Okay?"

"Okay. Aunt Cassie, can you fix my tie?"

"Only if I can have a Snickers."

With an exaggerated sigh, Izzy said, "Fine." She fished out the candy, handed it to Cassie, then turned her back to her. Cassie retied the back of the costume, then gave her niece a swat on the behind. "Thanks!" And she was off to catch up with Zack.

"Your mom had a really hard time with you being gone," Cassie said as she unwrapped the candy, her eyes on Izzy's retreating form as they strolled forward. "Mary talked with her about it a lot. I eavesdropped."

"I know. She didn't understand why I couldn't stay with her, and I couldn't understand why she wouldn't leave with me. It's always been an issue for us and now..." She let the sentence dangle and then was quiet. Cassie bit off half the candy bar and handed the remainder to Emerson, who popped it in her mouth. They walked in silence for a moment before Emerson clapped her gloved hands together once and said, "You know what? This is depressing. Talk about something fun. Tell me something about you. How did you end up with the store? Tell me that."

Cassie glanced at her face, seemed willing to change the subject for Emerson. "Okay. Well, I don't know if you remember, but Henry Bickham owned The Sports Outfitter when we were kids." At Emerson's nod, she continued. "I always thought it was a cool store, but Mr. Bickham was kind of old and stodgy."

"I remember that, too," Emerson said with a chuckle.

"I'd always enjoyed classes like economics and statistics and business in high school. I did well in them."

Emerson made a face that said she thought exactly the opposite of such classes.

"I went to Syracuse and majored in business, not really sure what I wanted to do exactly, but knowing I loved business. I managed to do okay, which was surprising considering how homesick I got." Cassie scoffed, perhaps slightly embarrassed.

"Syracuse is a good three and a half hours away. That *is* pretty far."

"I thought I needed to get away from my family, but I missed Lake Henry more than I can even put into words." Cassie shrugged. "Call me crazy, but it's true."

"I get it."

"You do? You, who moved three thousand miles away?"

Emerson's shoulders moved when she chuckled. "I didn't say I didn't miss it. I just needed to get the hell out. But no changing the subject. What happened next?"

The kids trotted down the walkway of a house and on ahead as Cassie waved to them. "Well, I graduated and came back here, and honest to god, I was so relieved to be home that I couldn't imagine leaving again. I think that's part of why I jumped into a relationship with Mike. Unfortunately, there are not a lot of business opportunities in a small town like this."

"I can imagine."

"So Mike and I had just gotten married. I was bartending at The Slope and working part time at The Sports Outfitter, but I was getting restless." Cassie shook her head. "I have no idea what prompted it, but I started to really pay attention to the store. I watched inventory and sales, what pulled customers in. I studied other stores, what they were doing, measured their success. I made a list of things I'd do differently if the store was mine. I was trying to work up the courage to sit down with Mr.

Bickham and go over my ideas with him when word started to go around that he was retiring."

"What luck." Emerson bumped her with a shoulder.

"Right?" Cassie laughed. "But don't think it was easy-peasy. I had to apply for a business loan, and my parents helped me out a bit. Mr. Bickham was old school. And old fashioned. Selling his store to a girl was not high on his list of things to do before retiring. It took me a long time, tons of research, and a boatload of schmoozing before he even considered it."

"I bet you wore him down," Emerson said, poking the inside of her cheek with her tongue.

"I totally wore him down." Cassie laughed. "I had a whole file full of ideas and numbers. I didn't want to give him my entire plan in case he didn't like it. I was more interested in showing him that I could keep the place afloat, that he wouldn't retire and see his life's work go out of business two months later."

"That's pretty impressive. You were what? Twenty-five?"

"Almost."

"Like I said. Impressive. You should be proud of yourself."

Cassie smiled warmly. "I am. It isn't always easy. Retail hours suck. Luckily, there's an awesome apartment on the third floor that I rent, so I'm never far from work. I can be there any time."

"But you're the boss."

"True. I've owned it for three years now, but I still have a hard time making my employees work on days I don't want to cover myself."

"That's what bosses do. That's the benefit of being the boss."

Cassie grinned. "I know. This conversation can go around and around."

They approached the local park that butted up to the beach. Dozens of people milled around. There was a bonfire, hot cider, donuts, and a community center which, tonight, was decked out in paper bats, strings of orange lights, and adults dressed as witches and goblins coaxing the kids into the haunted house. Speakers were set on the deck, and loud creaky door sounds and horrifying screams echoed along the beach.

"Aunt Cassie, can we go in?" Zack asked. The oval around his eyes left visible by his ninja mask stood out starkly in the dark.

Izzy came up behind him. "Please?" she asked, drawing the word out for several seconds.

"All right. Go ahead. But come right back here when you get out. Emerson and I will be standing in this spot. Zack, you are in charge of your sister. Hold on to her. Understood?"

They were running away before she finished her sentence, shouting yesses over their shoulders. Cassie shook her head.

"Want some cider?" Emerson asked.

"Love some."

Emerson left and was back in a few moments, two steaming paper cups in her hand, and two donuts balanced on top of them.

Cassie grinned as she approached. "Now that takes talent," she commented, indicating Emerson's balancing act.

"You'd better believe it. That was *not* easy. Not to mention, the guy at the counter kept looking at me funny."

Cassie craned her neck to see who the culprit was. "Oh, that's Jake." She smiled and waved at him. "He works one of the slopes. He probably recognized you. You're still a bit of a celebrity around here, you know."

Emerson grunted and sipped her cider.

Cassie studied her for a beat as she took a bite of her donut. Even in the firelight, Emerson could feel her eyes. "Why do you do that?" Cassie asked.

"Do what?"

"Shrug off your fame. This town loved you. They still do. You're a hometown hero."

"I'm a hometown failure."

Cassie shook her head, turned back toward the haunted house, "Only in your own eyes," she said softly. Emerson stared at her, but Cassie waited her out, and Emerson looked away without comment.

The kids came running to them, saving any further discussion. Zack was pumped. "Wow! That was awesome!" he claimed. "I saw Jeremy and David in there, too. And there was this mummy with blood on his mouth. And Leatherface with a chainsaw."

"How do you know who Leatherface is?" Cassie asked, shocked. "You're *nine*."

Zack shrugged and went on describing the various scares. "Can I go through again? Can I?" Cassie nodded and he was off like a shot. Izzy, meanwhile, was very quiet, and slipped her hand into Cassie's, leaning close. Gordie sat next to her and she pet his head absently.

"Iz? You okay, honey?" Izzy nodded, but said nothing. Cassie squatted down to meet her wide blue eyes. "Was that too scary?" Emerson heard Cassie ask quietly so as not to embarrass the girl. At Izzy's nod, Cassie wrapped her up in a hug and kissed the top of her head. "No worries, baby. Gordie won't let any monsters get you. Right, Gordie?"

On cue, Izzy looked at the dog and he promptly bathed her face in kisses until she giggled and squealed his name.

Cassie stood up, glanced at Emerson, and muttered, "My sister's going to kill me."

Before Emerson could reply, a woman called Cassie's name and hurried up to them. She was plump and blonde, her dimpled face open and friendly. "I just wanted you to know... oh, I'm sorry. Am I interrupting? Look at me, just barging in like a bull in a china shop." She giggled. "I'm so sorry."

"No, no problem at all," Cassie said. "Ginny Chatsworth, this is my friend Emerson Rosberg."

"Oh," Ginny said, her eyes widening in recognition as she held out her hand. "It's nice to meet you. I'm so sorry about your mother. She was a fixture around here. Really nice woman."

"Thank you," Emerson said as she shook hands. "I appreciate that."

"Anyway, Cassie, I just wanted you to know those skates are perfect. Jordan is ridiculously happy with them."

Cassie tilted her head and raised her eyebrows. "You need to learn to trust me, Ginny. I would never steer you wrong." To Emerson, she explained, "Ginny's daughter plays hockey on the team I help coach."

"I learned my lesson," Ginny promised. "I'll never doubt you again. Well, I've got to go find my other kids. I think they're on their third trip through the haunted house. Nice to meet you, Emerson."

"Wow," Emerson commented as she watched Ginny hurrying away. "Did she take a breath? At all?"

"She rarely does," Cassie said. "I'd like half her energy. That's all I need. Really. Just half. I'd be okay with that."

They met each other's gaze and smiled.

Cassie looked down at her niece, still cuddling Gordie. "Iz, do you want the rest of my donut?"

"Okay." Izzy took the offered pastry and immediately shared it with the dog.

Cassie closed her eyes and sighed.

The second half of the walk around the lake went much like the first, though the kids had begun to slow their pace. Emerson was still cold, but she was also surprised by how much she was enjoying Cassie's company, so she was willing to make the sacrifice. They stopped in front of a brightly lit house and watched the kids run up the driveway as three others came down. Cassie glanced at Emerson and furrowed her brows.

"What?" Emerson said, catching the look.

"Your ears are red." Before Emerson could comment, Cassie took off one glove, reached up, and grabbed Emerson's ear between her fingers. "You're freezing. You should've worn a hat or something. Here." Cassie took the bright yellow fleece band off her own head and, over Emerson's protests, stood on her toes to put it on her. "Stay still," she ordered, tugging and fixing until it was on correctly. It was warm from Cassie's own body heat, and Emerson felt it immediately. Cassie dropped her hands from Emerson's head, but let them linger on her shoulders, their faces mere inches apart. "Better?" Cassie asked softly.

Emerson swallowed and nodded, and they stayed that way for a long moment. Finally, Emerson cleared her throat and said, "But what about you? Now your ears will get cold."

Cassie made a face, let herself down off her toes. "I'm used to this weather. You, on the other hand, are a lightweight." She gave Emerson's shoulders a squeeze, then stepped back as the kids came down the driveway, much less exuberant than an hour ago. "You guys getting tired?"

Izzy nodded. Zack looked reluctant to admit it, though it was obvious. Their bags were fat and bulging with candy.

"I think you've got enough treasure there to last until Easter," Emerson commented.

Cassie pulled her phone from her pocket. "Let's keep walking, and I'll text your mom that we're just about done. Okay? She'll meet us."

Fifteen minutes later, a minivan slowed to a stop on the road next to them and the passenger side window hummed down. "Hey, anybody want a ride?" Emerson glanced over at the woman in the driver's seat who was the spitting image of Cassie. Her face was a bit rounder and her hair a couple inches shorter, but other than that, they looked like twins.

"Mommy!" Izzy cried and bounced on her toes. She held up her bag. "Look!"

The side door of the van slid open, and the kids piled in. Cassie glanced at Emerson, her voice low, her eyes warm. "Do you want a ride back? Or do you want to keep walking?"

Emerson's knee was aching steadily. She'd be limping in a matter of minutes. But the idea of another twenty minutes alone with Cassie was much more appealing than a ride in a minivan of kids and being dropped off at her door. "I'm fine to keep walking, but it's up to you." The smile Cassie gave her was all the proof she needed that she'd made the right decision.

As if reading their minds, Chris said, "Do you guys want a ride?" She ducked her head a bit and added, "You must be

141

Emerson. Hi. I'm Chris. Sister of the rude chick standing next to you who neglected to introduce us."

Emerson laughed and lifted a hand in greeting. "Nice to meet you."

"We're going to walk, Chris," Cassie answered. "Thanks, though."

"What do you guys say to Aunt Cassie?" Chris tossed over her shoulder at the kids in the back seat.

"Thanks, Aunt Cassie," they said in unison.

Izzy climbed back out of the van, held up her arms for Cassie, who gave her a big hug. In return, the girl handed her another mini Snickers. She hugged Gordie and kissed the top of his head. Then she moved a step over and held her arms up to Emerson.

Shocked, Emerson glanced at Cassie's smiling face before bending down and hugging the girl tightly. "Thanks for letting me trick-or-treat with you," she said quietly.

"You're welcome," Izzy whispered. Then she climbed back into the van and buckled herself into her booster seat. As the kids waved, the door slid shut, and Chris drove them away.

Cassie took a big breath and blew it out. "Alone at last," she said, then looked away quickly at Emerson's raised eyebrows. "How are you doing? Warm enough?"

"I'm good."

Cassie unwrapped the candy, and as before, bit off half of it and gave the other half to Emerson. Then she tucked her hand into the crook of Emerson's arm, and they began walking, keeping their pace slow, as if neither of them wanted the evening to end. Their shoulders rubbed. Emerson tightened her arm to her side, securing Cassie's hand there. Even Gordie strolled along easily.

"Thanks for coming with me tonight," Cassie said. "I hope it wasn't too boring."

"It wasn't boring at all," Emerson said and meant it. "I'm glad you asked me. Even if my ears did almost freeze off."

Cassie barked a laugh and pushed against her. "You were ill-prepared, Ms. Rosberg, and you know it. You need to come by my store and get yourself some proper cold-weather gear if you plan to hang around here much longer." She was quiet for a beat before adding, "Do you? Plan to hang around?" Then she quickly put up her hand. "No. No, don't answer that. It isn't my business. I just…" Cassie swallowed, looked out at the lake. "I'm just having a good time is all." She seemed to be struggling with something more she wanted to say, but she kept quiet and continued walking.

"I've had a great time, too," Emerson told her, aware that she'd started to favor her left leg, but hoping Cassie didn't notice.

She did.

"Emerson, your leg." Cassie stopped walking, turned and looked up at her. "You're limping."

Emerson shrugged. "It happens. I'm fine."

"You're not fine. You're *limping*. I kept you out too long and made you walk too far in the cold. I'm so sorry. You should have said something." She pulled out her phone. "I'll text my sister and get her back here to drive us."

Her concern was touching, and Emerson grasped her arm. "Cassie." She waited until Cassie made eye contact. "I'm fine. It's okay. It happens often. It just means it's time for me to sit soon. You didn't *make* me do anything. I'm a big girl. All right?"

Cassie didn't look convinced, but she said, "All right. But let's get you home and put that leg up."

"I like that plan."

"Here. Lean on me." She took Emerson's arm and draped it over her own shoulders. She held Emerson's bare hand with her gloved one. Her other arm wrapped around Emerson's waist, Gordie's leash held loosely in that hand, and they stayed that way for the rest of the trek, stepping in tandem, moving almost as one entity. They walked slowly. It was obvious Emerson was consciously trying to keep her full weight *off* Cassie, but neither of them said anything. And neither of them moved away.

By the time they approached the walkway that led down to The Lakeshore Inn, Emerson was limping pretty good and trying to clench her jaw without drawing Cassie's attention. They walked slowly down the sidewalk, passing by the main building, tossing a wave to a couple staying in one of the second floor rooms who was out on their balcony watching the water. Cassie stayed very close, still holding Emerson's hand, keeping Emerson's arm around her, ready to catch any stumble or break any fall that might occur. Gordie trailed slightly behind them, as if understanding that getting stepped on or fallen on was a possibility.

At the door, they stopped. Emerson faced Cassie and spoke quietly. "I really had so much fun tonight."

"In spite of your aching knee?" Cassie asked hopefully, keeping her hands on Emerson's arms, maintaining contact, much to Emerson's delight.

"In spite of my aching knee." Emerson glanced out at the lake, searching for words. She wet her lips and looked back at Cassie. "Truly. I would've just stayed here alone and…" With a shrug, she said simply, "This was so much better. Goblins and ghosts and…thank you."

"You're welcome," Cassie whispered.

They stood like that, face to face, Cassie's hands still on Emerson's arms, for what seemed like minutes, but was probably mere seconds. Emerson's senses were suddenly on overload, everything felt...bigger. The brisk air, the gentle lapping of the water, the hushed whispers of the balcony couple who were no longer visible, the feel of Cassie's warm breath on her face, smelling like chocolate, the comforting weight of Cassie's hands on her arms. Before she realized it, she was leaning in slightly as Cassie slowly raised up on her tiptoes. Her eyes drifted closed, as did Emerson's...

The sound of the door pulling open was like a gunshot, and it startled the two of them so much they each jumped. Even Gordie woofed in surprise.

"There you are," a woman said from inside Emerson's cottage. Cassie and Emerson each blinked at her as she held up a cell phone and tilted it back and forth in her hand as she looked at Emerson. "It doesn't help you to have this if you don't take it with you, sweetie. I tried to call."

"Claire." It was all Emerson could manage. She was completely taken aback. What the hell was Claire doing here? It took all her strength not to rudely ask the question out loud.

"Hi, baby." Claire leaned forward and pecked Emerson's lips with her own. Emerson felt Cassie stiffen, then take a subtle step to her right. Away from Emerson. "God, it's freezing out here. You didn't tell me this place got so cold so early in the season, Em. Come in so I can close the door before we all catch pneumonia."

Emerson turned her eyes to Cassie, who took another small step away and looked at the ground.

"We've got to get going," Cassie said, too loudly. She nodded down at Gordie, who was sitting politely and waiting for this new person to notice him.

"Are you sure? Would you like to come in for a drink?" Emerson was nothing if not a good hostess, and there was an internal battle going on in her head. Part of her wanted Cassie to stay. A big part. The rest of her wanted to get Cassie as far away from Claire as possible. Immediately.

"No, thanks. I'm good." Cassie was already backing away. "Get inside and get off that leg, okay?"

Emerson nodded. "I will." Claire had gone quiet behind her.

Cassie inclined her head once. "Okay. So." The silence grew, and she finally cleared her throat and said simply, "Goodnight." Then she turned and hurried up the walkway, Gordie trotting along next to her. Emerson watched until they were out of sight, continued to stare after them until Claire called her name. Then she closed her eyes, counted slowly to five, and went inside.

"Who was that?" Claire asked. "You didn't even introduce me."

"What are you doing here?" Emerson asked instead of answering as she closed the door behind her. She did an admirable job, she thought, of not sounding accusatory. She stepped out of her shoes, unzipped her jacket. As she turned to hang it up, her back to Claire, she pulled Cassie's headband from her head and held in front of her nose, the scent of Cassie's citrus shampoo filling her nostrils. Then she jumped as Claire spoke from directly behind her.

"Seriously. Who was that?"

Emerson shook her head. "Nobody. Just a woman who helped out my mom. She's nobody."

That seemed to placate Claire. "I felt terrible that I wasn't able to be here for your mother's funeral," she said, wrapping her arms around Emerson and pressing her cheek between Emerson's shoulder blades. "Then I heard about that fiasco at McKinney Carr and thought you could use some support." She stepped back and when Emerson turned to face her, she held her arms out from her sides. "Ta da! Here I am!"

Emerson forced a smile, then walked directly to the kitchen where a bottle of Cabernet stood open and breathing, a half empty glass with a lipstick smear standing next to it. "I see you found the wine."

"I didn't think you'd mind."

Emerson didn't speak. Instead, she poured herself a healthy glass and took it into the bedroom where she tried not to focus on Claire's enormous suitcase now propped in a corner. She found her pills, shook one out, and downed it with a big gulp of the wine.

"You know, getting here was not easy," Claire was saying as Emerson peeled off her clothes and changed into more comfortable flannel pants. She found a long-sleeved T-shirt in her mother's drawer and pulled it over her head, smelling it as it slipped past her nose. "I didn't realize I'd have to drive three hours from the airport. If I had, I'd have called you to pick me up."

Emerson kept herself from scoffing aloud, thinking, *That would* not *have happened.* She then immediately felt guilty. Claire had come a long way to see her. Rearranging her work schedule wasn't easy, and Emerson knew this.

"But I wanted to surprise you." Claire was still talking. She body-blocked Emerson as she came out of the bedroom. "Aren't you glad to see me?" Her bottom lip protruded in an expression she clearly assumed was endearing. Emerson tended to think it was childish.

With a deep sigh, she tried to relax and said, "Of course, I am."

Claire took the wine glass from Emerson's hand and set it on a dresser. Then she slid her hands up Emerson's arms, and wrapped her own arms around Emerson's neck. "Well, then, give me a real kiss, lover."

Their mouths met, Claire projecting her desire in seconds, pushing her tongue against Emerson's. Emerson forced herself to relax, to go with it. Behind her closed eyelids, Cassie's face loomed, and Emerson's heart rate kicked up a notch. She took Claire's face in her hands and sank into the kiss, feeling Cassie's skin against her palms, Cassie's soft lips beneath hers, Cassie's whimpers being swallowed by Emerson's mouth.

When she remembered who she was kissing, she pulled back, dropping her hands from Claire's face. Claire's eyes were cloudy, her cheeks flushed, her chest heaving. "Now that's what I'm talking about. Wow."

Blinking until her vision cleared, Emerson took a step back, snatched her wine off the dresser, and headed into the living room. "I have to sit down," she mumbled, her knee throbbing. She dropped onto the couch and propped her foot up on the coffee table, her entire body sighing with relief. She took a large sip of wine and held it in her mouth as she let her head fall back against the headrest and tried not to think about where her mind had just gone.

Zero Visibility

She hadn't even been here for two weeks and this fucking town was messing with her head already.

CHAPTER THIRTEEN

"I ALMOST KISSED HER."

Jonathan sputtered, trying not to dribble his coffee down his chin and onto his very expensive Ralph Lauren sweater. "You did *what?*" he asked once he'd gotten himself under control.

"You heard me." Cassie sat at her desk where she'd been most of the morning. She wasn't sure why she'd told Jonathan about the previous night. She knew what his reaction would be. He didn't disappoint.

"Jesus, Cassandra. What's gotten into you? Her? The Ice Princess? Really?"

Cassie shook her head and gazed out the window at the steel gray sky. The first snowfall was predicted to arrive this week and for the first time in years, she wished it would hold off. The idea of curling up in front of her gas fireplace alone was less than appealing. "I wish you'd stop calling her that," she said quietly.

"But it's so fitting."

"It's really not." Cassie dropped a hand onto Gordie's head, pet him absently as she continued to stare into the distance.

Apparently, Jonathan agreed to disagree with her because he let that one go. "Well, she is stunningly good looking. At least I can see why you'd be attracted to her. And pray tell, why did you *not* kiss her?"

Cassie looked at him and tried to gauge whether he really wanted to know or he was just pacifying her. Surprisingly, she didn't care. She needed to talk this out, and Jonathan was there. He'd do. "Her girlfriend showed up."

Jonathan stared at her for a full five seconds before he spoke. "Wait. What? Her girlfriend is here? In Lake Henry?"

"Well, my regular friends don't kiss me on the mouth in greeting, so I'm going to go with yes, it was her girlfriend, and she's here."

"Huh."

"Yeah."

"Was she pretty?"

Cassie cocked her head at him. "Really?"

He shrugged. "What? I'm curious."

"She was beautiful," Cassie said with a sigh as she thought back to the evening before and the woman who'd so rudely interrupted what had been an amazing night, surely about to get better. Chestnut brown hair that fell in waves around her shoulders, and light blue eyes that darted from Emerson to Cassie and back. An outfit that consisted of pricey tailored slacks and a light blue sweater that looked like it was meant only for her. Cassie shook the memory away and realized she was irritated with herself that it never occurred to her Emerson might have somebody. "Very put together. Pretty blue eyes. Gorgeous hair. Expensive clothes." *The anti-Cassie*, she thought but refrained from saying aloud.

"Has she been here the whole time?"

"I don't think so. Mary would've said something." Cassie thought back to the previous night. "And you know what? Emerson seemed as shocked to see her as I was."

"Oh, the surprise visit. Those are always fun. Not."

"Right? Anyway, I have no idea what's going on. It was all so weird. We had a fun night. She was surprisingly great with the kids. She got really cold at one point, but she never complained because…I think she was enjoying herself. I know I was."

Jonathan nodded, studying her, and didn't say anything for a long moment. Finally, he spoke. "You're really starting to like her, huh?"

"She's *nice,* Johnny. And she's so damn sexy…" She let her voice trail off for a moment. "I have no clue if there's much beyond that, but I do know that I had a really great night with a beautiful woman for the first time since the shit hit the fan with Vanessa. I spent the evening with a very attractive, intelligent, interesting woman who seemed to be enjoying my company. It felt good."

"And there was enough chemistry that you wanted to kiss her."

"And she wanted to kiss me. Don't forget that part. She wasn't exactly pushing me away."

"Well. Maybe you need to do some research."

Cassie furrowed her brows. "What do you mean?"

He stood, tossed his empty Starbucks cup into her wastebasket. "I mean talk to her. Ask her what the deal is. How else will you know?"

Cassie pinched the bridge of her nose. "Or I could just leave it alone. Things looked pretty cozy between them, and I'm probably just grabbing on to whatever I can since I'm single and hating it." She looked down at Gordie's eyes. "Right, Gordo?"

Jonathan shook his head and opened her office door. "You are such a girl."

"But you love me anyway," Cassie called out as he went into the hall.

"Lucky for you." The door clicked shut.

Gordie wandered to his round dog bed in the corner, turned in a circle five or six times, then settled down with a happy groan. Cassie sipped from her coffee cup, making a mental note that she needed to bring coffee to Jonathan later, as he was three visits up on her. There was a mountain of paperwork that needed to be done, as well as a list of phone calls she needed to make, but all she could manage to do was gaze out the window at the lake and rehash every second of last night.

When she'd invited Emerson to join her and the kids, it had been fairly innocent. Cassie was smart enough to recognize when she found somebody physically attractive, but she'd kept that in check. Emerson wasn't staying in Lake Henry. She'd made that abundantly clear more than once. So Cassie had been pretty sure she'd taken that attraction and shelved it. She had no idea when the switch had flipped, but she'd had a great time, and when Chris had shown up to get the kids, she wanted nothing more than to spend more time with Emerson. And the look in Emerson's blue eyes had said the same thing.

Jesus, had she become a complete failure at reading people? At interpreting body language? They really couldn't have been much closer on their walk. They'd strolled as slowly as possible so they wouldn't get to the end of the journey so soon, and being up against her, having Emerson leaning on her... She shook her head slowly. She'd been so drawn to Emerson...and it seemed the feeling was mutual.

Why hadn't Emerson mentioned having a girlfriend? She said she dated. Is that what she'd meant? That she was *dating*? Now? Currently?

Cassie remembered the woman's eyes ping-ponging back and forth between her and Emerson. Had she known there was something there? Had she seen it? Did she have any idea that if she'd waited five more seconds to open the door, she'd have caught them with their mouths fused together?

And with that thought, Cassie pictured it, as she had a hundred times last night as she tossed and turned in her lonely bed. Emerson had a great mouth. Those lips…

"Jesus Christ," Cassie muttered, shoving back from her desk harder than necessary. "Come on, Gordie. I need distraction. Let's go downstairs and sell some stuff. Wanna?"

The store was somewhat busy for a Tuesday mid-morning. The kids were in school, but a few tourists were still around. Not nearly as many as in summer and early fall, and not nearly as many as during ski season, but it was steady enough. This was the very tail end of the foliage season, or the season of the "leaf-lookers," as the locals called it. People from parts of the country that didn't have the amazing trees that changed color with the seasons flocked to the northeast just to see the leaves. And Cassie had to admit, it was beautiful. But it was just about over. Most of the trees had started to drop their leaves, and in another week or two, most of them would be bare. The landscape would go from blazing oranges, yellows, and reds to dull and boring brown.

She and Gordie headed down to the first floor to see how things were going. She checked in with Frannie, who nodded to her questions as she rang out a customer buying gloves. Then she sidled past a couple more customers in the aisle and headed down to the lower level to check in with her mom. Gordie found her first, zipping across the room to her. As Cassie headed toward the back door to peek out at the lake, she saw her mother making a weird face at her. Cassie squinted at her and held her arms out to the sides in a silent, "What?" Her mother gestured to her left with her eyes, then widened them. Cassie was confused, but when she looked in the direction her mother pointed, it all became clear.

Vanessa walked toward her.

"Shit," Cassie muttered under her breath. Then, "Hey."

Vanessa stopped next to her. She looked exhausted. Dark circles accented the undersides of her eyes and her normally glossy hair was dull and yanked back into a messy ponytail that looked like it had been done at the very last minute. "Hi." Vanessa's eyes darted around the room. Luckily, there were no customers on this level at the moment. Cassie sent up a silent thank you to the universe.

Cassie waited. When Vanessa said nothing more, she raised her eyebrows and turned her head slightly, an expectant look on her face.

"The kids' costumes looked great," Vanessa finally said, her voice quiet.

Cassie nodded. "Yeah, they did good." After a beat, she made a face and asked, "When did you see them?"

"Last night." Vanessa's eyes finally met hers, and they were crackling with...something. "We walked right past you, but you didn't see us."

Cassie searched her memory banks, but came up empty.

"Well, you didn't see me. The kids were busy knocking on doors."

That made more sense to Cassie, but she felt a little pang of guilt. "I'm really sorry, V. You should have said something, gotten my attention."

Vanessa barked a laugh that sounded inordinately loud in the quiet space as she glanced out the back windows. "No, I don't think so." She waited a beat, then turned her gaze back to Cassie. Her eyes were filled with unshed tears as she asked in almost a whisper, "Are you seeing her?"

Oh, Jesus, Cassie thought, rubbing her forehead with her fingertips. That's what this was about. "Vanessa," she said, and Vanessa cringed, then lashed out, still quiet.

"*Don't.* Don't you say my name like that. Like you pity me. Please, Cassie. I can't take that."

Cassie grasped her arm and led her to the back corner of the lower level of the store. She kept her voice low, but imploring. "Vanessa. We cannot keep doing this. We can't. You've got to stop."

"I know. I know." Tears tracked down her cheeks, but to Vanessa's credit, she kept herself mostly under control. She looked back into Cassie's eyes and said, "You didn't answer my question."

Cassie made a quiet guttural sound in her throat. "No. Okay? No, I am not seeing Emerson. She's with somebody."

Vanessa studied her face, and Cassie wanted to hide. She did her best to school her features, but Vanessa knew her better than anybody. "But you wish she wasn't. You wish she wasn't with somebody," she stated simply. "Don't you?"

Cassie clenched her teeth and looked away. "I am not going to do this with you."

Vanessa looked down at her feet, and they were both quiet for a long moment. When Vanessa looked up, her eyes were clear and she was doing her best to look perfectly fine. If Cassie didn't know her so well, she might not have realized how much pain she was hiding.

"You're right," she finally said with a sniff as her eyes traveled the store, looked anywhere but at Cassie. "I can't keep doing this. I know. I'm sorry. It's just been really..." Vanessa let the sentence dangle for a moment while she worked hard to keep control. With a clear of her throat, she went on. "It's been really hard, but I'm working on things. I'm working on me." She cleared her throat and added, "I've been on the internet doing some research like you suggested." With a humorless laugh she said, "Hey, better late than never, right?"

Cassie reached out and squeezed her upper arm gently. "Vanessa." Her voice was barely a whisper.

Vanessa swallowed, gazed out over the store, cleared her throat again, and again, to her credit and Cassie's surprise, held on to her composure. "I hope you understand that ultimately, I just want you to be happy." Her eyes finally returned to Cassie's and she whispered, "I love you, Cassie, and I just want you to be happy. That's all."

Cassie didn't know what to say, but Vanessa saved her from doing so by giving her a quick peck on the cheek before she turned away and left out the back door. Cassie watched her get in her car, start the engine, and drive away without a backward glance. She sucked in a lungful of air, slowly, and held it for a beat before letting it out just as slowly. Then she rubbed both hands over her face as if this would help scrub off all the stress. When she looked up, her mother was walking toward her.

"You okay?" she asked gently.

"Can this day get any worse?" Cassie asked.

Suddenly, the front door alarm went off, shocking both of them back a couple of steps and letting them know somebody was trying to leave the store with an unpaid item.

"Apparently, it can," her mother said.

"Son of a bitch," Cassie muttered, taking the stairs two at a time.

Katie Parker watched from across the store as Cassie dealt with the police and the shoplifter. It was moments like this when her pride in her daughter surged, when she was so obviously not a child, when she was so blatantly a grown woman who could take care of herself, her life, her business.

But Katie was a mother before anything else, and when she saw one of her children confused or hurting or defeated, it squeezed her heart in a way that no non-parent could ever understand.

Katie liked Vanessa Turner. She always had. She'd known her for years. Jim had taught her in school so many years ago, and she was a good girl. She'd settled down with a local boy, had kids, and was a fixture in Lake Henry...at the PTA, at sporting events with her kids. She was known around town as a reliable, nice girl. She was kind. She was beautiful.

She was in love with Cassie.

Katie had known it long before Cassie had ever told her. They're not kidding when they say, "a mother knows." A mother *knows*. She always knows. It's a mother's job to be in tune with her kids. It didn't hurt that Cassie was never good at hiding anything, try as she might. Katie even knew that Cassie's marriage to Michael would never last. She knew from the time Cassie was nine years old that she preferred girls. And she was fine with that. Jim had taken a bit more persuasion, but ultimately, he wanted his little girl to be happy and if spending her life with another woman was what would make her that way, he could accept it.

Vanessa Turner had been a surprise.

Cassie's signature on her divorce papers had barely dried before she began talking about how much time she was spending with Vanessa, how much fun they were having, how much they had in common. All her talk was very innocent, nothing at all suspicious, but a mother knows. Katie *knew*. Cassie was seeing Vanessa (she didn't know what else to call it.). That was clear to her. She had no idea how far it had gone at the time, but Cassie had definite feelings for this woman who was married with children. Honestly, that was the issue Katie struggled with: the married with children part. Cassie was not a home wrecker. That's not the kind of girl she was, not the kind of girl she was raised to be.

They were discreet. Katie had to give them that. She was fairly certain that nobody had ever suspected the affair. Mostly because this was Lake Henry, small town of the Adirondacks, and nobody's mind would go there without some serious pushing. But when Cassie was home, she talked about nothing else. Vanessa this, Vanessa's kids that. On the one hand, it was wonderful to see her daughter so happy…her constant smiles, the high, healthy color in her face were beautiful things for a parent to witness in her child. It was such a nice change from the stress she went through over ending her marriage to Michael. But Katie was worried. And more than that, she was disappointed in her daughter, which she hesitated to admit.

One night, she did.

They'd had Sunday dinner with the family, and it had been very nice. Chris and the kids had to get home so Trevor could study for his math test the next day, and Cassie had stayed behind to help Katie clean up the kitchen. It wasn't long before Cassie had started talking about a show she and Vanessa were going to see the following weekend. Katie listened as long as she could before it burst out of her.

"What are you doing?" she asked her daughter quietly.

"What do you mean?" Cassie dried a dish, put it in the cupboard, still smiling.

Katie stopped washing, turned to her daughter. "*What* are you doing?"

Cassie held a wet plate in one hand, a towel in the other, and furrowed her brows at her mother. She shook her head quickly and asked again, "What do you mean?"

"She's *married*, Cassandra. *That's* what I mean. She's a married woman with two kids and a life. What are you doing?"

Katie watched her daughter's face lose the joy it had been holding for so long, and she hated that she was the one who pulled it away. She also read Cassie's thoughts, saw Cassie realize that Katie knew *exactly* what was going on between her and Vanessa, that there was no more masking it.

Cassie rolled her lips in, bit down on them, obviously searching for the right words. After long moments, she spoke. "I know, Mom. I know. We've talked about it a lot. I don't want to push her. You know?"

It wasn't what Katie had wanted to hear, though if pressed she wasn't sure she could even articulate exactly what it was she would have preferred Cassie say. "I don't like it," she said.

"I know. I know. I don't either."

Katie shook her head and said it again, more to herself. "I don't like it."

"It's not ideal. I know," Cassie told her, a reassuring tone in her voice. "It won't always be like this. You'll see."

But time went on. More than a year. Nearing two years. Nothing changed but the light in Cassie's face. It dimmed slowly. She talked about Vanessa less and less. Katie began to worry. Finally, one day when Cassie had begged off of a Sunday family dinner, Katie decided to bring a dish directly to her apartment. When Cassie'd answered the door, her eyes were red-rimmed and her face was blotchy and puffy.

"What's wrong?" Katie asked, pushing her way through the door.

"Nothing. I'm fine," Cassie had lied.

"Cassandra." Katie set her dishes down and turned to her daughter. "You've been crying. What is it?"

Cassie had studied her feet, then moved her gaze to the window, then focused on Gordie, who sat at her feet looking as worried as Katie. Katie gently touched Cassie's chin, turned her face so their eyes met. The tears overflowed immediately.

They sat on Cassie's couch as evening moved on to night while Cassie cried in her mother's arms. Katie held her tightly, initially surprised by how much more intense these emotions were than the ones when she'd decided to divorce Michael, and she knew then that her daughter's heart was truly broken. Cassie had uttered only one sentence the whole time.

"She's never going to leave him."

Katie was not surprised. She was hurt that her child was hurting. And she was angry. She was angry with Cassie for getting into this mess in the first place. She was angry with Vanessa for stringing Cassie along. She was angry at all of it. But she kept her anger in check, and she did what she needed to do to help her daughter heal. That hadn't been very long ago. Cassie told her she'd been tapering things off with Vanessa for a couple months before the actual breakup. That had only been, what, a month ago? Maybe two? And in that time, two things had become clear to Katie: Cassie was moving on. Vanessa was not.

Or maybe she was. She'd seemed to have ahold of herself when she left today, which was more than Katie could say for the last couple times she'd seen her.

She watched now as Cassie shook the hand of Tommy Goran, the police officer helping her with the shoplifting situation. He'd graduated two years ahead of Cassie, and they were friends. Cassie smiled at him; he grinned back, a little smitten as he always had been when it came to Cassie. Katie couldn't help but shake her head and smile to herself. *Oh, no, Tommy. Don't get sucked in. She's got her eye on somebody else.*

Emerson Rosberg.

Chris had called Katie this morning, and now she knew all about the Halloween date. She smiled to herself and shook her head as she recalled the conversation when she'd asked Chris how Halloween went.

"The kids had a blast with Aunt Cassie," Chris had said. "And methinks Aunt Cassie had a blast with Ms. Emerson Rosberg."

"What do you mean?" Katie had asked, puzzled. "What was she doing with Cassie and the kids?"

Chris chuckled. "Mostly shivering. A lot. But when I offered to give them a ride home in my warm, toasty car, they both declined. Apparently, they preferred to walk home. Alone. Together."

Emerson Rosberg. Former darling of Lake Henry. Notorious hard-head. Somebody who fled when the going got tough.

Cassie's track record was not the most impressive. A boy she was more comfortable and familiar with than in love with.

A married woman with children. And now a self-centered loner who lived three thousand miles away.

"Oh, my baby girl. Where did you get such lousy taste in partners?" she muttered under her breath. But she couldn't work up a smile. None of this was funny. If Cassie really did fall for Emerson, there would be no way to catch her when she inevitably crashed to the ground.

Katie was worried all over again.

CHAPTER FOURTEEN

IT WAS TIME FOR CLAIRE to go. She moped around for much of the morning, knowing that with a four o'clock flight and a three-hour drive to Albany, she needed to get on the road by eleven at the latest. It was already after ten, and it was obvious she didn't want to leave. She looked sad. She acted sad. She clung to Emerson like they were the two sides of Velcro.

Jesus Christ, just go already, Emerson wanted to shout.

The guilt hit her immediately every time that sentence crossed her mind, and she felt terrible, because Claire had been a whirlwind of accomplishment in the two days she'd been there. The half-empty living room and the stack of neatly labeled cardboard boxes in the corner were testament to that. So what was Emerson's problem? Claire had buckled down and gotten busy doing exactly what Emerson had been dragging her feet on for over a week. Why did she feel so unsettled about that?

She was yanked out of her own thoughts by Claire's arms snaking around her from behind. "Are you *positive* you don't want me to stay longer?" she whispered against Emerson's neck. "I'm sure I could work it out."

Emerson swallowed, trying not to sound too adamant when she said, "Oh, no. Really. You've done so much already. I can't ask you to stay and do more."

Claire moved around to face her, keeping her arms around Emerson's torso. "Well, you *could*..." She let the sentence dangle as she pressed her lips to Emerson's.

They hadn't had sex during the visit, despite her many attempts, and Claire wasn't happy about that. She'd made it clear last night, and she made it clear now as she did her best to get Emerson going, using her tongue, her fingers. Emerson let her for several long moments before gently extricating herself and holding Claire at arm's length. God, she was a beautiful woman, but it just wasn't there for Emerson. It never really had been, and she was pretty sure they both knew it. They'd had fun. The sex—when they'd had it—had been pretty great. But they didn't really go any deeper.

Claire would argue. Emerson knew that, and she did *not* have the energy for it, so she took what she realized was the coward's way out. She sent Claire home with a kiss and a smile, and vowed she'd deal with it later. Somehow.

Claire's blue eyes held hers for a long moment before she dropped her arms from Emerson's shoulders and took a step back. She looked for another moment, nodded once, and pulled up the handle on her suitcase. The expression on her face was shuttered now, and Emerson was both relieved and saddened by that.

"I'll walk you out," she said quickly as Claire moved past her to the door.

At the rental car, Claire popped the trunk, and Emerson swiftly picked up the suitcase and deposited it.

"So, I guess that's it," Claire said, and the double meaning wasn't lost on either of them.

"Thank you so much for your help," Emerson replied, taking Claire in her arms and hugging her tightly. "I mean it." She felt Claire nod against her shoulder and hug her back, but she said nothing as she got into the driver's seat. "You know where you're going, right?"

Claire nodded again, and tilted her iPhone from side to side to show the map app she had opened. She pulled the door shut and keyed the ignition. After a beat, she powered down the window and gazed up at Emerson with those light blue eyes. With a clear of her throat, she said softly, "You take care of yourself, Em. Okay?"

Emerson nodded once. "I will. You, too."

The window slid up as Claire broke their eye contact. Then she slowly followed the drive up to the street, didn't look back or toot the horn, and was gone.

Emerson felt a pang of loss she didn't expect. Added to her mother's death, the stress of the packing and decision making, and on top of the offer from Arnold Cross that she still hadn't studied, Emerson was suddenly and unexpectedly overwhelmed by emotion. A lump she could not swallow down sat like an apricot in her throat. She hurried into the cottage when she saw Jack Grafton in the distance, walked straight into the bathroom, shut the door just to make sure she couldn't be seen through any windows, sat down on the toilet seat, and wept like a child.

"What the hell is wrong with me?" she whispered into the empty bathroom. "What the hell is wrong with me?"

It took Emerson a long time to pull herself together.

She was not a crier. She'd tempered that long ago, before her teens. Her father had taught her early on that crying would get her nowhere on the slopes, and if the cameras or reporters caught her teary-eyed, they'd use it to their advantage and she'd end up being the Skiing Crybaby or something equally horrifying. As young as she was, it had stuck, and she'd trained herself to tamp down her emotions, to stay stone-faced during a race. So much so that people had made comments about how stoic and expressionless she was for somebody so young.

Of course, she'd carried that into adulthood, more than one relationship ending with her partner tearfully accusing her of being emotionless.

"Thanks, Dad," she muttered now from the toilet seat, reaching behind her to grab a tissue and blow her nose. She stood and checked herself in the mirror, the red in her eyes and the puffiness of her cheeks unfamiliar sights. She leaned her hands against the counter and studied her face in the mirror, closely. Her eyes were an icy blue (another thing that solidified the stoic look she'd perfected all those years ago). She studied them. Were they cold? She supposed if you didn't know her, you might think so. But it was a pretty blue, a light sky blue color. And she wasn't always cold. She could be warm. Sometimes. She grimaced and moved on to her skin. She had great skin. This, she knew. She took care of it, used copious amounts of sunscreen in L.A., and had just enough of a tan to make her look healthy. No blemishes. One mole, a small one just under her left eye. That was courtesy of her mother, who'd had one in the exact same place. Her light blonde hair came from the Swedish side of her family. She liked the short cut, liked that it was no-muss, no-fuss, and that had come from her skiing days as well. It was so much easier to wear a helmet when she didn't have a pound of hair to shove up into it. She looked closely. She was pretty sure she had a few more years before it started to fade, as blonde hair tended to, and perhaps begin to gray. Then she'd have to think about color or letting it go brassy and dull.

She stepped back, studied her entire presence from the shoulders up, and for the first time in ages she wondered what people thought when they looked at her. Did they find her attractive? Approachable? Standoffish? Intimidating? She was tall. She had those eyes. Her face was often expressionless. Intimidating seemed to be the best choice, which didn't necessarily make her happy.

What did Cassie see?

That thought immediately yanked her from her reflection, and she stepped out of the bathroom as if the tile floor had just become excruciatingly hot. In the middle of the living room, she sighed and looked out the window. The sky was gray. The trees were losing leaves like crazy, many of them already bare. Even the lake water looked cold somehow. Winter was coming.

Almost unconsciously, Emerson rubbed her hands over her upper arms, goosebumps breaking out along her bare skin. She'd already rummaged through her mother's clothes, but with the size difference, her mother's sweatshirts had sleeves that ended in the middle of Emerson's forearms. No, if she was going to be here for a while longer, she'd need some warmer clothes.

She knew exactly where she could find some.

Emerson had decided to walk to The Sports Outfitter for two reasons. One, she planned to buy some things—including a pair of hikers—and didn't think trying to carry them back to the cottage on her bike was a smart idea. Two, if she drove her mother's car, by the time she found a parking space, she'd have to walk almost the same distance anyway.

It was cold. Emerson's phone said it was in the low forties, dropping down into the thirties tonight. The thought of the fireplace and a nice glass of red wine later was incredibly appealing as she made her way along the cobblestone sidewalk. Up ahead, she could see a tiny bird of a woman struggling with her garbage can, which seemed to be about three times her size. Emerson hurried forward and took the handle of the can from the woman who, up close, seemed to be in her seventies and must have weighed about ninety pounds on her heaviest of days.

"Here, let me help you with that," Emerson said, using her foot to kick the can back onto its wheels. "Where would you like it?"

"Oh, you're so sweet. Why do they make them so big? There's only me, for crying out loud. How much garbage do they think I create in a week?" She turned and headed down her driveway. Emerson grinned and followed her, pulling the can behind her.

"Right here would be great." The woman pointed to a corner of pavement next to her small garage.

"There you go." Emerson turned the can so the lid opened easily from the front.

"Thank you so much."

"Sure." Emerson started back up the driveway when the woman spoke again.

"You're Caroline's daughter, aren't you?"

Emerson turned, nodded.

"She was a good woman, a real nice lady, your mom. Shame, what happened." She waited a beat, then held out her hand. "I'm Joan Norris."

Emerson took the offered hand, which felt like a child's in hers, the skin papery soft, the bones delicate. "Emerson Rosberg."

"Caroline talked about you all the time, you know."

That damn lump was back, and Emerson swallowed hard.

After a moment, Joan Norris waved a dismissive hand. "Bah. Life. Anyway. Thanks for helping me, Emerson. You're a good girl, just like your mom always said." With that, she turned and moved toward the front door of her small waterfront house.

"Any time," Emerson replied, not sure if Joan heard her. She followed the driveway back up to the street and continued on her way, hands jammed in her pockets, shaking her head at the surreal feeling that seemed to engulf her so often lately.

Main Street wasn't terribly busy today. If she remembered correctly, this was sort of between seasons. The summer was gone, the leaf-lookers were tapering off, but it wasn't quite ski season yet (though they'd be getting ready to make snow on a couple of the mountains if they had to). It was nice to walk down the sidewalk straight instead of sideways to dodge the throngs of people moving from shop to shop.

The Sports Outfitter was on the left hand side of the street right on the lake, and it sat side by side and shared a building with a small, classy-looking boutique called, fittingly enough, Boutique. The building was a nice, solid brown brick and looked to be three floors. A driveway led to the back and when Emerson curiously followed it, she found a surprisingly large parking lot.

"Huh. Could've driven after all," she muttered. Her eyes tracked the dock that stretched out into the water and as she reached the bottom of the sloping driveway, she saw the bank of windows that lined one side of one floor of Cassie's store. Through those windows, she could see brightly colored kayaks, life preservers, and various water equipment. *Impressive.* She headed for that door.

Emerson hadn't realized how large Cassie's store was. She only vaguely remembered being inside maybe once or twice when old man Bickham had owned it. This bottom floor seemed to have everything a customer could possibly want for working on or playing on the lake. She wandered aimlessly up an aisle of flippers, goggles, and wetsuits, touching them randomly. There was only one customer on this floor, and he was looking at kayaks. An attractive older woman manned the counter, alternating between glancing down at the paperwork in front of her and up at Kayak Man and Emerson. She looked somewhat familiar, but Emerson couldn't place her.

After a few minutes of browsing, Emerson headed for the stairs and climbed up to what was essentially the first floor. The front door spilled onto the sidewalk of Main Street, and a neon sign hung from the window next to it, blinking "Open" in red and blue letters. This floor was busier. Not busy, but there was a handful of customers wandering around, fingering clothing, gazing at the shoe display on the back wall. Something cold and wet touched Emerson's hand, startling her. She looked down and saw Gordie, tongue lolling, mouth open wide in what could only be described as a smile.

"Hey, buddy," she said quietly and scratched his head. "What's going on?"

Rather than answering her, he sat down and allowed her to scratch him some more. Luckily, they were next to a rack of sweatshirts, so Emerson scratched with one hand and shopped with the other. She found two she liked, tossed them over her arm, and looked down at Gordie.

"Okay. Shoes next." They walked to the back wall of the store and Emerson studied the larger-than-expected selection of hiking boots and shoes. She had a Merrell brand in her hand when a soft voice issued from behind her.

"Good choice. Those are my favorites."

Emerson turned to meet Cassie's brown eyes, warm as usual, but slightly less so today. She had her hands clasped behind her back and seemed to be purposely standing a bit away from Emerson. "Hi there," Emerson said, unable to keep the smile off her face. "Just the woman I was looking for."

"Really." Cassie arched a skeptical eyebrow.

"Yes." Emerson held up the shirts, then the shoe. "I'm shopping. For warm clothes. Because I'm freezing my ass off."

Cassie craned her neck, made a show of looking around the store. "Where's your…friend?"

It was that moment that Emerson realized she hadn't even introduced the two women. She closed her eyes and shook her head, irritated with herself. "She's gone."

"Gone?"

"Yeah. Gone. Home. Back to L.A."

"I see." Cassie glanced at the shoe. "You want to try those on?" With a quick squint at Emerson's feet, she said. "Tens?"

Emerson nodded, and was about to say something about lucky guesses, but Cassie was off, Gordie on her heels. Emerson watched them disappear through a door in the back wall and pressed her lips together. It never occurred to her that Cassie would be so…chilly. Though after the way Monday night ended for them, she didn't know how she could think Cassie would *not* be chilly.

"Ugh," was the only thing she could think, and so she said it out loud. The woman shopping next to her gave her a curious glance.

Cassie was back in a few moments with a box. She handed it to Emerson without a word and went off to help another customer. With a sigh, Emerson sat down and tried on the shoes, which were a perfect fit and ridiculously comfortable. She put them back in the box, then went to the front of the store to grab a recyclable shopping bag in which to put her purchases. Her credit card was about to take a beating.

She wandered for nearly an hour, grabbing a few things here and there: a pair of warm gloves, a fleece hat, a blue V-neck sweater she didn't need but couldn't resist. The whole time, she kept watch on Cassie out of the corner of her eye. She was terrific with her customers. Fun, approachable, fair. She was just as kind to her employees, helping out when necessary, taking over in order to send somebody on a break. It was one of those breaks when Emerson made her move. She'd heard Cassie talking about the cashier—whose name was Frannie, Emerson had picked up—taking her lunch in ten minutes. So Emerson wandered for that long, but not too far. The second Cassie had relieved Frannie and sent her off to eat, Emerson headed to the cash register and plopped down her goodies.

Cassie's eyebrows went up. "Wow."

"Yeah, like I said. I'm cold." Cassie chuckled and began ringing. There was no small talk, so Emerson jumped in. "I think I'd like to do the mountain path you mentioned."

Cassie looked up at her, then back down at the purchases. "Yeah?"

"Uh huh."

"It's gorgeous. You can ride to the public access building where the parking lot is, then take the elevator the rest of the way up. It's a stunning view."

"I vaguely remember, but it's been years. I'd like to see it again."

Cassie gave a nod, focused on her work. "You should do it."

"I could use a tour guide. Would you come with me?" The words were out before Emerson allowed herself any time to think about it.

Cassie's head snapped up. "Excuse me?"

"Come with me. It's been way too long. I don't know the trail. And what if I hit a tree or ride over a cliff? Who will help me?" Emerson gave a half-smile to go with her half-shrug.

Cassie chewed on her bottom lip, clearly weighing the pros and cons. Emerson held her breath. She refused to analyze why she wanted to spend more time alone with Cassie, refused to think about it and what it meant. So she waited. Cassie chewed. Emerson waited.

"When?" Cassie said finally, scanning the last item Emerson was buying and giving her a total.

Emerson blinked at her. She hadn't thought that far ahead. "Um, tomorrow?" She handed over her credit card.

Cassie glanced at the wall behind her, ran her finger down a sheet of paper taped there. "I'm free after two." She then turned back to the register, swiped the card and waited.

"Perfect. I'll pick you up here at two-thirty?" Emerson took the receipt, signed it, and gave it back.

Cassie handed the bag across the counter to her. As Emerson grabbed it, Cassie continued to hold it. "It's a tough trail, not for the faint of heart. Sure you can handle it?" The challenge in her eyes was tough and daring and—*God help me,*

Emerson thought—sexy as hell, and Emerson grinned at her while the air between them all but crackled.

"Oh, I can handle it."

"We'll see. Tomorrow then." And with that, she let go of the bag, and looked past Emerson, done. "Can I help who's next please?"

But it was okay. Emerson didn't allow herself to feel dismissed as she left the store with her new stuff. Instead, she somehow felt like she'd done what she'd intended. Which was so weird because she had no recollection of wanting to ask Cassie out.

Wait. What?

Was that what she'd just done?

CHAPTER FIFTEEN

THURSDAY DAWNED COLD AND cloudy and didn't seem to be in any mood to warm up. But the sun shone brightly through the clouds here and there, which was helpful, and by noon, it was in the high forties. Emerson was glad for her new purchases as she tried to decide what to wear on the ride. More than two hours early.

"Ridiculous," she muttered under her breath, annoyed with herself for being so excited. She tossed her new sweatshirt onto the bed and forced herself into the living room to the couch and the mess she'd left there last night. On the coffee table, she had spread out the papers Brad Klein had given her, papers that detailed the offer from Arnold Cross. She could pretend all day long that the whole document made sense to her, but honestly, the legalese made her brain hurt. Klein had highlighted the pertinent information…the money lines, mostly, but that was bookended by so much double talk and Latin that Emerson had gotten to a point where she'd just shake her head and reach for her glass of wine. Shockingly, the Zinfandel hadn't magically cleared it all up for her.

The offer was fair. That was the bottom line. Glancing up now, she saw Jack Grafton out the window, walking by carrying a ladder and heading toward the giant maple that grew about halfway between the cottage and the lake. It had a very dead branch that was sure to come splitting down during the next high wind. The hand saw in Jack's grip was a good bet he was going to take care of it. Emerson watched him, wondered what he would do if he no longer had his job here. He had to be in his seventies. His demeanor was completely off-putting. Who would hire him? Would he simply retire? Emerson realized she didn't know a thing about him. Did he have a family to support or was he alone? Did he *want* to retire or would retirement be a curse to him?

That train of thought chugged her right into the station of What To Do About Mary. Her biggest obstacle in all of this. If Emerson sold The Lakeshore Inn, Mary would more than likely lose her job as well, because it was pretty clear that Cross would incorporate it with the larger building across the street and make it all one entity again. He most likely wouldn't need Mary. And she was in the same boat as Jack. Not quite as up there in age, but certainly no youngster. Would she retire? Could she afford to? Did she wish to? Could Emerson live with being responsible for sending two long-time employees— and friends—of her mother's directly to the unemployment line?

The pile of boxes Claire had filled, taped shut, and labeled with a Sharpie stared back at Emerson as she sat. They were neat and tidy, but she had no idea what she would do with them next. She had made no further progress, and every time she thought about it, she became more annoyed with herself. She couldn't just stay here indefinitely, surrounded by boxes of her dead mother's things. She had to do something, to take care of this mess so she could go home. She *had* to get home. There was an apartment to deal with. Rent to pay. A job to find. Jesus, she hadn't even begun looking for a job, not even online. It was like Lake Henry was this tiny bubble that held her here and sucked away any desire to take care of her life on the west coast. The need to bust out of it was a big one.

She rubbed both hands over her face, up and down, up and down, like somebody waking from a long sleep. Then she moved to her short hair, rubbing her hands over her head, scratching her scalp in the hopes that would help clear her mind. Of course, it did not. Instead of hauling her ass up off the couch and getting to work packing a few boxes before she met up with Cassie, she stayed where she was, looking out at the lake, enjoying the sporadic sun glinting off its surface, unexpected relaxation sinking her further into the couch cushions. She could see Mr. Gruffton in her peripheral vision climbing his ladder. She lifted her socked feet, set them on top of the papers that littered the coffee table, and crossed them at the ankle. She slowly willed her body to relax, and she stayed that way for a long time.

Cassie thighs felt like she had battery acid flowing through her veins as she pedaled, but she would not be stopped. It wasn't a race. She knew this. But she refused to take it slow, refused to admit out loud that, though she'd run the trail more than once, she hadn't done so in ages, and she'd never actually biked it. No, she was not giving Emerson Rosberg any reason at all to think she couldn't handle this trail.

To her credit, Emerson was keeping up with her, but her breathing came in ragged gasps; Cassie could hear them. At last glance, Cassie could see the sweat dripping down from Emerson's temple in one sexy rivulet along her ear. Instead of reaching out to catch it with her finger—which is what she really wanted to do, and which would also have sent them both crashing to the ground in a heap of limbs and bike parts—she had pushed harder, putting more space between them, forcing Emerson to push harder to keep up.

There had been little to no talking from the time Emerson had picked her up until now. Cassie wasn't sure what to say. No, that was so not true. That was a total lie. She knew exactly what she wanted to say. There were so many things she wanted to say.

Why didn't you mention you had a girlfriend?
How long have you been together?
Why did she go back home so soon?
Do you live together?

And most importantly, *Why didn't you mention you had a girlfriend?*

Cassie shook her head and pushed harder.

Their last water break was almost an hour ago, and she was ready to stop. Thank god they were nearly to the parking area, as Cassie was reasonably sure her lungs were about to explode in her chest. She stood up on the bike once again—a position she was in more often than not on this trail—and pushed with all she had until the path broke free of trees and spit her out onto blessed asphalt. She squeezed her brake handle and came to a stop for the first time in what felt like hours, swung her leg over and off the bike, and flopped down onto the ground like her bones had disintegrated. Only a few seconds behind her, Emerson did the same thing, but did not stop at a sitting position, and instead lay completely out on the ground on her back, her lungs heaving.

"Holy shit," she whispered. "You just tried to kill me."

Cassie surprised herself by laughing, and pulled her water bottle out. "Didn't do a very good job, did I?" She drank deeply, then handed the bottle to Emerson, who seemed in no hurry to sit up and grab her own.

"'A' for effort, though." Emerson took the offered bottle and raised up onto her elbows to drink.

A few cars pulled in and out of the parking lot, which was adjacent to an old-looking building of dull gray brick and concrete that was built right into the side of the mountain. More people trickled out than entered, and Cassie glanced at her watch. It was after four o'clock and at this time of year, with the temperature dropping, the amount of tourists was smaller than a month ago and smaller than it would be a month from now. There was also the sign at the entrance, the one that gave the tourists a hint to what they would see. Or, as in today's case, not see.

Visibility: Zero

Cassie'd had a feeling it would be this way when she woke up that morning to the fast-moving clouds, and she'd actually thought about rescheduling the bike ride to a more palatable weather day. But then she remembered that woman kissing Emerson on the mouth right in front of her and how foolish she'd felt for enjoying their time so much on Halloween, and she decided. *Screw it. If we don't see anything, we don't see anything. She doesn't want to be here anyway.*

Still, this was the best time of year to go up: when there were hardly any tourists. Cassie stood and pulled her bike upright. "What do you say? You up for going to the top?"

Emerson had an arm thrown over her eyes, which she now moved just enough to peek at Cassie. "There's an elevator, right? I don't have to expend much effort to get there, do I?"

Cassie couldn't help but grin. "No, you wimp. No effort at all except walking from here to there." She pointed at the door to the gray building, then held her hand out to Emerson. "Do you need me to carry you? Here, I thought you were this athlete in tip-top shape." She tsked and shook her head, which got exactly the reaction she'd hoped for.

Emerson playfully slapped her hand away. "I can manage, thank you." It took some effort, but she stood and picked up her bike, then followed Cassie across the road to the bike rack to lock the bikes up.

They passed a family of four, as well as an Asian couple and a group of college-age kids leaving as they made their way inside and to the elevator where a young redheaded man stood sentry.

"Hey, Kevin," Cassie said with a grin. "Busy today?"

"Hi, Cassie. No, not really." He pointed to a second sign just like the one outside the entrance. "You're not going to see much up there."

Cassie waved a hand. "That's okay. I promised my friend here we'd go to the top of the mountain and that's what we're doing. Emerson Rosberg, this is Kevin Stiles."

Kevin's eyes widened slightly as he held out his hand to Emerson. "Wow. It's great to meet you, Ms. Rosberg."

"Please. Emerson." Emerson shook his hand.

"Kevin works one of the slopes as well on ski patrol," Cassie informed her. "He's a great skier."

Emerson gave him a nod as he stepped back and waved them into the elevator. "Enjoy. I think you two will be the only ones up there. Watch your step."

The doors closed them into the small car and they were silent for several moments. Emerson swallowed, then said quietly, "I'm kind of amazed by the number of people who still recognize me."

Cassie looked at her for a long beat before saying, "Emerson. You were famous. You're a legend here. Lake Henry is proud to call you its own. The people here love and respect you. Don't you see that?"

With a shrug, Emerson wet her lips, but said nothing more.

The doors slid open and the two stepped out of the sheltered area onto the rock surface of the top of the mountain. The clouds were thick and there wasn't much to see aside from the trees that covered the sides of that mountain and the steps down that had a rope "fence" along them. Emerson pointed at them.

"Oh," Cassie replied as she carefully stepped along the rocks. "Yeah. People can walk down the steps if they don't want to take the elevator."

Even though they couldn't see much, there was something peaceful about having the top of the mountain to themselves, even for a few minutes.

Cassie inhaled deeply, blew it out, and asked, "Want to sit down?" She pointed to a flat rock that jutted out a ways. "That's my favorite spot."

"Perfect. Show me."

Cassie was cautious in her steps, and Emerson followed behind her, watching her feet. Once out to the farthest part of the rock, Cassie lowered herself to the ground and held out a hand for Emerson, who took it for balance, then sat next to her, close enough so their legs brushed against each other. The clouds swirled around them.

"This is like being in the middle of cotton candy," Emerson said, amusement tinging her voice.

"Except you can't actually eat it. Which sucks."

"Exactly. Bummer."

"I loved that stuff when I was a kid," Cassie said with a grin. "I still love it, but it kills my teeth."

"Mine, too. It's a cruel trick age plays on us."

"One of the many."

They sat in companionable silence for a long moment, just breathing. Just being. The clouds floated by, the air soundless. It was Cassie who broke the silence and she knew she was going to go there only a split second before she did.

"How come you never mentioned your girlfriend?"

There. It was out. Despite the fact that she wished she'd thought about it before opening her mouth, she felt instantly lighter, like she'd finally pushed the weight off her shoulders.

Emerson turned those ice-blue eyes on her and held her gaze. Then she wet her lips again and said simply, "I don't have a girlfriend."

Cassie squinted at her. "Excuse me? Then who was the gorgeous woman who kissed you on the lips the other night and might as well have draped herself all over you?"

Emerson continued to look at her, and one corner of her mouth lifted almost imperceptibly. She raised an eyebrow and said, "If I didn't know any better, I'd say you sound almost jealous."

Cassie's eyes sparked. "I am *not* jealous. I was just curious. Why in the world would I be jealous? I have no reason to be jealous."

Emerson shook her head. "No, you don't. Claire is not my girlfriend. We've been dating for a while, but that's all." She looked down at her hands and then back out into the misty clouds. "Besides, it's over now."

"Oh."

"Yeah."

"I'm sorry," Cassie said, knowing she really wasn't.

"No reason to be."

"Okay." They were quiet, and there was no sound except the gentle wind and the occasional bird. It was a beautifully calm, serene moment. The air was cool, chilly even, but warmth radiated from the place where their bodies touched. Warmth that was rapidly turning to heat. Eventually, Cassie turned to Emerson, cleared her throat, and said softly, "So. No girlfriend."

Emerson turned to her, met her eyes and replied, just as quietly, "No. No girlfriend."

It was just a couple of inches between them, and Cassie needed only to lean slightly to cover them, which she did before she could second-guess herself. Her lips pressed into Emerson's, tentatively. She retreated slightly, not quite sure. But Emerson was sure, and she lifted her hand to the side of Cassie's head, gripped her, and drew her in closer. Their mouths melded, soft lips against soft lips, gently exploring, keeping an uncertain pace at first. Cassie pulled back just a little, looked into Emerson's eyes. Seeing no caution, no trepidation, nothing but the haze of desire, she dove back in, this time more firmly, reveling in the slight saltiness of Emerson's skin. She grabbed the strings hanging off Emerson's hood and pulled her closer. They kissed deeply, thoroughly, lips parting, tongues coming into play. When Cassie felt Emerson's hands in her hair, she let a groan slip out, something Emerson must have liked because she pushed into Cassie more, wrapped an arm around Cassie's waist and pulled her even closer.

God, had anything ever felt this good?

The question zipped through Cassie's mind as she felt warmth on her face, a gentle heat that confused her and caused her to withdraw slowly and open her eyes. Emerson followed suit. What they saw made them both stare.

The clouds had suddenly blown off the mountain, and the sun shone brightly on them. In a matter of moments, their view went from the inside of a cotton ball to a breathtakingly stunning landscape of trees, sky, and mountains as far as they could see. Cassie turned around to look behind them and watched in awe as the bank of clouds simply floated away.

"Oh, my god," Emerson said in a near whisper, as if afraid her voice would spoil the moment.

"I know," Cassie said. "That does *not* happen often."

It was at that moment that she noticed their hands, locked together between them, fingers entwined, as if nothing else had ever been so normal.

"This is beautiful," Emerson said.

"It is. I know I live here and can see this any time, but the truth is I don't get up here often. And when I do, it still takes my breath away every single time."

"I bet."

They sat, hand in hand, hip to hip, shoulders brushing, and simply enjoyed the view. There was no sound from them but their gentle breathing, nothing to pull their attention. Cassie was certain she could sit just like that, next to Emerson, holding her hand, for hours, it was that peaceful.

Off to the right, the top of the ski lift at Mount Hank had become visible, the man-made metal jutting up almost offensively, marring the view of nature. They both turned and saw it at the same moment, and Cassie could feel Emerson stiffen slightly, then turn away from it and look the other way. Cassie studied her face…the almost imperceptible bump on the bridge of her nose, the smooth skin of her cheek, the mole below her left eye, the soft, downy blonde hair along the front of her ear, then down the side of her neck, at least what Cassie could see before the fabric of her sweatshirt obscured the view. She was so drawn to Emerson, it was like a physical pull. It scared her, but at the same time, didn't, which made no sense at all in her head. All she knew for sure was that she wanted to know everything about this woman. Everything.

"Emerson?" she asked quietly.

"Hmm?" Emerson pulled her gaze back to Cassie, the ice-blue eyes suddenly seeming warmer than Cassie thought the first time they'd met.

"What happened?"

Emerson's brows met above her nose. "What do you mean?"

With her eyes, Cassie gestured back to Mount Hank, to the ski lift. "That day. What happened?"

Emerson swallowed audibly and forced her gaze back to the ski lift. She stared at it for a long time, as if that would help her be able to face the memories with less pain and anger. She closed her eyes and stayed that way for so long Cassie thought maybe she'd crossed a line, had asked something she shouldn't have, that Emerson wasn't going to answer at all. Then she spoke. Slowly and deliberately.

"I was an idiot. That's what happened. I was young and I was cocky and I was stupid. I'd done too many runs as it was that day, but my time was bad, and it was screwing with my confidence. I knew I could go faster. I knew it. If I could just do it one more time, take one more run, I'd make it. It was snowing hard and getting worse. My coach wanted to be done. He was worried that I wouldn't be able to see where I was going. My father even wanted to be done, which never happened. But I was so tired of other people telling me what to do. I was almost nineteen, and I decided in that moment, on that mountain, that I was going to be the boss of me. The visibility was terrible, but I was just freaking out about my time. I didn't want to go into the championships with doubts. I needed to be in control. I was going to take one last run, and I was going to best my time."

Cassie barely breathed as she watched Emerson's face. She gazed off into the distance as she talked, the mix of emotions playing out across her features like a movie. Emerson inhaled heavily, let it out slowly, glanced down at her lap, scratched her forehead.

"I was so stupid." Emerson's voice had quieted to barely a whisper. "I don't remember a lot of the run. I was flying, I remember that. I felt so free and alive. I was going to beat my own record; I could feel it. And then…" She shook her head at the memory. "I don't even know what happened. One minute, I was gliding down the run like my skis were rockets, blinded by speed in the swirling snow, and the next, I was lying in a heap, tangled in the snow fence, my legs all twisted. I couldn't feel the pain at the time. I think I went into immediate shock. The rest of it is kind of a blur."

Cassie shook her head, murmured, "My god."

"I remember bits and pieces. My dad's face in mine, shouting at me, except I couldn't hear him. The ski patrol loading me up on their stretcher. The snow blowing hard, landing on my face as I lay there. I have no recollection at all of the ambulance ride or the first day in the hospital. They rushed me into surgery immediately. My knee was destroyed."

The lump in Cassie's throat wouldn't go down, no matter how many times she swallowed. The thought of what Emerson must have gone through, watching her dreams slip slowly away while she lay there immobile had to have been heart wrenching, and Cassie's eyes welled up in sympathy.

"Over the next year, I had three more surgeries. Pins, metal, plates. My dad took me all over. The best hospitals. The best orthopedic surgeons." Emerson smiled bitterly. "I'd made a real mess of things. It was pretty clear, despite how kind and smiling the doctors and nurses were, that my skiing career was over. Just like that. One run. One stupid teenage mistake." She shook her head. "When I finally came back here, I couldn't face anybody. My father made it clear that he had no reason to stick around either. My mother fussed over me so much I wanted to scream. I'm sure I did. The shaking heads…the questioning eyes asking how I could have been so reckless. How could I crush the dreams of Lake Henry doing something so selfishly stupid? And the pity…" She closed her eyes and shuddered. "The stares of pity were the absolute worst. I couldn't take it. Everybody who looked at me was just so…disappointed."

"They felt awful for you," Cassie said quietly.

"I know, but it made me feel like a leper. Like a huge failure. Like they were all whispering behind their hands, 'That's Emerson Rosberg…she had such potential…' I have never cried so much in my life as I did those six months I was stuck in the house recovering. I could have been out and about a lot sooner, but I just couldn't bring myself to face anybody."

"So you left."

"I did. I had never failed at anything in my life. Ever. So I ran." Emerson's voice was tinged with defensiveness. "It was all I could do if I wanted to keep my sanity."

Cassie nodded slowly, trying to understand, but she was unable to picture herself leaving her entire life and family behind. "Why Los Angeles?"

Emerson laughed without humor. "It was as far as I could go from here and still be in the U.S. And my dad was there on and off. Since he was familiar with the city, he helped me get settled before jetting off to his next adventure. And his next wife."

"Your mom must have been crushed when you left." Cassie said it gently, trying hard not to sound accusatory, because she knew firsthand that Caroline had indeed been crushed. She missed her daughter terribly.

"I wanted her to come with me."

That was news to Cassie. "You did?"

Emerson turned to meet her gaze. "Of course I did. I didn't intend to just run away from *her*. I intended to run away from this town. These mountains." She pointed at the ski lift. "That. I'd hoped that she'd come, too."

It was so interesting to see it all from a different angle. Cassie had never thought about the possibility of Emerson not actually wanting to leave her mother behind. She was pretty sure the rest of the town hadn't either. As far as most people were concerned, Emerson had run away and left Lake Henry and Caroline behind without so much as a glance over her shoulder.

"But she always said that Lake Henry was in her blood, that she was part of it and it was part of her."

Cassie nodded, having heard Caroline say that exact thing. She'd nodded then, too, because she felt exactly the same way.

"And I think I understood that," Emerson went on. "But I couldn't share it. I didn't want to. Everywhere I turned in this town, I saw failure and disappointment."

"And you do understand that that's your issue, right?" Cassie squeezed Emerson's hand in her own, kept her voice gentle. "That it's not reality? That nobody in Lake Henry saw you as a failure?"

Emerson cocked her head, her expression skeptical.

Cassie held up a hand, palm forward. "I get the pity thing. I do think people felt terrible about what happened to you, and keeping that expression off your face is hard. But nobody saw you as a failure, Emerson. Nobody."

"And you know everybody in town?" Emerson asked with a chuckle.

Cassie gave the same answer she'd given last time. "Pretty much, yeah." She was serious. "People didn't know how to approach you. I remember. I was sixteen at the time. They didn't know you; you were this familiar stranger, this untouchable, revered piece of our town. Nobody knew what to say, so they kept their distance, gave you space. But when you left, we lost our tragic hero."

Emerson studied her, then hummed a response and was quiet.

They sat in comfortable silence for a long while after that. The sun sank lower in the sky and the breeze picked up, but neither of them was in a hurry to move. The change in weather had brought the tourists back and soon there were another dozen people milling around, ooo-ing and ahh-ing and taking pictures of the view and of each other. All it took was a shared glance to understand it was time to go.

They stood up together, their hands falling back down to their sides.

CHAPTER SIXTEEN

AT SEVENTY-THREE, MARY O'Connor was no spring chicken. This was a fact that became clearer to her each morning as her muscles ached and her bones crackled and ground together while she hauled herself out of bed promptly at six a.m. Not that she even needed the alarm clock since Caroline died. She was awake long before the alarm. Some nights, she'd gotten no sleep at all. She'd simply lain in bed and vacillated between being angry that Caroline was gone and being absolutely devastated.

Had she been this emotional when her husband, Bill, had passed away? She wondered this often, and had no idea why. Honestly, her brain had begun to take strange pathways at night, especially if she made it past one or two o'clock without sleeping. She wondered about Bill, about where he was, if there really was a life beyond death. She wondered if she made the right choice to not have children, especially now that she was alone. She wondered if she should have traveled more often, seen more of the world instead of being so completely content to stay in her little Adirondack Mountain town.

Mostly, she wondered what would happen next. Emerson would sell the inn. She was certain of that. What other option was there? She could leave it open, let Mary run it, hire one or two other people, and check in from afar. But that wasn't Emerson. She hated this town, hated being here. Frankly, Mary was surprised she'd stuck around this long. More than a week. Nearly two! It was shocking. If only she'd thought to make this long a visit while Caroline was still alive.

Caroline.

The tears started again, and she wiped them away angrily as she washed her face in the small bathroom sink, then chose her clothes for the day. She lived barely a quarter of a mile down the lake from the inn, so she didn't need a lot of time to get herself up and ready before walking down the cobblestone path to the inn's office, the smell of Caroline's famous blueberry muffins catching her nose before she even opened the door.

God, she missed that woman. Her best friend, despite their age difference. People tended to think Mary was younger than she actually was, when in reality, there was actually a sixteen-year gap between the two women. Still, Mary never thought of Caroline as a daughter. She was a friend, the best one she'd ever have. How was she going to go on without her?

Bracing herself against the bathroom wall, she slowly sank down to the toilet seat and allowed herself a good cry. This had become the regular morning routine. Get out of bed, brush her teeth, wash her face, cry her eyes out, get on with her day. She expected it to be better by now, though that was probably silly. She had quite literally lost her best friend. That wasn't something one recovered from quickly, especially at this age.

When she was finished, she pulled herself together, got dressed, filled Bill's old green travel mug with coffee, and locked her little house behind her.

It was November, and the smell of fall was melding into the smell of winter. There was no doubt. The earthy scent of leaves and wet dirt filled her nostrils, a smell she'd loved her whole life. The trees were almost bare, and pretty soon, the mountainsides would be brown, then white. Many people mourned the loss of summer, the leaching of all color from the trees, reminiscent of death in many ways. Not Mary. She loved the impending winter. Hell, you couldn't really stay in Lake

Henry full-time if you didn't. Many locals despised the tourists, but Mary enjoyed them. She and Caroline would laugh over the various guests at the inn, try to figure out their stories. She loved talking to people from faraway places, and they got a lot of them. Last year, they'd had a couple from New Zealand, and the year before, a man from Turkey. There were also countless guests who'd returned yearly, over and over again, a testament to how Caroline ran the place, how she took care of her guests.

Now, that would all change.

She pulled her coat tightly around her as an unexpected chill shook her body.

Mary greeted various neighbors as she walked, nodded a hello to Joan Norris sitting on her side deck despite the cold of the morning, waved to cars that drove past. She knew almost all the locals. How could she not? She'd lived in Lake Henry her entire life, and she would die here, and she was okay with it. Content. She'd never wanted more.

But that was supposed to happen first. She was supposed to go *before* Caroline.

Okay, maybe she *did* think of Caroline as a bit of a daughter every now and then.

The smell of blueberry muffins was the first thing Mary noticed as she slid her key into the lock of the main office, and for an instant, she almost believed it had all been a dream, that Caroline had not died, that she was in the kitchen right now making muffins for their guests. Boy would they laugh about this later today!

But no. It wasn't Caroline making muffins. It was Emerson, and she glanced up and smiled at Mary when she walked in. "Good morning."

Mary stood and simply blinked. It was all so surreal. Emerson there in the kitchen. Emerson already dressed and baking. Emerson saying good morning. Mary cleared her throat and found her voice. "Good morning," she replied, moving to the sink to leave her mug there.

"I was up early and came in here to start the coffee. I thought I might as well throw in a batch of muffins." She gestured to the freezer. "You're almost out. I'll make some more this afternoon."

Then she smiled, and for a split second she looked so much like Caroline that Mary almost burst into tears right then. But she held it together, swallowed twice, and nodded once. "Okay." Before she could say any more, a polite bark sounded from the front desk. Then the kitchen door opened and Gordie came in like a shot, his entire body wagging with joy at not one, but *two*, people in the kitchen he could lavish his love on. It was amazing how quickly the dog could elevate her mood, and Mary felt the corners of her mouth pull up into a smile as she squatted slowly down to Gordie's level and let him shower her with kisses. Her heart felt instantly lighter.

"Good morning," Cassie said cheerfully from the doorway.

Mary looked up to see her smiling across the kitchen at Emerson, who was smiling back. All this smiling. It was strange. Not for Cassie. That girl was rarely without a smile. But the *way* she was smiling, and the *recipient* of that smile, that was strange.

"Morning," Emerson said back. "Muffin?"

"I thought you'd never ask." Cassie crossed the kitchen and took a warm blueberry muffin from Emerson's outstretched hand, their fingers lingering a titch longer than necessary, their gazes holding tightly to each other.

Hmm, Mary thought as she stood, her knees cracking and popping, the sound so loud it actually pulled Cassie's attention.

"Mary, have you been taking your arthritis medicine?" she asked as she stretched out a hand to help.

"Yes, Mother, I have," Mary replied with a laugh.

"Hey, don't you smart mouth me," Cassie said, pointing at her and grinning. She took a bite of her muffin, made some noises of enjoyment, and gave Emerson a thumbs up. "How are your legs today?" she asked.

Emerson grimaced. "Let's just say I'm really glad there are no stairs in the cottage."

Cassie laughed, then took another bite of her muffin. Once it was down, she turned to Mary and said, "I have a couple hours and came to help. What can I do?"

Mary gestured for her to follow into the front room. Looking over her shoulder, she saw Cassie look back at Emerson.

"I'll find you later," Cassie said, pointing at her.

"I'm counting on it," was Emerson's playful reply.

Uh-oh, Mary thought this time. It wasn't that both girls were lesbians. Mary had made her peace with that long ago. She didn't understand it, but she was a woman who enjoyed harmony and love and she didn't see what all the fuss was about when people protested same-sex couples. Why just last night, she'd seen an ad for a new reality show that had straight couples marrying at first sight. How did that not mess with the "sanctity of marriage," but two men or two women who loved each other deeply did? Mary would never understand that; she and Caroline had had many a discussion about it. But no, that wasn't what worried her. What worried her was that Caroline would not like this. Emerson and Cassie? Oh, no, she wouldn't like this at all. Caroline wouldn't be worried about Emerson, her daughter. She wouldn't be trying to protect her daughter from Cassie. No, Mary knew Caroline well, and she was very certain about this fact: Caroline would be trying to protect *Cassie* from her daughter. Emerson was too much like her father, and poor Cassie didn't stand a chance.

They were interrupted twice by people checking out, but nearly half an hour later, Mary had gone over a quick list with Cassie regarding rooms needing to be cleaned and laundry needing to be washed, and returned to rooms awaiting new guests. Cassie nodded, taking it all in, asking few questions.

"You do know how much I appreciate all the help you've been giving me, especially since Caroline's been gone, right?" Mary asked quietly, her eyes on the computer screen.

Cassie squeezed her shoulder. "I do."

Mary turned and made eye contact. "I mean it."

"I know."

The kitchen door swung open and Emerson peeked out at them. "I've got a batch of muffins in. I'm going to grab a quick shower. I should be back before they're done, but if you hear the timer, could you just take them out?"

Mary waved in acknowledgement without looking back at Emerson. When she glanced at Cassie, Cassie's eyes were glued to the now-closed kitchen door. Mary slid the two keys for the empty rooms across the counter to her and said simply and poignantly, "Careful there."

Cassie blinked at her, but said nothing.

"Oh, that's no big deal at all," Mindy Sullivan was saying as she examined the front tire of the bike Emerson was renting from her.

"You're sure? Because I don't want to screw up your merchandise. I'll gladly pay for any damage."

Mindy shook her head. "No way. It's fine. I'm going to replace the rim. No problem. Happens all the time."

"I didn't realize that path was as rough as it was."

"The one up Jones Mountain?" At Emerson's nod, Mindy chuckled. "Yeah, that one's a bear. I'm surprised you didn't do more damage than bend the rim. Did you make it all the way?"

"I did. Just ask my quads. They've been quietly crying all morning."

Mindy looked at her with even more respect. "Nice. You're in great shape then. Most people stop about three quarters of the way up and have to walk the rest of the way." She raised her hand. "Me included."

Emerson was still inexplicably basking in that compliment when the bell over the door rang and a vaguely familiar looking young man walked in.

"Hey, Mind. My chain here?"

"Got it this morning," Mindy said and disappeared into the back room.

The man smiled at Emerson. "Hi again."

Emerson squinted at him. "I'm sorry, we've met, right?"

"Well, sort of, yes. On Halloween. You were with Cassie and her niece and nephew."

His face finally clicked for her. "Oh! You sold me the cider."

"I did." He held out his hand. "Jake Collins. It's nice to officially meet you."

"Emerson Rosberg," Emerson said as she grasped his large hand.

"Oh, I know."

Mindy returned, handed a package to Jake. "Of course he knows who you are. You're our famous skier. Careful, he's going to try to recruit you to work for him this season."

Jake laughed, but nodded in agreement. "She's right. Don't know how long you're staying, but we'd be happy to have somebody of your stature at our slope. You'd bring in the customers, that's for sure."

Emerson now remembered Cassie saying something about Jake working at one of the ski slopes. "Ah, well, thanks for the offer, Jake. I'm not staying, though."

"Too bad," Jake said, disappointed.

"Emerson's got herself a life in the City of Angels, Jake. I don't think we compare with our one main road, subzero temperatures, and tiny shops." Mindy said it with a chuckle as she clicked keys on her computer, and though there was no malice or sarcasm in the statement at all, Emerson still felt a little sting at the words.

Later, after the bike had been repaired and she'd taken several very slow laps around Lake Henry, she still wondered about Mindy's words. Why did they bother her? Were they true? She couldn't seem to shake the feeling they left with her.

It was too cold to be riding. She'd made that observation when she'd been too far away to turn back, so she'd completed her ride, more for her head than her body. Now that she was back in the cottage, her hands were like ice, and her ears were numb. The remote for the fireplace sat on the coffee table, and she clicked it on as she passed. In the bathroom, she ran the bath water as she stripped out of her biking clothes, deciding to soak in a hot tub a little earlier in the day than she normally would. She'd just settled into the nearly-scalding water and closed her eyes when her cell rang.

With a sigh, she picked it up to look at the number, then answered. "Hello, evil stepmother."

"Hey there, pain in my ass."

"Twice in less than two weeks? To what do I owe this pleasure?"

Marlena's soft laughter rumbled over the phone line. "I'm just checking on my ex-stepdaughter. Is that a crime?"

"Not at all. You know I'm always happy to hear from you."

"How's it going? You doing okay?"

"Well, let's see. I just took a glorious ride around the lake on a bike—even though I turned blue from the cold—and I am now soaking in a hot bathtub, which is delicious. If I lean slightly to my left and crane my neck a bit, I can see the lake out the window from here. The only thing missing is a glass of wine, but that's because it's not even dinner time yet and I don't want to be that single woman who drinks wine in the afternoon." She finished with a soft laugh.

"Sounds like a nice day."

"It was. Oh, and I made blueberry muffins this morning."

There was a pause on the line, then Marlena said, "I'm sorry, do I have the wrong number? I was looking for Emerson Rosberg, city girl, lover of all things warm and sunny, can barely fix herself a bowl of cereal in the kitchen. *That* Emerson Rosberg."

"Ha, ha. Very funny."

"Seriously, Emmy, you sound good. Are you?"

Emerson inhaled deeply, let it out slowly. "It's strange being here in her house. I admit that. It smells like her. Isn't that weird? I don't even know what the smell is, only that it's her." A lump threatened to close her throat, and she was quiet.

"I think that's perfectly normal." Marlena's voice was tender. "Smell is a very powerful sense. Even now, whenever I smell Old Spice aftershave, I instinctively look around for my grandpa, and he's been gone for ten years."

"I should have been here more." Emerson's voice caught. "I was a terrible daughter."

"Oh, Em."

"It's true. Everybody here tells me how wonderful she was and how proud of me she was, and I couldn't manage to give her more than an occasional phone call." *Where the hell was this coming from?* she wondered, swiping angrily at the tear running down her cheek. Marlena was the only person in the world she felt safe enough to talk to about such things, but Emerson had surprised even herself.

"I know it seems that way, but you can't beat yourself up over something you can't ever change. That's a good way to drive yourself crazy. You just need to enjoy your time there, in your mother's space. Soak it in." She waited patiently while Emerson sniffled and pulled herself together. Then finally, she asked, "Blueberry muffins, huh?"

"I kick ass at blueberry muffins."

"I can't believe you never made those for me."

"Next time I see you. Promise."

"I'm going to hold you to that. So, what else have you been up to?"

"I took a great bike ride up Jones Mountain yesterday with Cassie." She described to Marlena how the view had gone from zero visibility to perfectly clear. "We could've sat there for hours. It was gorgeous."

"This is the same woman you were with on Halloween?"

"Yup. I bent the rim on the bike, but Mindy fixed it, and while I was at the bike shop, a guy from one of the ski slopes offered me a job." Emerson laughed at the memory. "It was bizarre, but in a cool way."

"Sounds like it. Making any progress on packing?"

"A little, but not enough." Emerson sighed. "I don't know why. I just can't seem to get moving."

"It's not an easy job. You'll get to it when you're ready."

"You think so? Because I can't stay here forever. I've got to get back home."

"To what?"

Marlena's question surprised Emerson into momentary silence. She studied the toes of her right foot as they peeked out of the surface of the water.

Marlena went on. "Sounds like you've got more going on there than you ever had in L.A. You should hear yourself. I've never heard you sound this...healthy."

Emerson furrowed her brow. "What are you talking about?"

"Em. You've made friends. You've got a cute little house to stay in. You've even got a job offer. And let's not forget the love interest. I'm making air quotes around that, just so you know."

Emerson shook her head even though Marlena couldn't see it. "You're wrong."

"Am I?"

"Yes." She sounded touchier than she meant to.

"Okay. I'm wrong then. But if I am, you have to do something for me."

"What's that?"

"Be careful."

"What does that mean?" Emerson asked in confusion.

"With Cassie. You like her. I can tell. I know you, remember?" Marlena's voice was firm now, as she pulled out her I'm-your-stepmother-not-your-pal voice that she used on Emerson when she was younger and needed a little straightening out. "And I'm guessing she probably likes you, too. But if you have no plans of staying, you need to tread carefully or you're going to hurt that girl. Be careful. That's all I'm saying." With a playful lilt in her voice, she said, "Your history does not show evidence of longevity, sweetie. You're like your dad that way…a pretty new girl every six months or so."

Emerson let that sit for a moment, and suddenly all the lightness of the day evaporated until she felt heavy again. "Okay." It was all she could think of to say in response.

At her change in tone, Marlena's volume increased a bit as she said, "Honey, I'm just teasing you."

"I know," Emerson said, and forced a chuckle as she tried to keep things light, but Marlena's words sat heavily in the air.

They chatted for a short while longer, but it wasn't the same. Emerson was monosyllabic and Marlena apparently became tired of trying to milk words from her. They hung up with Marlena promising to check back in a day or two. Emerson was left soaking in the bathtub for a long while. The water went from hot to tepid, then from tepid to almost chilly before she shook herself out of her thoughts and lifted herself from the tub. Her fingertips were wrinkled, and she was no longer relaxed. In fact, she felt just the opposite. Stressed. Tense. Irritated. Trapped.

Trapped.

That was a big one, one that didn't sit well with her, and she suddenly felt the urge to set things in motion, finally, so she could get the hell out of Lake Henry. She needed to pack. She needed to sit down with Klein and Cross and bang out the sale of her mother's properties. She needed to forget about the fact that Mary and Jack would probably lose their jobs. She needed to roll her eyes at the idea of working at a ski slope. She needed to not think about Cassie. Or Cassie's rich brown eyes. Or Cassie's infectious laugh. Or Cassie's soft lips.

No! Stop it.

Scrubbing the towel over her face roughly, she put her thoughts in order, picked up her cell, and dialed the neighbor who'd been taking care of her apartment. She wanted to let him know she'd be home soon. She needed to get things taken care of and get the hell out of this godforsaken town.

She'd stayed too long already.

Emerson was quiet during the car ride, but Cassie was beginning to learn that sometimes, that's how she was. Not everybody talked as much as Cassie did. Not everybody needed to process things out loud. Michael had reminded her of that several times during their relationship, and at first, Cassie was stung. Eventually, she realized that he was simply stating a fact, and she made an effort to be more cognizant of how others might be different from her. So instead of prodding her to talk, they drove in silence for a while, Gordie standing up in the back seat, his whole body thrumming with anticipation of this twice-monthly trip.

The Cotter's Ridge Rehab Center was about thirty-five minutes from Lake Henry. Every other week, Cassie borrowed her mother's car and she and Gordie piled in and drove to Cotter's Ridge where they spent an hour or two with the patients. Gordie was a certified therapy dog, and the residents at the center always seemed to light up whenever he set foot in the door.

She'd called Emerson earlier and was instantly aware of a severe mood change on her part. After some prodding, she'd managed to glean that Emerson was at a loss at what to do with all Caroline's clothes. Cassie suggested she bring some of them to the rehab center, as they worked with many different hospitals and organizations who were sure to have use for them.

So now, they sat in near-silence, the only sound being the low hum of the radio as Sara Bareilles sang mournfully about Manhattan.

At the center, lights shone brightly, and people milled around, medical staff in colorful scrubs, residents using canes, walkers, or wheelchairs. Many of them waved at Cassie when she and Gordie entered. Emerson followed.

"Hey, Cassie." A tall, African-American woman in bright orange scrubs raised a hand in greeting, then came over to them, immediately squatting to give love to Gordie.

"Hi there, Nina." She gave them a few moments, then said, "This is my friend, Emerson Rosberg. She has several bags of clothes out in the car for donation. Can you help her get them to the right place?"

Nina stood and shook Emerson's hand. "Of course. We can always find people or places who need the donation." With an arm outstretched toward the door, she said, "Lead the way."

Cassie handed the keys to Emerson. "We'll start making our rounds." With a tug on Gordie's leash, she headed down a hall. "Come on, boy."

For the next hour and a half, Cassie took Gordie from room to room. Some people wanted to chat. Some didn't want to say anything at all; they just wanted to pet Gordie. It always amazed Cassie, the way they would instantly calm, the way running a hand along his thick, soft fur could relax a person who might be on edge. Countless studies proved it to be true, but it was still an amazing thing to behold.

And Gordie, bless him, seemed to know why he was there. He tempered his excitement, his jumping, his licking, and remained calmly focused. He would hop up on a bed and lie down or sit next to a wheelchair and just…be present while he was scratched and stroked and talked to. Not for the first time, Cassie thanked the universe for sending her Gordie.

It wasn't until they were wrapping up that Cassie realized Emerson had not caught up to them, and she felt guilty for not seeking her out. She and Gordie often lost track of time when they were at the rehab center, and she wondered if Emerson was sitting in the car, annoyed and waiting for her. She was grimacing at the thought when she turned the corner to the common room and saw the back of a familiar blonde head sitting next to an old man in a wheelchair. Very little hair sprouted from his head, and what was there was a powdery white. He had one leg wrapped in a knee brace and propped straight out in front of him. Something made Cassie stop there and listen rather than interrupt.

"You're kidding," the man said. "You're too young."

"Apparently not," Emerson replied with a grin.

"What happened? If you don't mind my asking."

A shrug. "Skiing accident. I was dumb. You?"

"Fell off a ladder. I was dumb, too."

Cassie smiled at the sound of Emerson's warm chuckle as she asked, "How's it going?"

"Hurts like a son of a bitch," the man growled. "Pardon my French."

"It'll get better. But I'll tell you this: you have to do the exercises the physical therapist gives you. You *have* to."

The man waved a dismissive hand and scoffed. "That punk is trying to kill me. I know it."

"It feels like it, doesn't it? I know what you mean." Emerson shook her head. "I called my PT Nurse Ratched. I swore to god, her goal every session was to see how quickly she could make me cry. The woman was a sadist."

The man grunted as he gave a nod.

Emerson went on. "But." She stopped until the man looked at her. "I did the exercises. I was determined that she was not going to win the battle, that I would eventually be able to walk with no problems. And *then* I would kick her ass. Pardon my French."

"And what happened?"

Emerson stood up, walked to the far wall of the room and back. "I can walk with no problem."

"Did you kick her ass?"

A smile slowly spread across Emerson's face. "I did not. Know why?"

"Why?"

"Because the first time I walked like this, Nurse Ratched cried."

"She what?"

"She actually cried. I kid you not. She was so happy for me that she got all teary." Emerson sat back down and lowered her voice. "You can't really kick somebody's ass when they're crying."

The man shook his head. "Nah, you can't. Just makes you look like the asshole. Pardon my French."

Emerson laughed then, and Cassie felt it in the pit of her stomach. It was a joyous sound that tickled her heart, and she was immediately sad she didn't hear it more often. Ice-blue eyes caught Cassie's brown ones, and she gave a little wave.

"My ride's here," she said, standing. "You take care of yourself, Mr. Kendall. Okay?" She pointed a finger at him. "Do the exercises."

Mr. Kendall gave Emerson a salute. "Yes, ma'am." He grasped her arm before she could walk away. "You know, I'm going to be here for a few weeks. Stop by again if you're in the neighborhood."

"I will." Emerson gave his hand a pat, then walked up to Cassie and Gordie. "Ready to go?"

Cassie nodded, and they filed out the front door, waving to Nina as they left.

Once they got situated in the car and were on their way back to Lake Henry, Cassie spoke. "That was pretty amazing."

"What? Gordie and the patients? I'm not surprised at all that he's a great therapy dog."

"No, silly. You and that man."

Emerson furrowed her brow before catching on. "Oh, Mr. Kendall? He had a knee replacement last week."

"You were great with him."

Emerson shrugged.

"I mean it." Cassie laid a hand on Emerson's arm to emphasize as she repeated, "You were great with him. Not everybody has that. Building a rapport with somebody who's depressed or in pain...it's not easy."

"I guess all my time in rehab and PT helps me. It was a long time ago, but I can still understand where they're coming from, what they're feeling, how angry they can get. I think it helps to talk to somebody who actually *gets it*, you know? Instead of people who are just trying to pacify you." She was quiet for a beat before adding, "I know the medical staff means well. The doctors, the nurses, the physical therapists. But nobody can *really* understand that kind of pain and frustration unless they've actually been there, actually experienced it for themselves."

The tone of protection in her voice had Cassie glancing at her, at the clean lines of her face, at the slight downturn of her eyebrows, at her hands in her lap, long fingers folded together, and she felt something inside. Something warm, something tender. Cassie wanted to touch her face, to run her fingertips along Emerson's smooth skin. When Emerson met her eyes, she smiled gently and returned her gaze to the road, keeping her hands on the steering wheel.

"Thanks for bringing me with you," Emerson said quietly.

"Thanks for coming." This time, Cassie gave in and reached across to take one of Emerson's hands in her own. To her delight, Emerson entwined their fingers and squeezed.

CHAPTER SEVENTEEN

FRIED CHICKEN WAS CHRIS'S specialty. Or it was the only thing her kids would eat. Cassie wasn't sure. All she knew was that every time she came to dinner, Chris made fried chicken. Which was okay because it was fantastic.

Trevor had come in from hockey practice forty minutes ago. Thirty minutes ago, he'd turned on the shower. It still ran.

"How long do fourteen-year-old boys spend in the shower these days?" Cassie asked her sister, and popped a baby carrot into her mouth as she chopped vegetables for salad.

Chris rolled her eyes. "Don't get me started. I don't even want to know what he does in there." She made a face. "If I have to choose between him taking hour-long showers or not showering at all, I'll put up with the showers. Did you smell him when he came in?"

Cassie grimaced. "I did."

"Yeah, nothing can wilt fresh flowers or peel the paint off the walls like teenage boy sweat. You should smell his sneakers."

"I'll pass, thanks."

Chris topped off their wine glasses. "So how's life? I feel like I haven't seen you since Halloween."

"That's because you haven't." Cassie grinned and touched her glass to her sister's. "Life is good. Practice is going well. I've got a couple new girls who aren't bad."

"Enough for a team this year?"

Cassie gave a snort. "Of course not. They'll play with the regional team."

"Hockey isn't really a girl's game."

"Really? We're going to go there? Again?" The twinkle in Cassie's eye took any sting out of the words. It was an age-old argument they'd had since they were kids and Cassie had wanted to play on the boys' team.

Chris laughed. "No, let's not go there. You know I'm right. I'll accept that." She ducked as a baby carrot flew by her head. "Hey! Don't let my kids see you throwing food. They'll think they can too."

They continued working in tandem to prepare dinner. Chris's husband was working a late night, so it was just the sisters and the kids. Cassie loved having dinner there. She loved the atmosphere of the happy home, so much like their parents' house where they grew up. Chris had done a fabulous job raising her kids and maintaining her household. It wasn't large, but it was roomy enough, and the love was palpable. Cassie wanted nothing more than the same kind of life Chris had: happy marriage, a home, love.

Chris glanced out the window over the sink as she stood at the stove turning chicken in the pan. "It's getting dark fast. Man, fall flew by."

"I know. I feel like the leaves turned colors for a week and that was that."

"So much for the fall tourist season." Chris shrugged. "I heard the view from Jones Mountain has been less than stellar as well. Bad for business, Mother Nature. Bad for business."

"We had a great view the other day," Cassie commented, shucking the seeds and membranes from a green pepper.

"We? Who's we?"

"Me and Emerson. We rode the bike trail up Jones yesterday. Then we took the elevator up to the top. The visibility sign said zero, so we weren't expecting much. We got up there and the clouds were pretty thick. We sat down and all of a sudden, they just blew away. Literally, they just blew away, and we could see for miles. It was unbelievable."

Chris was nodding, but the expression on her face was... odd. Cassie chose to ignore it.

"Then she went with me to the rehab center. You should have seen her with this old man who was having knee issues. She was amazing. She just...*talked* to him. Like, person to person instead of talking down to him. It was awesome."

Chris continued to say nothing as Cassie squinted at her.

"What?"

"What what?" Chris replied.

"What's that face for?"

"I'm not making a face."

"You are totally making a face."

"Am not."

"Chris." Cassie set the knife down and cocked her head sideways.

Chris sighed, but kept her eyes on the chicken. "I guess I'm just wondering what you're doing."

"What do you mean?"

"With Emerson. What are you doing?"

Cassie shrugged nonchalantly. "Nothing. I've spent some time with her. Is that a crime?" She sounded way more defensive than she'd hoped, and she knew immediately that her sister had picked up on it.

"Of course not. I just want you to be careful."

"Of what?"

Chris looked at her now, exasperated. "Of *her*. I know you, Cassandra. You fall fast and you fall hard and you're already well on your way with this woman."

Cassie picked the knife back up, turned her back to Chris, and chopped peppers viciously. "You don't know what you're talking about."

"Fine, Cass. Fine. You're absolutely right. I don't know what I'm talking about. I haven't known you for all of your twenty-eight years. Let's go with that. Just keep this in mind: she leaves. She runs away. You know this. It's what she does. Don't think for a second she won't do it to you."

Izzy came running into the kitchen at that moment, which was a good thing because Cassie had no reply. Instead, she looked down at her little niece and asked if she'd washed her hands for dinner yet.

"Nope. Will you help me?"

"Sure." Anything to get out of the kitchen and away from Chris's words.

Too bad they hung with her no matter which room she moved to.

She leaves. She runs away.

Did Cassie expect anything other than that?

Of course not. Of course she didn't. She knew all about Emerson. She'd been friends with Caroline for years, damn it. Caroline always talked about her daughter, about how much she wished Emerson would visit more, about how much she despised Lake Henry and all it represented for her, and about how she'd probably never come back. Ever. Because she left. She ran away.

It's what she does.

That was fine. That was absolutely fine with Cassie. She wasn't stupid, for Christ's sake. Did people think she was? Did they think she was unaware of what was going on? Did they think she wasn't treading carefully? She liked Emerson. So what? It didn't mean there was anything more than that.

Cassie looked up from the sink into the mirror. Her brain tossed her a flash of memory, she and Emerson sitting atop Jones Mountain, kissing deeply, the warm wet of it... Cassie closed her eyes, groaned quietly, and muttered an F bomb. The tiny gasp from her hip startled her, and she looked down into Izzy's horrified eyes.

"You said a *really* bad word," her niece whispered.

Cassie pressed her lips together in a straight line and held Izzy's gaze. "I know," she whispered just as quietly. "I know I did. I'm sorry. But I really, really meant it. Can it be our little secret?"

Izzy gave it serious thought before nodding once. "Okay. But don't say it again."

"I won't. Promise." Cassie shook her head, reached for the towel to dry her hands, then followed the little girl back to the kitchen. She kept her mouth shut tightly, but the same word echoed through her head just as loudly as if she'd been reciting it proudly with every step.

She was quiet at dinner. Too quiet, she knew by the way Chris kept glancing at her. Trevor was his usual, sullen teenage self, but the littler kids teased and chattered on, unaware of the tension between their mother and their aunt. Chris listened to them and responded to them as only a mother who has mastered the art of multi-tasking can, because she kept just as much attention on her younger sister across the table. Cassie knew she should say something, let Chris off the hook; it was obvious she was worried she'd pushed Cassie too far. But instead, she let Chris stew a bit, mostly because she was stewing as well and didn't think she should be alone in her misery.

Chris was right about Emerson. If Cassie was going to be truly, brutally honest, she had to admit that. Emerson's track record spoke for itself. And so what? It's not like there was anything between them. They'd kissed. Big deal. They weren't in a relationship. They hadn't even talked about anything remotely close to that. They were friends. That was it.

She rolled that around in her head for a moment, trying it on for size. *Emerson is my friend. My friend. She's my friend. That's all.*

The scoff she made aloud had Chris looking at her yet again.

Were the walls closing in on her?

Emerson lay on the couch in the cottage and wondered at the question. It had grown dark long ago, and yet here she lay. Still. She'd done very little and there seemed to be a battle going on in her head between her conversation with Marlena the day before and her conversation in the car with Cassie last night. Her brain felt weird. Full. Heavy. Confused. And ridiculously tired. How could that be? How could she feel so tired, so drained, just from recalling a couple of conversations? It didn't seem possible.

The blue light on her cell phone had been blinking steadily from the coffee table for the past couple of hours, indicating she had voicemail. Emerson had turned off the sound, not wanting to deal with anything else today. Now, knowing it wouldn't just disappear on its own, she blew out an exaggeratedly loud breath and flopped her arm out to pick up the phone. She dialed in her code and was soon listening to Brenda, her ex-colleague from McKinney Carr.

"Haven't heard from you, Emmy, and wanted to make sure you were doing okay. Listen, I got hired by Jensen Pharmaceuticals and they're still looking for people. I gave them your name and told them I'd have you call. It's a nice setup. Not as big as McKinney Carr, but they seem pretty solid and steady. Anyway, they're familiar with you, they know how great your sales were, and they're interested in you." She rattled off a name and a phone number, along with a website address, and told Emerson she should contact them immediately.

With a put-upon sigh, Emerson skipped to the next message. It was from Claire.

"So, we're done then? Is that it? I was hoping I'd misread the signals you sent so clearly when I left. But you haven't called since, not even to *thank me* for all the work I did while I was there." Her voice was icy. Brittle. Emerson couldn't blame her. "You know, you could have talked to me, Emerson. I thought we had something good. Something that worked well for both of us. But god forbid you get out of your goddamn head once in a while and have a goddamn conversation with somebody. Oh, no. Not Emerson Rosberg, the high priestess of non-emotion. You're such a coward." She was on a roll now. Emerson should have just deleted it without listening to the rest, but for some reason, she felt like she deserved to hear every last, furious, pained word. "I will miss you, Em. I will. I'll miss the great sex we had." Her voice softened slightly. "It *was* great. You thought so, too. I know you did. That was the only time I ever thought you were completely with me, but now I know that was only me hoping. Hoping that you were with me and not off someplace in your head. Someplace else. With somebody else. I could never be sure with you." Claire paused, and Emerson could almost picture her collecting herself, regaining her composure. "I wish you well, Em. I do. I hope you figure it all out. Whatever it is you're looking for, I hope you find it." She paused again, then sighed. "Goodbye, Emerson."

Whatever it is you're looking for.

Was she looking for something? Emerson shook her head, shrugged, not wanting to dwell. But dwell she did.

Whatever it is you're looking for.

"I'm not *looking* for anything," she said to the empty room, and a heat began to spread through her, one that came with anger. She stood up too quickly and had to reach out to steady herself against the head rush that hit after lying down for so long. The only light in the room came from the glowing fireplace, and she decided she liked it that way. Stomping over to the wine rack, she chose an Argentinian Malbec, took it into the kitchen, and opened it. As she poured, she muttered, "High priestess of non-emotion? Really? That's nice, Claire." But she realized she wasn't angry at Claire. She was angry at herself. She'd just listened to two very important voicemail messages, and yet neither of them had much effect on her. Why wasn't she jotting down the name and number of the guy from the pharmaceutical company…what was the name of it again? Jesus, she didn't even retain *that*. Why didn't she feel something, anything over Claire's message? Shouldn't she feel angry? Hurt? Guilty? If nothing else, she *should* feel guilty for the way she'd treated somebody who cared about her.

"What's the matter with me?"

Unsurprisingly, no answer came.

She downed a large swallow of wine and went to the window to gaze out at the lake, almost impossible to make out in the dark. The moon was no more than a sliver of white in the sky, and was sharing very little light with the earth. She could see the outlines of bare branches looming over the water. That's how it was in the Adirondacks, she remembered. One minute, it was fall and then like the snap of fingers, the leaves were gone and winter was closing in. Just like the walls of the tiny cottage.

The anger took hold then. Emerson was suddenly hit with a white-hot feeling of rage that bubbled up from deep inside her. She set the wine glass down on the counter, as she was afraid she might hurl it across the room. Using both hands, she braced herself against the edge of the counter and let her head drop down between her arms.

"What's the matter with me?" she asked again, this time through clenched teeth. Squeezing her eyes closed, she tried to focus. This had only happened once before, when she'd been told the surgeries on her knee had been less successful than predicted and that the doctors wanted to replace the entire thing. Marlena had been around then, and she'd coached Emerson through the fury, talked to her, urged her to search her brain, her heart, and pinpoint exactly what she was angry about, who she was angry with. Marlena told her to find it, take it out, handle it, examine it from all angles until she had full control. She remembered how it had worked then.

What am I angry about? Who am I angry with?

Simple questions, really, but she skipped the easiest one and dug deeper.

My father.

She'd never really admitted to that before. Fredrik hadn't completely abandoned Emerson, but once her potential to be a skiing sensation was gone, he'd lost interest in her. Sure, he called every so often. He told her he loved her. She said it back because it was true. He was her father and she loved him. But since the accident, he hadn't been there for her. At all. He sent her money. He phoned once every month or two. That was about it. She was never first on his list; he was. He always had been. A very clear memory hit her then, one she recalled from her time of rehabilitation, when she'd worked with a physical therapist and ended up in angry tears more often than not, the pain was so excruciating. She remembered lying on a mat, the physical therapist pushing against her artificial knee, forcing her to bend it and twist it. She grit her teeth so hard she was certain she'd cracked a couple molars, and all she wanted was her father to be there, encouraging her. He was the only one who would understand the loss she'd suffered. Her mother was there, but she didn't ski. She didn't really get it. Fredrik would. But he'd jetted off to Sweden to do color commentary on a race and couldn't be bothered to help his daughter while she watched the only thing she ever thought she'd do evaporate before her eyes. And at that moment, she remembered thinking that when she had kids, she would never, ever let them think they weren't first on her list. They would always be first and she'd make it clear to them. She'd sworn it then and she felt even more strongly about it now.

Rocking forward and back slowly, still braced against the counter, she let herself continue to feel the anger. Still not wanting to face the obvious source, she dug some more.

Cassie.

That surprised her, and she furrowed her brows a bit. Why was she angry with Cassie? It was a silly question, because she already knew why, she just didn't want to admit it. Cassie made her think, made her wonder, made her reevaluate. Emerson didn't want to be here. She didn't want to hang out in Lake Henry. She wanted a quick trip. Easy in, easy out. That's how she'd planned it. But then she'd met Cassie. Cassie, who'd been nice to her when Emerson was less than inviting. Cassie, who'd taught her about hockey and made her laugh. Cassie, who'd loved Emerson's mother, who'd acted as a surrogate daughter for Caroline when her real child couldn't be bothered to visit. Cassie, who had kissed her senseless, and then had shown her the most beautiful view Emerson had ever seen.

Cassie, who made her feel.

She remembered holding hands in the car yesterday, how natural and comforting it had felt. Emerson slapped a hand on the counter and actually growled deep in her throat.

Cassie, who made her *feel*.

My mother.

That was the next source of her anger. Not at all surprising, really. Still, the admission caused emotion to roll through Emerson like a storm. She continued to rock forward and back as she felt the tears fill up her eyes, clog her throat. She was angry at her mother for dying on her. Of course she was. It was a perfectly normal and understandable reaction to the death of a parent so young. Emerson gripped the counter so hard her fingers hurt, and the pain in her chest felt like it was going to split her ribcage open. Caroline was gone. She was never coming back. And that admission led to the big one.

Myself.

Swallowing hard, Emerson let that anger continue to roll through, hoping it would abate soon. *I am angry for not being here. I was a lousy kid, and now I will never be able to fix it. I can never make up for my failings as a daughter. My mother is gone and I was not here for her. I was never here for her. And I get to live with that. For the rest of my life, I get to live with that.*

Still clenching her teeth, Emerson let it all sit. She felt nauseous, but she embraced that as well, and simply concentrated on breathing. In...out...in...out. It took several long minutes, but soon, she could feel her racing heart begin to calm. Her grip on the counter slowly eased. Her ragged breathing evened out, and her rocking slowed bit by bit until she was still.

Slowly, she let go of the counter and stood straight. She felt infinitely better. Marlena had been right about facing her anger. Examining it helped. It allowed her to understand it, to pinpoint the sources and figure out why it ate at her. Feeling much better, she picked up her wine and took a small sip. Carrying the glass with her, she went back into the living room and took a seat on the couch. It was still dark, the cottage still lit only by the soft glow of the fire. She sipped again and continued to be still until she felt completely calm.

The blinking blue light caught her eye, and she reached for her phone. A call must have come in while she was busy having her nervous breakdown. Hoping it wasn't more vitriol from Claire, she punched in the numbers and listened as Cassie's gentle, lilting voice spoke to her.

"Hey there. I'm so sorry I didn't get a chance to catch up with you this morning like I had hoped. Today was ridiculous at work. There were a couple of issues that needed my attention and I got stuck there much longer than I expected to. Then I had dinner at my sister's. I'm home now and exhausted. I've got hockey practice in the morning, but maybe we could get together for some coffee or something after that? Okay. Call me back if you get a chance. Oh! I have two tickets to a show next week. My friend Jonathan and his boyfriend can't go and he gave the tickets to me, so I need a date. It's a play, but that's all I know. Tempting, huh?" She chuckled, which was an adorable sound. "I think that's it." A beat. "Call me back, okay? Bye, Emerson." The last two lines were said very softly, almost intimately, and Emerson felt them in the pit of her stomach. And lower.

She quickly erased the voicemail, then sat with the phone against her lips, her eyes staring off into the middle distance, her own taunting voice echoing in her head. *Next week? A date? I don't think so, Cassie. It's time you learned what most people already know about me. I am not the dating kind. I'm just like my father.* Reaching a decision, she hit the Call button, scrolled for a contact, and dialed. She reached voicemail, which she expected, as it was after business hours. At the sound of the beep, she spoke.

"Hi, Brad. It's Emerson Rosberg. I'd like you to set up a meeting for me with Mr. Cross for Monday. I've looked over his offer, and I think I'm ready to sign the papers."

CHAPTER EIGHTEEN

A LIGHT LAYER OF SNOW had fallen overnight. Not really enough for the kids to get excited about the season's first snowfall, but enough to have left a dusting of white on everything in Lake Henry, making the whole town look fresh, clean, and sparkling in the morning sunshine.

Emerson was being a coward and she knew it full well. She was not happy about it, and her sour expression said as much to anybody who looked at her face as she hurried down Main Street to The Sports Outfitter's front door and pulled it open.

It was fairly quiet inside. Popular music emanated from hidden speakers, but the volume was low, as if worrying about disturbing the crisp and gentle morning. Stomping the light flakes of snow off her hikers, Emerson walked toward the back of the main floor where the same vaguely familiar woman she'd seen before stood behind the register focused on the computer screen. Emerson cleared her throat.

"Well, hi there," the woman said cheerfully. "What can I do for you?"

"Um, is Cassie here?"

The woman shook her head. "I'm afraid not. She's coaching hockey practice this morning. She should be back around eleven, though. I'm her mom. Can I give her a message?"

Cassie's mother. Jesus Christ, didn't that just figure? No wonder she looked so familiar. Emerson could see it now, despite the difference in hair color. Cassie's eyes were the same rich brown as her mother's, and the angle of their eyebrows was identical. Their build was also very similar—a confident posture. Glancing down, she noticed they had the exact same hands.

"Emerson?" Cassie's mom prodded when Emerson went for a long moment without speaking. Emerson's eyebrows rose and Cassie's mom chuckled. "Of course I know who you are, honey. Most of the town does. Did you want me to give Cassie a message?"

"Um…" Pulling herself back to the present, Emerson fished in her pocket and pulled out the bright yellow fleece headband Cassie had lent her on Halloween. Emerson had held on to it for…god knew what reason. "This is hers. She let me borrow it. I just wanted to make sure she got it back." She set it on the counter before Cassie's mom could reach for it, muttered a "thank you," and turned away. She could feel eyes on her back as she hurried to the door and pushed through, feeling almost as though she couldn't breathe until she reached the fresh air outside. Once on the sidewalk, she turned and looked back at the store, the clean, streak-free windows, the bright lettering in neon colors announcing a big sale on ski equipment, the number above the door.

The number above the door.

The address of Cassie's store, of the building where she lived and worked, of the building that housed her entire life.

The number above the door.

217.

"Oh, fuck," Emerson whispered. "Oh, no, no, no…" She shook her head slowly back and forth as she backed away from The Sports Outfitter and walked as fast as she possibly could toward the Lakeshore Inn without actually breaking into a full-out sprint.

Could things possibly get any worse?

God damn, it was cold.

Another couple of years and it was going to be time to retire someplace warm. That thought didn't used to zip through Arnold Cross's mind, but it had lately, especially the past winter. It had been brutally cold. Not so much snowy as bitterly frigid. He wasn't getting any younger, and neither was the missus. She was already talking about the pros and cons of Florida versus Arizona. He would let her research for a while before he told her in no uncertain terms that he would never live in Florida, that armpit of the country. He hadn't worked his tail off his entire life to make money so he could live in a place with undrinkable water and bugs the size of cinder blocks. Not to mention the humidity. No thank you. He was all for the Southwest. Arizona was a possibility. San Diego was even better. But he'd let his wife read up on all of it before he gently began steering her toward the other side of the country. By the time she settled on San Diego, she'd think it had been her idea to begin with.

Cross got out of his car and stood in the parking lot, looking out at the water, 217 Main Street at his back. It was a fabulous setup with a dock reaching out into the lake and plenty of room for boats to be anchored. Of course, he'd build up the dock so it was wider, more substantial, not just a four-foot-wide plank path leading out onto the water. He'd build a much bigger one that opened up into a huge seating area out onto the lake. Maybe he'd even install a seasonal bar right out here for the summers. People could steer their boats right up to the dock, tie off, grab a cocktail. There was plenty of space for that.

Turning to face the building, he assessed it. Two separate retail spaces, both three stories plus basement levels. He knew the top floor was a spacious apartment, so only slight changes would be necessary when he transformed the whole thing into condos. He could go the upscale route and just fashion it into two separate three-story units, complete with basements. They'd be pricey, but gorgeous. Or he could get more bang for his buck and convert it into eight smaller units, two on each level. Or he could go with six, two on each level from the first floor up and combine the basement levels for a restaurant, opening up to the water.

He rubbed his hands together and smiled. So many options.

That was both a blessing and a curse when it came to renovating property. If he had few options, decisions were easy, obviously. When there were several ways to go, outside parties had to be consulted. Designers, financial analysts, and so on. Too many fingers in the pie could be stressful, but often that was the best way. After decades in the business, Cross was aware of this. Most people would send their contractor in, not bother with worrying about it. But not Arnold Cross. He liked to go in first, get the lay of the land, weigh his alternatives, and then he'd have to think about it.

From the outside, the building's structure looked sound. There was no telltale crumbling of foundation corners, no obvious shifting in the framing. The roof was old. He'd need to replace that soon. He pulled a small notebook and pen from the inside breast pocket of his suit jacket and jotted a few things down. Then he told his driver to sit tight, and he walked slowly around to the front of the building, examining every aspect of it with a trained eye.

He nodded his satisfaction as he left the parking lot behind. He liked that there was so much space for cars. Parking was at a premium in Lake Henry, and a lot this size was money. He jotted another note, reminding himself to take little to none of the lot when renovating. If restaurants went in the basement level, they'd need outdoor seating—a no-brainer when right on the lake—but he'd make sure to steal as little of the parking as possible. Condos with their own off-street parking would garner more money.

The location was lovely, right smack in the middle of the business district of Lake Henry, and the main reason he'd jumped at the chance to buy it. Structures on the outskirts were still nice, there was still money to be made, but this was the equivalent to being in the center of Manhattan. Everything of importance was within walking distance with the exception of the slopes and the bobsled run, and to use either of those things, you'd have equipment to carry, which meant you'd drive anyway. The ice rink, all the major restaurants, shops, and bars could be reached on foot, as could the beach and the park.

The storefronts were classy and neat, the windows clean, and the sidewalk swept. Boutique stood on the right, the type of shop filled to the rafters with useless trinkets and knick-knacks that cost way more than they should and served little to no purpose. Cross's wife could be lost in there for hours and drop hundreds of dollars. He'd take a look in there next. On the left was The Sports Outfitter, a nicely maintained sporting goods store that was fairly busy every time Cross had been by. He felt a tiny pang of guilt that he'd be closing the place down, but Lake Henry didn't need more stores. It needed more living space.

He pulled the door open and went inside, happy to get out of the cold and into the warmth of a bustling shop.

"Hey, Mom." Cassie pulled off her gloves and unzipped her jacket as she walked up the aisle of the basement level of the store.

"Hi, Sweetie. How was practice?" Katie was arranging the paddle display to make room for the extra ski poles that wouldn't fit upstairs. During the winter months, the water equipment section of The Sports Outfitter became the overflow for ski paraphernalia.

"It was good, but I've got to run up and get an order placed. Brian Turner is running the booster club for the boys' team and he wants to order ski hats and scarves, but he's so ridiculously disorganized." She shook her head as she shucked her jacket. "I just told him I'd take care of the design and colors and such."

"Brian?" Katie asked. "Vanessa's husband?"

Cassie nodded.

"Isn't that going to be…awkward for you?"

Cassie shook her head. "I don't think so." At the look of skepticism on her mother's face, she reached out and squeezed her shoulder. "It's okay, Mom. I'm okay. Don't worry." With a reassuring smile, she turned away and headed straight up to her office the back way, wanting to avoid any customers or employees until she could take care of the order.

As she sat down behind her desk, she realized what she'd told her mother was the absolute truth—despite the look of doubt Katie had shot her. She was fine where Vanessa was concerned. It still stung. It was still a little bit difficult, but she was okay. She was moving on, and that was a good thing. A very good thing.

She tried to ignore the fact that she had something (or more accurately, someone) else to focus on.

A couple of catalogs in her filing cabinet would help her find the right items for the booster club, and she yanked a drawer open and flipped through a bunch. Picking three, she took them back to her desk and glanced at the security monitors as she sat down. A particular face caught her eye, and she did a double-take. Focusing on the small, rounded body of Arnold Cross, she watched him carefully as he zipped quickly through her store, jotting notes into a palm-sized notebook.

"What the hell?" she asked aloud, then watched him for several more moments before narrowing her eyes and pushing herself out of her chair.

Less than a minute later, she tapped him on the shoulder. When he turned to meet her gaze, a look of dread shot across his face, though he seemed to work hard to push it away.

"Can I help you, Mr. Cross?" Cassie asked.

"Ms. Prescott." He held out his hand and Cassie, having been raised with manners—and aware of the clientele milling through the store—shook it quickly.

"I've been watching you on my security cameras. You've been taking notes. Can I ask why? What are you doing here?" He scanned her, seemed to take in her stormproof pullover, her Ripstop nylon pants, and her all-weather hikers. Then he tucked his notebook back into his breast pocket and met her eyes. "Mr. Cross?" she prodded.

With a regrettable sigh, he said simply, "I'm taking notes on the building, as I am going to own it soon."

She blinked at him. Simply stood and blinked at him, as if he'd spoken in Latin or Hebrew. A wave of panic flushed through her. After a moment, she stammered out, "I—I don't understand."

Cross cleared his throat, kept his voice low and controlled, almost as if he was being conscious of not embarrassing her. "The owner of this building is deceased, and the remaining family has decided to sell. I am going to buy it. On Monday. I don't mean to intrude, Ms. Prescott. I was in the area on other business and just thought I'd stop in to take a closer look. I apologize for the inconvenience."

With that, he pulled his trench coat closed and belted it. Cassie still stood unmoving, trying to comprehend what he'd told her, but the words just kept jumbling in her head. When she finally glanced up at him, she was surprised to see the apologetic look on his face, like he was sorry he'd told her.

With a nod, he left her standing there and pushed through the doors. She watched out the window as he was jostled by passersby. He hurried around the building, but she did not follow. Why would she? What good would it do?

She couldn't move anyway.

"Did you know?"

Jonathan jumped at the sound of Cassie's voice. He'd been absorbed in a printout from the previous month's sales and had his back to the counter when she blurted her question. He gave a quick glance around the store, then spoke quietly. "Good morning to you, too, Cass. Good lord, are you trying to give me a coronary?"

"Did you know?" she asked again.

He narrowed his eyes at her, obviously studying her face, noting the panicked worry that creased her forehead. "Did I know what? What is wrong with you?"

"Caroline Rosberg owned this building." Cassie bore into him with her eyes, waiting for an answer. He couldn't know. He would have told her. But it was the only thing that made sense.

"What?" Jonathan was completely confused now, Cassie could tell by his expression. He rounded the counter, grasped her by the elbow, and steered her into the office behind it. There was a one-way mirror so he could see the store from his desk. He kept one eye on it and then glanced back at Cassie. "Sit down and tell me what the hell you're talking about."

Cassie stayed standing, but relayed the previous few minutes to him. "He said the owner of the building is deceased and the remaining family wants to sell. Who else could he be talking about? Who else around here has died recently? Emerson keeps referring to her mother's stuff as the inn and 'some property.'" She made air quotes to emphasize her point.

Jonathan rolled it all around in his head. "So…the Burgermeister Meisterburger is going to buy this building. That's essentially what you're saying, right?"

"That's what I'm saying."

"And Caroline owned the building? Patrick pays the rent, and I know it goes to that agency. I guess I never really thought about it. I had no reason to."

Cassie dropped heavily into a chair. "Why didn't she tell me?"

"Who? Caroline?"

"Emerson! Jesus, Jonathan. Stay with me here."

Jonathan held his hands up, palms forward. "Hey, don't get mad at me. I warned you about her." He put his hands on his hips and stared out the one-way glass for a long moment. "Cross builds condos. I'm probably going to lose my store," he said, more to himself than Cassie.

"Me, too. I mean, we've got leases, right? So he can't just kick us out. But once they're up..." She shook her head. "I can't believe neither one of them told me. I feel sick." She rubbed a hand across her stomach as they sat in silence. Then Cassie stood abruptly, startling Jonathan, and muttered, "You know what? This is bullshit." She stormed out of the office.

The air was biting. It was the first day of the season that Cassie actually noticed the cold, and she cursed at the frosty air as she stormed down the street with no coat on. Head down, eyebrows furrowed, she plowed down the sidewalk like a steamroller, not really noticing how people jumped out of her path, made way for her. She heard a couple of mumbled greetings, but she did not respond. She didn't want to snap at innocent bystanders, so she kept her eyes glued to the sidewalk ahead and moved along with great purpose.

A casual walk from The Sports Outfitter to the Lakeshore Inn took about ten minutes, but Cassie made it in half that time. She bypassed the main building and stomped down the pathway to the little cottage that used to be Caroline's sanctuary. She banged at the side door loudly, not caring who heard her.

With no immediate answer, she raised her fist to bang again, but the door was pulled open before she had the chance.

Emerson seemed surprised to see her. That much was obvious by the startled expression on her face. Cassie wished she didn't look so good in the worn jeans that clung to her body in all the right places, and the navy blue Reebok hoodie she'd purchased in Cassie's store just days before. To avoid the view, Cassie pushed past Emerson and into the cottage just as Emerson said, "Hey."

Boxes were everywhere. Some were packed and taped up neatly, labeled with black marker. Others stood open, half-filled with things that used to belong to Caroline. Instantly, Cassie was hit with a blast of sadness and grief that almost buckled her knees. Seeing Caroline's life boxed up made Cassie's heart ache. Then she remembered why she was here, and she spun on Emerson.

"Why didn't you tell me?"

Blonde eyebrows made a V above Emerson's nose. "Tell you what?" She stood tall, still, legs shoulder-width apart, her hands tucked into her back pockets. She looked completely at ease, which made Cassie angrier.

"That you owned my building? That you were going to sell it out from underneath me?"

Emerson's face ran the gamut of emotions then, from shame to apology to anger to…blank. Cassie watched the transformation with rapt attention and could pinpoint the exact second when Emerson turned off her feelings. "I didn't know until this morning." She abruptly crossed the room—not looking at Cassie—and began packing a box.

"You didn't know until this morning," Cassie echoed dubiously.

"I didn't. 217 Main Street was just an address."

"Just an address."

Emerson threw down the book she'd been ready to pack. "What, you're a parrot now? What do you want from me, Cassie?"

Cassie blinked at her in disbelief. "What do I want from you? Are you seriously asking me that question? I just watched Arnold fucking Cross wander through my store and take notes so he can better make the building into condos or whatever he's going to make it into that doesn't include my business. Or my apartment, *my home*. And all you can do is act all irritated that I'm upset about it?"

"Do you want an apology? Is that it? Fine. I'm sorry. I didn't know. Okay?"

Cassie flinched at Emerson's coldness, then watched in incredulity as Emerson went back to packing. Cassie opened her eyes wide and shook her head. "That's it? Really?"

Emerson turned to her and held her arms out to the sides, silently asking, *what more do you want?* Something shot across her face then, a fleeting glimpse of emotion, but it came and went so fast, Cassie wondered if she'd actually seen it. She waited a beat, but it didn't happen again, and Cassie's heart began to ache.

"I don't mean a thing to you, do I? The last three weeks? All the talks? The trek up Jones Mountain?" Cassie's voice dropped. "That kiss? None of it meant a thing to you, did it?"

Emerson opened her mouth, then closed it again. Her ice-blue eyes stared past Cassie, then down to the floor. Finally, she dropped her arms to her sides and looked at Cassie. "I don't know what you want me to say."

Disappointment washed over Cassie in one big wave, and she looked at Emerson with pleading eyes. "I want you to say you're sorry and mean it. I want you to say maybe we can talk about it, work something out. I want you to say you give a shit."

Emerson just stared at her.

"This town invested so much in you, Emerson. I know it was a long time ago, and you don't like to remember that, but it's true. Maybe it's time you return the favor, invest in the town now. Why not stay?"

Emerson shook her head, her mouth set in a tight line, and looked down at her feet.

Cassie stared for a long moment, willing it all to be different, willing Emerson to lift her head, to look at Cassie with those eyes, to show Cassie the warmth she'd seen yesterday with Mr. Kendall, the heart she knew was in there. She saw none of it now. Not a trace. Emerson's face was carefully blank and it infuriated Cassie almost as much as it broke her heart. To protect herself from the sadness, she let the anger surge up again, to take over.

"People warned me about you, you know, told me to stay away." Emerson's head snapped up at that, and Cassie pushed on, thrilled to get a reaction of any kind. "They did. They told me you were a runner, that it's what you do. You take the easy way out. When things get hard, Emerson runs away. They told me not to get too close, that I'd only get hurt. But I didn't listen. Oh, no, I couldn't be bothered because I thought there was something more to you. I was sure of it. But you know what? They were right. You don't give a shit about anybody but yourself, do you?"

"Do *not* make this my fault," Emerson snapped, her eyes flashing as she stabbed a finger in Cassie's direction. "What kind of businesswoman doesn't know who her landlord is? My mother owned the building; she never told you. That isn't my fault. I told you the moment I arrived that I wasn't staying. How does that make me a runner? Maybe this isn't about me. Maybe this is about you. Maybe you just like to go after things you can't have. Like me. Like Vanessa."

Cassie literally took a step back as Emerson's words sliced through her, unable to believe what she'd heard. She swallowed as her eyes welled up, crushed by the look of indifference on Emerson's face, the face she'd grown so fond of, and the hurt made her take a shot at the jugular. "God, you're so fucking cold," she said quietly. "Your mother was right about you."

She stayed only long enough to see the pain rip across Emerson's face, the tears pool in her eyes, before turning away, not wanting to see any more of the damage she'd caused. She slammed the door behind her and ran bodily into Mary, who was standing on the pathway, looking stricken. Cassie mumbled an apology, then quickly moved around the innkeeper and hurried up the walk. She'd done what she needed to do. She'd said everything she wanted to say. She'd stood up for herself.

So why, then, did she feel so horrible?

CHAPTER NINETEEN

EMERSON WAS EXHAUSTED, but could not sleep. She'd spent the rest of Sunday shifting from being angry at Cassie for the things she'd said, to being angry with herself for being the way she was, to being angry in general for knowing that Cassie had a point, to being angry that there was so much crap in her mother's house to pack. Though she preferred the anger to the pain, she wasn't clear on why she still felt it. In typical situations, she just felt numb. After years of pain pills, she'd become used to feeling nothing. This ire inside burned, made her uncomfortable and restless. She didn't like it, yet couldn't seem to shake it.

Your mother was right about you.

She closed her eyes, opened them again, stared at the ceiling.

Packing had been a giant pain in the ass. But she'd done it. The kitchen was packed up. The living room. The rest of Caroline's clothing–all packed. She'd taken a lot to the rehab hospital, but there were a few things Emerson was shipping to her place in L.A. A couple roomy sweatshirts, her slippers, and an oversized flannel shirt that had originally belonged to Emerson's grandfather. Emerson could still picture her mother throwing it on when she was chilly, its blue-and-black-plaid flannel threadbare in spots, the sleeves needing to be rolled up six or seven times before she could see her hands.

In bed now, Emerson was warm and comfortable, albeit wide awake, just as she had been for the past three-and-a-half hours. A glance at the clock told her it was barely six. The sky was still dark. The birds hadn't even awakened, the lake and trees silent outside the window. She got out of the bed, ran quickly to the window, and opened the curtains wide, then hurried back on her toes to avoid the cold floor, and dove under the covers. She wasn't ready to get out of bed yet, but wanted to watch the sun come up, if it had any plans to do so. Despite the early hour, it was brighter out than usual, thanks to the new snowfall that had blanketed the town overnight. Emerson propped herself into a not-quite-sitting position and just gazed out the window into the white stillness and beauty of Lake Henry beyond.

I wish you could see the snow, Mom. You'd love it.

Shifting positions in the bed, she winced as aching muscles made themselves known. Her knee wasn't throbbing, but it was definitely sore. She'd worked her ass off yesterday, staying busy being the only way she could keep her brain from alighting on all the things Cassie had said. Emerson was shocked by how angry the woman was. When Cassie left, Emerson had been seconds from bursting into tears, something she rarely did. Thank goodness Mary had then knocked on the door and entered, asked if everything was all right. Emerson had no choice but to tell her what was going on, so she'd pulled herself together and had done so. She told Mary all of it, even about the sale of the inn. Mary hadn't seemed surprised. Even she hadn't known which building Caroline had owned.

A quick phone call to Brad Klein had answered all of Emerson's questions. Apparently, the building had belonged to her grandfather, who'd been using the same rental agency for ages. Caroline had seen no reason to change things, and therefore, just left it all as it was, let it be run the same way it always had been when her father had been alive. The money went into an account from where any necessary maintenance was also paid for, and her accountant took care of it all. Caroline took a set amount from it each month, popped her monthly statements into a folder, and never looked any further into it. She had no need to.

How ridiculous that such a simple and innocent setup could cause so many problems later on.

Caroline must have lain in bed and gazed out the window just as Emerson was doing now, because she'd mounted a bird feeder just outside. Mr. Gruffton must have kept it filled, as Emerson had no idea where the birdseed was, but it was nearly half full now. Two chickadees and a handful of sparrows flitted around, taking turns at the seed, chittering in their little bird voices. Caroline loved birds, Emerson remembered now. A very vague memory of looking through a bird book when she was little struck Emerson then, flipping pages, scanning photographs, trying to find the bird with the right color and body shape. A lump appeared in her throat, and she had to clear it several times before it abated.

The emotion had been so close to the surface recently, and it was freaking Emerson out a little bit. She'd been focusing on the anger simply to keep the emotion at bay, but now felt like she might be losing the battle.

She was meeting with Cross this morning at nine. Concentrating on that helped her push the sensation of tears and sadness back into the dark recesses of her brain. She'd looked over the paperwork a dozen times now, and it all seemed to be in order. Klein had said the offer was more than fair, and she trusted him. He'd been her mother's attorney for many years. Caroline wouldn't have stayed with him if she didn't trust him to keep her best interests at heart.

Emerson was surprised at the early hour of the meeting, given Cross's long drive. He was clearly anxious to close the deal. And she was confident this was the right thing to do.

Wasn't it?

She flashed back to when she'd told Mary and how the innkeeper didn't seem upset, though Emerson detected a hint of...disappointment?

"Do you know what Cross plans to do with the inn?" Mary had asked quietly, not looking at Emerson.

"I don't." Emerson was a little embarrassed that she hadn't asked, though it wasn't really her business.

Mary gave a slow nod and said simply, "Well then."

She let Mary go through Caroline's things, told her to take anything she might want, anything that held memories for her. She took a corkscrew, a couple of wine glasses, a stack of books from the shelves, and a basket of yarn and knitting needles, chuckling sadly about how she'd given Caroline all the supplies for her last birthday and then attempted to teach her the craft, only to find out Caroline had no talent for it whatsoever and even less patience. Emerson had helped her pack everything up and watched with mixed emotions as she carried it back to the main office, her shoulders weighed down with her box of memories.

"It's fine," she said loudly now, suddenly throwing off the covers and jumping up. The need to shake this melancholy feeling was intense. Emerson dressed in sweats and a hoodie, stepped into Caroline's slippers, and went out into the living room. She clicked on the fireplace and just stood, looking at boxes, at the photos still on the wall—the last things she had to pack up—and bent backwards slightly to stretch her spine.

The next couple hours dragged by, and Emerson did anything she could to speed them up. She wanted to walk around the lake, but was apprehensive about who she might run into while doing so. Instead, she wandered down where the dock usually was (Jack had taken it out for the winter the day before), looked out over the water and took in the fresh air and early morning quiet. It seemed to settle her, even if it was only slightly. Then she took a very hot, very slow shower and didn't hurry to get dressed, ironing her pants and suit jacket, wishing she'd packed another, as Klein and Cross had both seen her in this one already. There was nothing to be done about that, though she was happy to have found a red silk blouse among her mother's clothes. It was tighter than Emerson would normally wear, but the blouse was exactly what she needed to go into this meeting with calm and confidence that she wasn't quite feeling. Red was her power color; she wore it often at work to close sales.

The clock finally made it to 8:45. She took one last look in the mirror, ran her fingers through her short hair, tugged on the hem of her suit jacket, and slipped into her pumps. Just a little mascara brought out her eyes, and she added a light coat of lip gloss. Her mother's diamond earrings finished the outfit, and for the very first time in her life, Emerson wished she physically resembled her mother a bit more. She'd always been very happy with her father's Swedish genes…her height, her light coloring. Today, she missed Caroline, and the thought made her swallow hard. Blinking rapidly, she pulled on a dressier wool coat she'd found in the closet, took one last look around the cottage, and closed the door behind her.

The day had dawned bright and sunny, the overnight snow melting slightly. She knew from her childhood that it wouldn't be long before the sun disappeared for days, sometimes weeks, on end. People would be out enjoying it as much as they could today, as if trying to store it up for the upcoming winter. She drove the opposite way around the lake so as not to drive past The Sports Outfitter. She'd been fairly successful at blocking out her entire conversation with Cassie, but now things were creeping back in. The edge in Cassie's voice, the sounds of anger and betrayal. Worse, the pain in her eyes. She'd tried to hide it by playing the tough guy, but Emerson had seen it, had known she put it there.

Literally shaking her head to rid herself of the memory, she followed the road around Lake Henry and within five minutes, came upon the parking lot for Brad Klein's office. A sleek, silver Town Car was parked in the lot, the neatly dressed driver holding a newspaper open across the steering wheel. He glanced up at Emerson, gave a curt nod, and went back to his reading. Cross had come early.

"Figures," Emerson muttered, again pulling her unnecessary briefcase out of the passenger seat. She waited until she was in the foyer of Klein's building—where nobody could see her—before she smoothed a hand over her hair, her chest, her hips. Deep breath in, slow breath out. "Let's get this over with," she said to nobody.

The office was still warm and inviting, not adjectives Emerson would normally expect to describe a lawyer's office, but it was true. Klein's receptionist was on the phone, but smiled when she saw Emerson and held up a finger, the universal sign for "hang on just a second." Emerson took a seat and let her gaze wander the room.

Nothing had changed since her last visit, though she was pretty sure the potpourri had been rejuvenated, as the smell of cinnamon seemed stronger than she remembered. The last time she was here, she hadn't had time to notice small things like the framed photos on the receptionist's desk. In one, two teenagers, both blonde, both with mouths full of metal, smiled at the camera. The other showed a German Shepherd lying in the grass, his friendly brown eyes full of love and trust. Next to that was a wooden sign painted navy blue. Its lettering was white.

"Never look back unless you are planning to go that way." –
Henry David Thoreau

Emerson stared at it, then read it again. She felt as if the words floated off the wood in a line, danced through the air, and morphed right through her eyes and into her brain, like they might in a cartoon. She was still staring at them when the receptionist hung up and spoke to her, but Emerson didn't hear her.

"Ms. Rosberg?"

Emerson blinked rapidly, pulled out of her trance by the woman's voice. "I'm sorry." She cleared her throat, collected herself. "I'm sorry. You caught me napping."

The receptionist smiled and pointed down the hall in the same direction as the last visit. "They're waiting for you in the conference room."

Emerson smiled. "Thanks."

Steadying herself at the door, she grasped the knob and turned it.

"Ms. Rosberg." Brad Klein looked handsome as always in a nicely tailored navy blue suit and striped tie. He held out a hand and shook Emerson's quickly.

Arnold Cross stood, and Emerson had to give him credit. It couldn't be easy for a man of his stature to stand in front of a woman of Emerson's and not feel...well, small. They shook hands, Emerson smiled, though she knew it didn't reach her eyes, and they all sat.

"Coffee?" Klein asked.

"No. Thank you." She set down her briefcase and felt... unsettled was the only word she could come up with. Her chair faced the window. Outside, the sun sparkled on the water of Lake Henry even as patches of white snow were still visible.

"So," Klein said. "We're here to finalize the sale of both the Lakeshore Inn and the rental property at 217 Main." He slid a few papers around on the table in front of him. He continued to talk and he and Cross bantered a bit back and forth, but Emerson only half-listened. She was too busy gazing out the window, watching the water and hearing words resonate in her head, which was weird because nobody had spoken them aloud.

Never look back unless you are planning to go that way.

"Ms. Rosberg?"

Emerson blinked, her eyes tearing slightly, and she turned her focus to Klein. It couldn't be that simple. Could it?

"Are you okay?" he asked with concern.

She looked at his face, only slightly lined, ruggedly handsome, clean shaven. He may have been smiling, but his eyes showed worry and something else she couldn't quite pinpoint, and for a moment, she got the impression he was not happy to be there.

Turning her head, she took in Arnold Cross. He *was* happy to be there. Very happy. Too happy. His smile was so wide, it was almost laughable, but even so, his jowls pulled the sides of his face toward his lap just enough to make his expression more artificial than he probably intended. Emerson's eyes darted from one man to the other as if she were watching a ping-pong match.

"Never look back unless you are planning to go that way."

That was it. The thought, *third time's the charm*, zipped through her head just as she felt something crack open inside her, and much to her horror, her eyes filled with tears. She pushed her chair back roughly and clamped a hand over her mouth as a sob threatened to bubble up and out from her chest.

Arnold Cross began sifting through papers, and wasn't looking at her as he spoke. "This is a very good day for you, Ms. Rosberg. Your family's hard work is about to pay off, and you are going to be a wealthy woman. Your mother would be proud."

"Ms. Rosberg?" Klein stood, his concern multiplying, and came around the table. "Emerson? Are you all right?"

Emerson held out a hand to hold him back as she looked up at him. "Would she? Be proud? Is this what she wanted?"

Klein cocked his head slightly to the side and said quietly, "I don't know. I do know that she loved Lake Henry. And that she wanted you to be happy." He reached for her.

"No," she managed, still pushing a hand in his direction. "No, stay there. I don't…I can't…" She sobbed one more time, eyes wide, and began to shake her head from side to side even as her breathing increased and her heart began to pound. Collecting herself enough to speak, she said, "I'm so sorry. I can't do this. I can't. I'm sorry. I have to go." She turned away from Arnold Cross, whose face had gone from overly joyful to angry betrayal in a matter of about three seconds. She thought she detected a ghost of a grin on Klein's face as she turned and fled his office, but she couldn't be certain.

Out in the lobby, she stopped and looked for an escape. Klein's receptionist stood, her forehead creased with worry as Cross's angry voice boomed from the conference room.

"Ms. Rosberg? Are you okay?" the receptionist asked.

Instead of answering, Emerson glanced one more time at the wooden sign with the Thoreau quote, then walked up to the receptionist and embraced her in a tight hug. She let her go and headed for the door, leaving the stunned woman standing there, wondering what the hell had just happened.

Emerson didn't run, but she might as well have. She ripped open the car door, threw her briefcase and coat inside, and flopped into the driver's seat where she then pounded on the steering wheel with open palms as she cried. Glancing to her left, she saw Cross's driver looking at her, completely perplexed, and she knew she needed to leave before he decided to come see if something was wrong. She wiped her running nose with her hand, started the car, and pulled out of the parking lot with more speed than was safe.

She couldn't stop crying.

It shouldn't have surprised her when she turned into the parking lot of Cassie's store, but it did. She jammed the gearshift into park and sat in the car, looking out the window at the back of The Sports Outfitter. Tears covered her cheeks and her nose continued to run, but she didn't stop to think. She got out of the car and marched across the lot into the back entrance.

Cassie's mom was at the cash register. When she looked up, her eyes widened.

"Is Cassie up there?" Emerson asked before the woman could speak and pointed at the stairs.

"Yes, but..."

Emerson headed for the stairs.

"She's with customers," Cassie's mom called out.

Emerson kept walking, determination in her steps even as she stumbled, tears still flowing. She clamped her hand over her mouth once again, hoping to keep the sobs from being too loud and attracting the attention of shoppers.

The customers didn't stop the emotion overflowing out of her, and her tears continued to run. It crossed her mind that she must look like a crazy person, hurrying falteringly down an aisle, pushing past those in her way. Her mascara was running in a big way, which she discovered when she took a swipe at her wet cheek and her hand came back streaked with black. She ignored the strange looks people gave her as she passed, pretended not to hear any of the whispers. She managed to swallow a couple of the sobs, but here and there, one broke free from her lips, causing heads to turn.

Cassie had four people in line, and she stood behind a register next to a college-age young man as they worked together to ring out customers. When her gaze landed on Emerson, her eyes went very wide. Emerson pushed her way to the front of the line.

"Emerson? Are you okay?" Cassie asked, concern and irritation battling in full view on her face.

"No. No, I'm not. I need to talk to you, Cassie. Please." Gordie suddenly appeared at her side, pushing against her, obviously worried.

Cassie looked around almost wildly, then held her arms out to the sides, palms up. "Emerson. I'm working. In case you didn't notice, it's pretty busy right now. Can it—." She stopped talking abruptly as Emerson broke into heaving sobs.

"Oh my god, what is happening to me?" Emerson said under her breath, bracing herself against the counter as she tried to catch her breath. Gordie whimpered in his throat. Emerson looked at Cassie and whispered, "*Please.*"

"Frannie!" Cassie called out. A redhead appeared in a few seconds. "Can you take over here and help Damian?"

"Sure. No problem."

Cassie moved around the counter past the customers who were too stunned to complain, grabbed Emerson firmly by the elbow and led her to the back stairway. "Gordie, stay." The dog sat, obviously not happy about it. To Emerson, she said, "Come on. Come with me." Taking Emerson's hand in hers, she tugged her up the stairs.

Emerson felt like she had begun to get a handle on whatever breakdown she was having, and by the time they reached the top floor, she was breathing almost normally.

Until Cassie opened the door to her apartment and pulled Emerson inside.

"Oh, god. *This* is your place?"

Cassie glanced back at her. "Um, yeah."

"It's beautiful. Oh, my god. It's so *beautiful.*" Realizing she'd almost sold it out from under Cassie, she felt the tears wash over her again, and she cried openly as she stood in Cassie's entryway. She looked up through blurry, wet eyes and asked again, "What the hell is happening to me?"

Cassie shook her head, her expression conveying sympathy and also that she was at a loss. "Here." She gestured to the small living area and the couch. "Sit down. I'll get you some tea."

Emerson sat, sobbed quietly, and tried hard to pull herself together. Cassie returned with a box of tissues, then disappeared again. Emerson could hear her moving in the kitchen, faint sounds of dishes and spoons emanating from behind a wall. She pulled a tissue from the box, blew her nose, then patted under her eyes as she tried not the think about how awful she must look. Puffy, red-rimmed eyes, streaking mascara, snotty nose. All those people in the store staring at her. She groaned and shook her head, then sat back against the couch cushions and looked around.

The apartment wasn't tiny, but it wasn't huge. It was, however, gorgeous. It had an open floor plan for the most part, except for the short breakfast bar that separated the kitchen from the living space. Two skylights let in the day from above, and a small gas fireplace occupied the corner of the room, positioned to warm not only the living room, but the makeshift dining area where Cassie had a table for two set near a window where Lake Henry could be seen in all its sun-reflecting glory. The hardwood floors were in great shape, the wood shiny and rich-looking. A doorway in front of Emerson gave her a peek at a bed covered with something emerald green and a pair of Nikes with their laces still tied strewn on the floor.

The wall next to the bedroom door was covered with photographs in frames of all shapes, sizes, and colors, and the fact that none of them matched made the collection more interesting than one would expect. Emerson kicked off her pumps, still sniffling a bit, and turned her gaze out the window.

"Here we go," Cassie said quietly. She had two mugs of tea, and she set them on the coffee table. A trip back into the kitchen produced a small creamer and a sugar bowl. "I wasn't sure how you take it."

Emerson swallowed, wiped her eyes again. They doctored their individual tea in silence. Emerson sat back. Cassie folded one leg up so she sat facing her.

"So," Cassie said. She took a small sip of the very hot tea, then perhaps thought better of drinking more and set it down. "What's going on?" Though there was definite sympathy and worry in her voice, Emerson could also see trepidation. She was bracing for some kind of impact, even if she was trying not to show it. Emerson closed her eyes, looked down at the tea in her hand, hating that she'd made Cassie feel that way around her.

"I am honestly not sure," she said after a long beat of silence.

"You're all dressed up."

"Yeah. I thought that was the right thing to do for a business meeting."

"With Cross?"

Emerson didn't meet her eyes. "Yes."

"And now you're a blubbering mess."

With a snorted laugh, Emerson nodded.

"In public."

"God, I know." She blew her nose again.

"How come?"

Emerson shook her head.

"Is it your mom?" Cassie asked quietly and reached out to lay a hand on Emerson's arm.

The lump that had never really left seemed to grow in Emerson's throat, and she swallowed several times as she nodded and her eyes filled with those godforsaken tears yet again. "A little, I think. Yes."

Cassie paused before asking her next question. "Do you think maybe you have some guilt about selling the inn and this building? That maybe she wouldn't have wanted you to?"

Emerson looked at her then. "I didn't."

Furrowing her brows, Cassie looked confused. "You didn't what? Feel guilty?"

"Sell. I didn't sell."

Cassie went still and blinked at her. "You didn't?"

"I didn't. I couldn't. I was ready to, and…I just couldn't. I'm not completely sure why, but I think I have an idea." She told Cassie about the saying on the receptionist's desk and how it kept coming back to her while she was in the conference room. "I kept thinking that it couldn't possibly be so simple as me stupidly letting my past shape my future, so simple that I read a quote and my whole life dissolved at my feet, but I couldn't shake it. It was like a…a sign. Well, it *was* actually a sign, but… you know what I mean. I couldn't shake the feeling that I needed to do something, I don't know, something *different* for a change, not take the same path I always take. I mean really, where has that gotten me?" Warm tears tracked down her cheeks, but she didn't care. She took Cassie's hand in both of hers. "I don't want to go back. I want to go forward. I have so many regrets in my life, Cassie. So many." She gave a humorless laugh. "Trust me, I am way too young to have all the regrets I have." She squeezed Cassie's hand, looked into her rich brown eyes, and said softly, "I don't want to add Lake Henry to that list. I don't want to add *you* to that list."

They were quiet for long moments, their hands clasped tightly. Finally, Cassie entwined their fingers, then looked up and asked, "What does that mean, exactly?" The question was gentle, free of any accusation.

"I don't know for sure," Emerson replied with a wan smile. "I just know that, for the first time in…ever…I'm just saying what I feel. Not what I'm supposed to say. Not what I think I should say. Just what I…feel." She thumped a hand against her chest. "I'm being completely honest. I don't know what it means. I'm just saying what's in my heart." Cassie nodded slowly. "For what it's worth," Emerson went on, "I have never been this honest with anybody. In my life."

Cassie was quiet for several seconds before replying, "Well, for what it's worth, I've never seen a woman cry so much. In my life."

They held each other's gaze for a beat before bursting into laughter.

"Jesus, right?" Emerson said. "That was so weird. I literally felt like something broke inside me, and all these emotions just flooded my system." She paused, pressed her fingertips against her forehead. "I think it might have been my mom." Her eyes welled up yet again. "And we're apparently not done." She grinned through the tears and gave Cassie a shrug. "See? I can't stop."

"Oh, sweetie. Come here." Cassie opened her arms and pulled Emerson into them, and they sat together on the couch while Emerson cried herself out and their tea got cold.

Cassie was just draping a blanket over Emerson's sleeping form on the couch when the light tap at the door came. When she opened it, her mother stood in the hall, looking expectant and more than a little concerned. Cassie put a finger to her lips and stepped into the hall, closing the door behind her.

"Is everything all right?" Katie asked. "You've been gone for over an hour."

"I know. I know. I'm sorry." She sidled past and headed down the stairs, Katie on her heels. "She's having a rough time."

"And she came to you?"

Cassie stopped in the middle of the staircase and turned to face her mother, who was two steps above her. "Yes, Mom. She came to me. I'm glad she did."

Katie pressed her lips together and Cassie knew her well enough to know she was reining herself in. "Okay. I'm sorry. I didn't mean to judge." Their eyes held. "I just don't want to see you get hurt."

Cassie's demeanor softened. "I know. Me neither."

"Come downstairs. It's a zoo."

Gordie was beside himself with joy at seeing her and stuck to her like glue for the rest of the day. The ski season had hit, as it usually did this time of year, and her mother was right; the store was a zoo. Cassie sent Frannie on her break and took care of a steady stream of customers for the next several hours.

The fact that her store was *not* being sold out from underneath her put an extra bounce in her step.

That, and Emerson was asleep on her couch.

CHAPTER TWENTY

EMERSON HAD NO CLUE what time it was when she opened her eyes, and for a brief moment, she had no idea where she was. She gave herself time...time to stretch out on the comfy couch, time to revel in the warmth of the blanket that had found its way over her and that smelled pleasantly of laundry detergent, time to remember the morning and how an emotional dam of some sort had split open inside her. Her eyes stung and her eyelids felt lined with sandpaper. She lay there for a long while and just breathed.

When she finally turned her head, she saw a stack of clothing on the coffee table and a note.

I thought some different clothes would be more comfortable than your suit. Help yourself to the kitchen. I'll be back to check on you in a bit. Cassie.

There was a smiley face next to her name. *Of course there is,* Emerson thought and it brought her own smile to her lips. The pile of clothing contained a pair of yoga pants, a well-worn Syracuse sweatshirt, and a pair of thick, warm-looking socks. Emerson was loathe to uncover herself, as the blanket was toasty and she loved the smell, but her pants had twisted around her hips and were restricting most movement. Her suit jacket was a wrinkled mess, she was sure.

Forcing herself up, she stretched her arms over her head and yawned widely as her eyes fell once again on the photographs on the wall she'd noticed earlier. It was a collage of different frames of varying sizes, all black. They told the story of Cassie's life better than any explanation could. Pictures of her and her high school friends decked out in the Lake Henry High colors of orange and black. A picture of Cassie and a handsome young man, both holding up bottles of beer in a toast to the camera. Cassie and her sister and their parents. Chris, a man who Emerson assumed was Chris's husband, and their three kids, then another with Cassie and the three kids. Cassie and Vanessa, arms linked, smiles wide and tooth-filled. Emerson lingered on that one for long moments. There were several shots of Gordie, from puppydom to present day. In every photo, Cassie's smile was wide, her eyes crinkled in merriment. She was happy. She was a happy person.

Emerson wondered what that must be like.

She almost laughed out loud ten minutes later because she felt *much* happier in the sweats than she had in the suit. The yoga pants were the perfect length on Emerson, which told her they must be much too long on Cassie. The sweatshirt was washed-soft, thick and warm, and the socks were perfect. How was it possible that the right clothing could make a person feel a hundred and fifty percent better?

And how was it that she felt so much…lighter? This moment compared to when she'd woken up that morning were at opposite ends. She felt like somebody had lifted all the weight from her shoulders. She was relaxed. She was relieved. She felt *good*.

"What is going on with me?" she asked the room.

As if in answer, the door opened and Cassie walked in with a big grin.

"You're up," she said as she shut the door. "Hi."

Emerson looked at her—really looked at her—for the first time that day. She wore black Nike wind pants and a pink fleece quarter-zip pullover. Her dark hair was pulled back and into a ponytail, a few stubborn wisps escaping to frame her face. Small gold hoops decorated her ears and her smile was warm, everything about her telling Emerson she was glad to see her.

"Hi, yourself." Emerson gestured to her own outfit. "Thank you so much for the clothes. This is so much better than my suit."

"I thought you might need something more comfortable, but I didn't want to wake you to have you change. You were sleeping so peacefully."

Only then did Emerson recall the last moments before she'd fallen asleep. She'd been crying—no, blubbering—on Cassie's shoulder. And Cassie held her the entire time. Emerson could feel the heat start in her chest, climb up her neck, and take up residence on her face. Even her ears grew hot.

"Oh, my god," she said and looked away. "I'm so sorry about that."

"Oh, no." Cassie hurried across the room and placed a hand on Emerson's upper arm, gave it a squeeze. "Don't be sorry. There's no reason." A reassuring smile crossed her face and the squeeze changed to a gentle rub. Cassie took a deep breath and changed the subject. "Are you hungry?"

"What time is it?" Emerson asked, thankful for the shift in gears and realizing she had no idea what time it was.

"It's going on three. You slept for a long time." Cassie moved to the kitchen, calling over her shoulder, "Things have died down in the shop, thank god. I was barely able to breathe, though I should never complain about being busy. I have to go back down in a bit, but I'm starving. How about a grilled cheese sandwich?"

"Grilled cheese sounds heavenly." Emerson followed Cassie into the kitchen. "Can I help?"

With a butter knife, Cassie gestured to one of the two stools under the breakfast bar. "Yes. You can sit there and talk to me while I cook."

"I can do that." Emerson sat and watched Cassie spread butter on bread.

"So, what happens now?" Cassie asked after a few moments. She kept her eyes on her task as she spoke.

Emerson propped her elbows on the counter and her chin in her hands. "I'm not exactly sure. I need to go back and talk to Brad Klein. He didn't seem at all bothered by my sudden change of heart, but Mr. Cross certainly was."

"The Burgermeister Meisterburger? Did his face turn red? Did he throw his fists up in the air and stomp his little feet?"

Emerson burst into laughter. "Oh my god, he *does* look like that!"

Cassie turned to her. "Right?"

When they finished laughing, Emerson went on. "I want to sit Mary down and talk to her about what she needs to keep the inn running. As for this building…I don't think anything needs to change."

Cassie stopped for a moment, then set the knife down and came around the breakfast bar. She wrapped her arms around Emerson and hugged tightly, whispering, "Thank you," quietly next to her ear. She let go, but Emerson held on to her arms.

"There is one thing, though."

Cassie cocked her head, waited.

"Will you be okay renting from a person who—I don't even know how to say this—kind of has a thing for you?"

"You have a thing for me?" She apparently tried to ask it seriously, but couldn't keep the grin from spreading across her face.

"I wasn't kidding earlier, Cassie. I don't want you to be something I regret missing out on." She swallowed, then cleared her throat.

Cassie stared at her for a beat, swallowed hard, then took in a shaky breath in and let it out slowly. She leaned in, captured Emerson's lips with her own and kissed her unhurriedly. Emerson let herself get lost in the feeling of Cassie's mouth on hers, of the softness of her lips, the warmth of her tongue. She slid her hand along the back of Cassie's neck, under her ponytail, and held her close. After long moments, Cassie finally pulled away. "We have to eat and I have to get back downstairs and if I keep kissing you, neither of those things is going to happen."

Emerson grabbed both sides of her face and kissed her again. Hard.

Long moments went by before finally, and with a reluctant groan, Cassie wrenched herself away and went back to the sandwiches, settling each onto the frying pan with a gentle sizzle. Emerson watched her work in happy silence, amazed at how comfortable she suddenly felt. She had no idea what had happened this morning, but it was kind of amazing.

Cassie dished the sandwiches onto plates, brought them to the counter, and took a seat next to Emerson. They ate quietly, occasionally smiling at one another. Her last bite of her sandwich in her hand, Emerson spoke.

"I have a favor to ask."

Cassie nodded for her to continue, chewing.

"There's so much to do, so much to deal with, and I just want to hide out a little while longer, enjoy some peace." She cleared her throat. "Can I maybe stay here tonight?" Before Cassie could answer, she held up a hand. "I can sleep on the couch—as we both witnessed earlier—so there's no pressure or anything. I just...don't want to go back yet and face all of my new, self-imposed responsibilities."

Cassie finished chewing and swallowed. "You can stay as long as you want. And you will *not* be sleeping on the couch." She stood and gathered their plates. Then she leaned close to Emerson and said, "You may not even be sleeping."

Emerson felt the heat again, felt her face redden and her palms begin to sweat, and this time, the heat moved down her body and settled as an insistent ache between her legs.

Cassie kissed Emerson's mouth quickly, winked, and took the dishes into the kitchen.

Cassie was exhausted. Bone-deep, aching muscles exhausted. The first big ski sale of the season was always chaos —in a good way. But wow, she was amazed she could still stand. Her feet hurt, her eyes burned, and her brain was tired. Gordie must have felt similarly tired, as he waited quietly at her feet while she opened the door to her apartment...though that changed when he caught the scent of somebody else occupying their space. He flew through the door and beelined to the bedroom.

Cassie didn't bother to try to stop him. She just smiled and kicked off her shoes, then followed her dog.

Emerson sat up in Cassie's bed, remote in one hand, Gordie's belly being scratched by the other. She wore one of Cassie's old Buffalo Bills T-shirts. Her face looked freshly scrubbed, and her eyes were clear and smiling.

I could get used to this, Cassie thought immediately, but dared not say it. The vision of Emerson in her jammies in Cassie's bed was something to behold. She leaned against the doorjamb, folded her arms across her chest, and just grinned.

Emerson looked up and saw her, put down the remote. "Hi there. Your dog is vicious, by the way."

"He is. He's just lulling you into a false sense of security. That's actually attack mode."

Emerson chuckled. "I'd better be careful then. How was work? You look tired."

"I'm beat. It was very busy." Cassie entered the room and took a seat on the bed where she could join in on the scratching. "Lots of sales. Always a good thing."

"Good." Emerson looked down, picked at the T-shirt. "I hope you don't mind. I borrowed some pajamas."

"I don't mind." Their gazes held, then Cassie gestured to the bed with her eyes. "Is there room in there for me?"

"I don't know. This shirt is pretty small."

"Ha ha. Be right back."

In the small bathroom, Cassie brushed her teeth and stared at her reflection. She was not only tired, she looked it, dark circles under her eyes, her skin sullen and dull. With a sigh, she washed her face and hands, put on deodorant, and spritzed a little perfume. She pulled the rubber band from her hair and let it fall around her shoulders. Then she reached for the worn Syracuse T-shirt hanging on the back of the door and pulled it over her head. Wearing only that and her panties, she turned off the bathroom light and opened the door.

Gordie had moved to his spot at the foot of the bed, where he would stay until he got too warm. Then he would jump to the floor and under the bed as soon as he was sure his pack was safe. It was the same routine every night.

Emerson turned to look at her and simply stared until Cassie shifted uncomfortably.

"You look amazing," Emerson said softly.

Cassie gave an amused shrug as she walked forward and stopped at the edge of the bed. "This shirt is about seven years old. It's from my college days and believe me, it has seen more than its share of beer and chicken wings." Her chuckle died in her throat as Emerson grasped her by the wrist and looked her in the eyes.

"You look amazing," she said again. "Come here." She pulled Cassie to her until she'd crawled across the bed to meet Emerson's mouth.

They kissed slowly, unhurried, like they had all the time in the world. And they did. Gordie hopped off the bed and then crawled under it as Emerson pulled Cassie closer, slid both hands up the sides of her neck, and dug her fingers into dark, loose hair.

"I rarely see you with your hair down," she whispered. "You're even more gorgeous, and I didn't think that was possible." Then she grasped Cassie's head and pulled her in for another searing kiss. It was blissful...soft, warm, and a little bit demanding. Cassie sank into it for long moments, and when she pulled back slightly to breathe...an enormous yawn pushed out of her.

Their gazes held for a second before they both broke into laughter.

Cassie covered her eyes with her hand. "Oh, my god, I'm so sorry." She felt her cheeks redden with heat.

"I guess I should work on my moves," Emerson said, but she was grinning, and she pulled Cassie in close. "You're tired. I get it. Here." She shifted and helped Cassie settle in against her under the covers, Cassie's head on her chest, Emerson's fingers digging gently into Cassie's hair, scratching her scalp. "Just relax and I'll do the same. We've both had a pretty tumultuous day."

"We have." Cassie snuggled in closer, burrowed her head up and under Emerson's chin, wrapped her arm around Emerson's middle, then exhaled a long, contented breath, let herself revel in the feeling of Emerson's fingers. "Oh, this is good."

"Yeah?"

"It's perfect."

"Good. Just close your eyes." Emerson reached for the remote and turned the volume down a couple clicks. Then she zipped through channels until she came to a rerun of *Criminal Minds*. When she looked down to ask Cassie if she minded the show, Cassie was fast asleep. Emerson smiled, pressed a kiss to the top of the dark head, and settled in.

Cassie didn't know what woke her up, but she lay in her bed with the unfamiliar—and wonderful—feeling of Emerson spooned behind her. The clock on the night table said it was 1:47, and she could hear Gordie gently snuffling in his sleep under the bed. She clasped Emerson's hand and pulled it up to her lips and kissed the knuckles, trying to remember when she'd last felt this utterly content.

To her surprise, Emerson shifted behind her. Her arm tightened a bit, then her fingers gently found Cassie's face and turned it so she looked into eyes that were a beautiful blue even in only the moonlight. Their gazes locked for a beat before Emerson lowered her mouth to capture Cassie's. Cassie's entire body was suddenly awake, alive, and flooded with sensation. She turned herself fully, and Emerson slid on top of her. They kissed deeply, almost roughly, tongues doing battle as their breathing became ragged.

They moved easily together. Seamlessly. That thought crossed Cassie's mind moments later as she lay under Emerson, stripped of her T-shirt, her painfully erect nipple in Emerson's mouth, Emerson's hand tugging her panties down over her backside. Seamlessly, as if they'd been making love together for years. She held Emerson's head to her chest, Emerson's short blonde hair like silk against her hand. She slipped it down Emerson's back, grasped the hem of the T-shirt, and pulled it up.

"Fair is fair," she whispered at Emerson's arched eyebrow. Then she pulled the shirt over Emerson's head and tossed it aside. "God, you're beautiful," she remarked, and meant it. Emerson's skin glowed, her breasts small and perfect, her shoulders broad and strong. Emerson's mouth came crashing down on hers then, and all thoughts were banished from her head, Emerson's mouth, Emerson's tongue, Emerson's hands the only things she could focus on.

Cassie felt her panties pulled the rest of the way down, and she helped kick them off. An involuntary groan escaped her as Emerson used her leg to separate Cassie's, then pressed her thigh up into Cassie's center. Emerson gasped, and pulled back to look in Cassie's eyes, moving her thigh very gently up and down, sliding through Cassie's wetness. Cassie swallowed hard and clung to Emerson's shoulders. Their eye contact never wavered. A few more moments of blissful torture, and Emerson shifted. She moved her body, spreading Cassie's legs farther apart, and settled her hips between them. Cassie bent her legs, lifted them, squeezed her knees against Emerson, and she groaned again, her eyes drifting closed.

Emerson nuzzled Cassie's neck, her lips and tongue finding the sensitive skin there and nibbling while at the same time, she slid her hand down Cassie's stomach and between her thighs. Cassie was soaked; she could tell by how easily Emerson's fingers moved, gliding against her flesh, causing waves of warmth to spread through her core, her legs trembling with it. Emerson found her mouth again and kissed her, firm and deep, as she pushed her fingers into Cassie, then slipped them out, gathering wetness before pressing back in.

Cassie felt her knees drop open, as if they had minds of their own and wanted to do everything they could to give Emerson more access. Emerson's breasts were in her hands now, and she cupped them, kneaded them, rolled the hardened nipples between her thumbs and forefingers, but her focus was split. Every time Emerson's fingers came out and slicked through her wetness before pushing back in, Cassie felt her orgasm draw a little bit closer. It was deliciously teasing, and shot a tingling sensation through her entire body each time. Her breath came in torn gasps whenever Emerson let her up for air, and *oh, my god, has it ever been this good before* was the only thought that she was able to comprehend. When she finally decided she could take no more, she wrenched her mouth from Emerson's and grabbed her wrist, stopping her from pushing back into Cassie's center. When Emerson met her gaze, Cassie simply whispered, "Please," then let Emerson's hand go. One side of Emerson's lovely mouth quirked up and she kept eye contact with Cassie as she began moving her hand again. Slowly this time, pressing, sliding, circling, watching Cassie's face, gauging her reactions.

The warm waves started up again, but Emerson kept moving, used her hips to push her hand more firmly against Cassie, and held her gaze. Cassie gasped a small breath, and her lips formed an O before Emerson gave her one more stroke, the stroke that pushed her over the precipice and pulled a guttural, surprisingly low-pitched moan from Cassie's throat. Her muscles tensed as she arched her neck and held onto Emerson as tightly as she could while colors exploded behind her eyelids.

Hours later, they lay entwined like vines of the same plant, their legs tangled together, Emerson spooned behind Cassie again, her warm breasts pressed into Cassie's back. Both of them were content, sated. Cassie could tell by the deep evenness of Emerson's breaths that she'd fallen asleep, and she loved that Emerson was comfortable enough to do so in her bed, wrapped around her like she was. Of course, the amazing sex had played a part, she was sure. Her brain tossed her a couple images, flashes of hands and mouths and legs, the sound of Emerson's orgasm still fresh in her head, the intake of breath and the quiet whimper. Cassie smiled. She couldn't help it.

But now she had questions. So many questions.

She wished she was the kind of person who could simply shut off her brain for a while. Take a hiatus. Breathe. Not worry. But the truth was, she wasn't that kind of person and never would be, and she knew this about herself. She made a mental note to make sure Emerson knew this about her. She should know going in. Vanessa had trouble with it, with Cassie rarely being able to just let something go, let it sit, leave it alone.

What happens next?

That was the big question. And she wanted to ask it so badly she had to clench her hands into fists and focus on keeping them in front of her rather than reaching back to wake up Emerson so she could ask.

She certainly wasn't naïve enough to believe that everything was magically perfect now between her and Emerson. Cassie was an adult, after all, and she'd been through her share of bumps and curves when it came to relationships. She was understandably wary. They weren't going to set up a house together and live happily ever after...at least not yet. Was Cassie being ridiculous to hope that one day they would? Because that's the kind of person she was; she wanted the happily ever after. She always had. How was it that she could absolutely see herself with Emerson for the long haul? How did that happen so quickly?

It scared the bejesus out of her.

Lack of naivety aside, there was nothing she'd like more than to throw herself completely into this relationship. Wait, could she even call it that? They'd had sex. That was all. Yes, it was amazing, mind-blowing, limb-melting sex, but it was just sex. There'd been no professions of love, no promises for the future.

Although.

Emerson did say she thought they had something worth exploring. Right? That was pretty huge coming from somebody like her. It was positive. It hinted at a future. But Emerson would still have to go back to L.A. All her stuff was there. She had an apartment, belongings, a car. What if she went back to L.A. and realized she wanted to stay there? Decided not to return to Lake Henry after all?

Emerson stirred in her sleep, and tightened her arm around Cassie's middle. Cassie snuggled backwards slightly and tried to shut off her brain. She closed her eyes, inhaled deeply, exhaled slowly, let her muscles and her brain relax.

Maybe it was enough to just breathe.

At least for now.

CHAPTER TWENTY-ONE

"WE'LL ALSO HAVE TO pay taxes at the end of the year," Mary said as she stood up from the computer. "Your mother did that each quarter. I know the accountant's card is around here someplace. It's the same guy you met with yesterday." She pulled open a drawer and began rifling through it.

Emerson scrubbed her hands over her face. She already had the accountant's card, but this break was much needed, so she let Mary search while she tried to focus on something other than numbers. They'd been going over things for almost four hours and her brain was full. Mary was fairly patient with her, but any changes Emerson suggested—no matter how slight— were met with all the acceptance and give of a slab of concrete. Adjustments were going to take some work.

The good news was that the inn was operating in the black, and there was no reason to think that would change. Emerson could see places where costs could be cut...simple things like buying cleaning solutions and such in bulk rather than running to the store to grab a bottle of detergent whenever they ran out...but she had realized over the past couple of hours that she'd need to introduce that type of thing gradually. Mary was not good with change. That much was obvious.

Emerson had met with the rental agency that handled Cassie's building. It didn't bring in a ton of money, but enough to warrant leaving it all alone, at least for the time being. She chose that option, simply because she was operating at capacity. Between meeting with Brad Klein to decline Cross's offer, going over things with the rental agency, sitting down with the accountant, and going over everything she needed to know about the inn with Mary and Jack, she was pretty sure she could fit no more information into her head without it exploding all over the counter in front of her.

Add to all of that, the subject of Cassie.

She was trying so hard, Emerson could see it. Cassie was a talker. She processed things verbally and Emerson could tell by looking in her eyes that she wanted to talk about them, the two of them, Emerson and Cassie and whether they had a future. It was such an important topic, it deserved all Emerson's attention. And she just couldn't give that right now. Every time she looked into Cassie's brown eyes, saw the silent plea there, she wanted to punch herself in the face. Cassie was such a good soul, had such a kind heart. Emerson would do anything to keep her from being hurt…yet here she was, doing the hurting. And she knew it.

Emerson cradled her own head in her hands. It was all so much. Too much.

"Hi, there."

The man's voice startled Emerson enough to make her jump. Then she pressed a hand to her chest and laughed.

"Sorry about that," the man said with a gentle chuckle. "Didn't mean to scare you. I just wanted to check out."

Mary took over as Emerson watched each computer keystroke she made, followed each step, but she got lost partway through, and pressed her fingertips into her eyelids instead.

I have to get back.

The thought had crossed her mind more than once over the past couple of days as new information was piled on top of old, things that needed to be tended to here in Lake Henry adding to the list of things in L.A. she needed to deal with. She'd already made her flight reservation for the next day, but if she could wave a magic wand, she'd go right now. She wasn't unhappy with the decisions she'd made, but she was rapidly becoming overwhelmed by the scope of everything there was to deal with, and part of her wanted to go back to LA, crawl into her bed, pull the covers up over her head, and forget all of it.

"Here are the applications for housekeeping." Mary's voice snapped her out of her reverie, and she was surprised to see the man was gone. She took the stack of papers Mary handed her.

"This many?" She had to be holding twenty-five applications.

"Not a lot of jobs come available in a town this small." Mary shrugged.

"Terrific."

Mary patted her on the shoulder. "Ain't easy being the boss lady, is it?" With a squeeze, she disappeared into the kitchen.

Emerson dropped her head into her hands.

The airport was surprisingly busy for a Wednesday morning, and Cassie wasn't sure if she should be happy or disappointed. She had insisted on parking and walking Emerson into the building, wanting to milk every last second with her that she could, and she felt like a lovesick teenager. It was a little embarrassing.

They'd talked about stupid, mundane things during the three-hour car ride, mostly because Cassie was afraid to ask Emerson the one question that was really on her mind.

Are you coming back?

The past few days had been a whirlwind of activity for Emerson as she tried to meet with everybody necessary to settle her mother's estate, and also learn about the new responsibilities she now had. The inn. The rental property. Emerson was now a business owner, and Cassie wasn't terribly clear on how Emerson felt about that.

They'd had little time together after their night of bliss. It had actually been a morning of bliss as well, as they hadn't been able to keep their hands off each other, and Cassie had stumbled down to work bleary-eyed and with sore thighs. Her mother had taken one look at her and had known exactly what she'd been up to; thankfully, she'd chosen not to discuss it. But since then, Emerson's time had been filled with people, advice, direction, numbers, paperwork, and suggestions, and by the time each day had ended, she'd fallen into bed nearly comatose. Cassie suspected Emerson was actually looking forward to going back to L.A.

That's what worried her.

Despite her breakdown, her pleas to not let Cassie become a regret, Cassie wasn't completely convinced that Emerson wasn't about to run again. When she put herself in Emerson's place, it was painfully obvious how much easier it would be to simply stay in California and run things by phone and computer. Emerson would never have to return to Lake Henry again. She could do that. She had done it in the past. Hell, in her shoes, Cassie couldn't say for certain that she wouldn't do the exact same thing.

Emerson finished checking in at the airline counter. Returning to Cassie, she hefted her computer bag onto her shoulder, and they walked to the security line, which was shorter than expected (and shorter than Cassie had hoped) and seemed to be moving along quickly.

"Okay," Emerson said, turning to her. "This is where I get off." She gave a lopsided grin at her attempt at humor.

Cassie's eyes welled up, much to her horror. She cleared her throat. "Okay. Travel safely. Text me when you land." She looked off to her left, her own voice in her head shouting *please come back, please come back, please come back.*

"I will." Emerson reached for her then and wrapped her in a hug.

Cassie held on as tightly as she could for as long as she dared, three more words banging around in her head, trying to find a way out, but Cassie kept them locked in tight.

They parted, neither able to look the other in the eye. Emerson shifted her bag onto her other shoulder. Cassie saw her throat move as she swallowed. "Bye," Emerson said hoarsely.

Cassie lifted a hand, moved her fingers, watched as Emerson entered the line and moved along quickly. She stood in the same spot as Emerson pulled her laptop from her bag, kicked off her shoes, and sent everything through the scanner. On the other side of the metal detector, she gathered her things, looked back one more time, waved to Cassie, and was gone.

Cassie stood still for long moments after that, aware that hot tears were coursing down her cheeks and not caring.

"Please come back," she whispered desperately. "Please come back."

CHAPTER TWENTY-TWO

DECEMBER HAD NOT ARRIVED quietly. Not this year. It had ripped into Lake Henry like an angry banshee, all howling winds and blustering snow. Vanessa stomped her boots on the floor to knock off any slush, then held onto Brian as she unzipped them and left them in the foyer of Jonathan and Patrick's gorgeous home.

"Oh, my god, look at you two!" Jonathan had his arms out and stood still, taking in the sight before him. He wore black dress pants, a very tight red sweater that made it clear how often he worked out, and a Santa hat. "You look fantastic. That dress looks like it was made for you." He kissed Vanessa on the cheek and gave Brian's hand a hearty shake. "Come in, come in. Merry Christmas. Drinks are over there. Hors d'oevres are everywhere. Make yourselves comfortable and be merry!"

Vanessa looked up at her husband, who grinned, then shrugged. "Shall we find a drink?" he asked her.

"Absolutely."

He held out his hand and she clasped it, using him for balance as she put on her shoes. His skin was smooth, his hand warm and strong.

Jonathan and Patrick had one of the most gorgeous homes Vanessa had ever seen. It was large and elegant without being ostentatious. In fact, it was inviting...something she found lacking in many large, expensive homes. The walls in the two-story entryway were cream, and the curving railing and bannister were a tasteful pairing of cream risers and railings with dark wood steps and spindles. A stunning crystal chandelier hung suspended from the high ceilings, and strings of lights, garland, and red velvet decorations gave the entire place the look of a Christmas movie set, twinkling and festive.

The crowd was already large, as Brian had a Friday afternoon meeting that had run late. Vanessa did not mind waiting for him, and that surprised her.

A lot of things surprised her lately.

Who knew that finding a therapist she could talk to openly would change her life? Who knew that talking to her husband with honesty and sincerity would change her life even more?

It hadn't been easy. She'd held out hope that she and Cassie would maybe resume what they'd had. She'd held onto that for what felt like ages, but in reality had only amounted to a few weeks. Because when she really thought about it, what was it that she and Cassie had? An affair. Plain and simple. Cassie wanted a commitment from Vanessa, and Vanessa knew she couldn't do that for reasons that confused her at the time. Still, she'd thought maybe someday...

Then Emerson Rosberg had entered the picture, and Vanessa watched her someday slowly evaporate before her eyes, like the lake mist on a summer morning. Anybody watching Emerson with Cassie knew there was something there, even if the two of them hadn't realized it.

Vanessa thought she would go mad from the giant mix of emotions that had her screaming at her kids for no reason and shutting her husband out completely. She had to do something before she imploded.

After spending a night online while Brian was away on business, she finally took the advice Cassie had given her more than once over the past year or two. She went online and got a real, educated handle on the fact that she was bisexual, that it was a real thing, not a cop-out, that she wasn't a person who couldn't make up her mind. The liberation was palpable, and she'd actually sat at the computer and cried. Big, wracking sobs of relief. After she pulled herself together, she read until her eyes felt like they were about to melt into her head. She did a little more research, found a reputable therapist two towns over, and booked herself an appointment immediately. She attended three sessions before she knew she needed to talk with Brian. She sat him down and told him everything, including about her affair with Cassie. Needless to say, he wasn't happy about what he'd learned, and his first question was, "Are you leaving me?" The beauty of therapy was that it had helped Vanessa understand two truly important factors: she loved her husband, and she wanted to make her marriage work.

It had been tenuous at first, and some days, it still was. He'd tiptoed around her like she might shatter into pieces, uncertain what to say or how to act, hesitant to touch her in any way, seesawing between being concerned and being angry. They were still working on things, but after three weeks, they were doing better. Now he held her or touched her nearly all the time. A hand on the small of her back. A finger toying with a lock of her hair. It was nice. And it was sweet. And she loved him more now than when they'd first fallen for each other.

They moved through the crowd of people slowly, sharing greetings and Christmas wishes. Brian laughed with a golf buddy as he handed a flute of champagne to Vanessa. She sipped and scanned the guests.

Anybody who was anybody came to Jonathan's and Patrick's Christmas party, and some people who were just people. It was the most talked-about event in Lake Henry, both before and after. Vanessa noted several skiers, the hockey coach, the mayor, three attorneys, a judge, and several business owners, plus many friends she knew from PTA meetings and Jeremy's hockey games. Barry Manilow and K.T. Oslin were singing *Baby, It's Cold Outside* on the stereo, and a warm fire crackled in the fireplace across the room. Vanessa sipped her champagne and smiled, her heart filling with contentment. Love for her town, love for her family and friends, love for the holiday.

The opening and closing of the door was near constant as guests continued to arrive, icy blasts of air pushing through the room, only to be disseminated by the warmth of the fire. Brian had tugged Vanessa closer to the fireplace and was deep in conversation with a guy who coached hockey when Vanessa looked toward the door and saw Cassie walk in.

Jonathan mock-squealed and threw his arms around her, shouting, "I thought you'd never get here!" Behind Cassie, Frannie from the store came in, said hello to Jonathan, then waved across the room to somebody and was gone. Cassie stayed in the entryway, laughing with Jonathan, and unbuttoned her long wool coat to reveal a stunning black dress that hugged her body like a lover. She, too, had worn boots like Vanessa, but shucked them in favor of a pair of low red pumps she pulled from a tote bag. They matched the red Bolero jacket and red Christmas earrings she wore. Cassie did not dress up often. She didn't enjoy the fuss it took, and she disliked wearing anything on her feet but sport shoes, but on those rare occasions when she made that effort, she looked gorgeous. Jonathan grabbed her hand and was tugging her toward the kitchen when Cassie met Vanessa's eyes. Cassie gave her a quick smile and a little wave, and then was out of sight.

Vanessa felt Brian stiffen next to her. She ignored the flip-flop her stomach did at seeing Cassie and instead, squeezed his hand and turned to meet his worried eyes. With a smile, she mouthed, "It's okay." It took a beat, but he smiled back, and bent forward to brush her lips with his. She sipped her champagne.

"What the hell took you so long?" Jonathan asked as he pulled Cassie along, stopping every foot or two to buss somebody's cheek or answer a question about food/drink/decorations.

"I had to get some paperwork done, and I wanted to get a couple orders placed before the holidays," Cassie explained. She wasn't really in the mood for a party, but after missing Jonathan's Halloween party, he was not about to allow her to miss this one. Honestly, she was tired and a little sad at the prospect of facing the impending holidays alone. She'd hoped to get a phone call from Emerson tonight, but no luck, and she was unhappy about that. She'd almost bailed, but Jonathan was important to her...and spending some time at a Christmas party was probably better for her head than being cooped up in her apartment alone, staring at her cell phone, willing it to ring. She went on with her explanation. "A lot of businesses shut down early, and I didn't want to take any chances. I told you all this. And I'm not *that* late."

"Late is late, Cassandra. There are no varying degrees. You are late or you are not late. You, my dear, are late." He stuck his nose up, doing his best impression of somebody haughtily irritated, and Cassie couldn't help but laugh. "Besides, I didn't want your present to spoil."

Cassie stopped walking, which pulled Jonathan to an abrupt halt. "We decided not to do presents this year."

"We did?" He feigned shock, pressing a hand to his chest.

"You promised." Cassie narrowed her eyes at him.

"Well, first of all, my dear, you look fabulous. I don't think I told you, but that dress? Ridiculously hot. Second, I will always do presents for my besties, even when I say I'm not going to. Don't you know me at all? Third, you can thank me later." He pulled her around the corner and into the open-concept kitchen/great room combination and held out an arm as if presenting an award. "Ta-da!"

Cassie followed the direction his arm pointed and her eyes fell on Emerson, standing at the counter dressed in a long-sleeved glittering dress of emerald green. She had a wine glass in one hand and was gesturing at Chris with the other, the two of them deep in conversation. Cassie's breath held in her lungs, and she simply drank in the beautiful sight before her, standing quietly, an enormous grin spreading across her face.

Chris caught her eye then and smiled, touched Emerson's arm, and gestured with her chin in the direction of her sister. Emerson turned and their eyes locked. For a long moment, everybody in the room disappeared and it was just Cassie and Emerson. As if tugged by a rope, Emerson set her glass down, came around the counter, and wrapped her arms around Cassie.

"My god, you look gorgeous," she whispered in Cassie's ear.

"I can't believe you're here," Cassie said, embarrassed to feel her eyes fill with tears.

Emerson pulled back to look at her face. "Hey, why are you crying? Should I go back to L.A.?"

"No!" Cassie nearly shouted, then laughed. "No. You should stay right here with me." She swiped at her face, pulled herself together. She dropped her voice so only Emerson could hear. "These are happy tears. I promise. It's just...I've been trying so hard to resign myself to spending the holidays alone. I got through Thanksgiving, and this morning I was just giving myself a pep talk that I only had two more holidays and I'd be home free. And you're here. *You're here.*" She went up on tiptoes and kissed Emerson's soft cheek. "I am so glad to see you."

The rest of the party seemed to move again, as if the music had stopped and started back up, all the guests had frozen in place and were animated once more. Jonathan was suddenly at their sides.

"Merry Christmas," he said to Cassie.

"You did this?" she asked.

"He's a pretty persuasive guy," Emerson commented. He had grabbed her wine glass from the counter and he handed it to her now. They clinked.

Cassie shook her head. "I never thought I'd see the day you two actually liked each other."

"Well," Jonathan said, picking an invisible piece of lint from his sweater. "I still think she's a bit of an ice princess."

"And he's sort of a whiney queen," Emerson said.

"To royalty," Jonathan announced, and they clinked again. Then Jonathan was off to tend to his guests.

"When did you get here?" Cassie asked, still stunned at seeing Emerson standing in front of her in the flesh. It had been over a month since they'd seen each other, since Emerson had returned to LA to take care of things there, since Cassie wondered if she'd ever see her again.

"This morning," she said, her eyes holding Cassie's. "God, it's good to see you." She quickly kissed Cassie's mouth, apparently not caring who saw.

"This morning?" Cassie's voice combined shock and hurt.

Emerson lay a warm hand on her upper arm. "Jonathan wanted it to be a surprise. It was fine. I holed up at the inn with Mary going over the receipts from the past month, looking over some ideas she has for spring."

Cassie recalled Jonathan having some weird business trip this morning. He left early and had to skip their morning coffee date. Two and two suddenly made four. "Jonathan got you at the airport."

"He did. We spent three hours in the car together and rather than kill each other, I think we're going to be pretty good friends." She sipped her wine as she glanced around the room at all the people milling about. "We had some pretty frank discussion."

Cassie grimaced. "This could either be a really good thing or my worst nightmare. I haven't decided yet."

Emerson laughed as Cassie's parents walked up to them and hugged Emerson.

It was all a bit surreal to Cassie. Ever since Emerson had sat down with Mary and Jack and hashed out details for running the inn, Cassie's parents had gained new respect for her, as had Jonathan. Her parents chatted with Emerson now like they were old friends as Cassie watched, almost removed.

Over the past month, she and Emerson had texted and e-mailed and talked on the phone, but the whole time, Cassie hadn't put voice to the questions she'd had after that first night, specifically: what happens next? Was Emerson coming back? Did she want to explore what they might have together the way

Cassie did? She hadn't asked then and the more time went by, the more reasons she found for continuing to not ask. Initially, it *had* been because she was trying to be cognizant of all Emerson had on her plate. The last thing she'd wanted to do was add to the pressure. Now? It was simple: she was terrified of the answer.

But Emerson was here now. That had to mean something. Didn't it?

The next few hours went by in sort of a dream-like haze. They mingled. They ate ridiculously delicious food. They drank fabulous wine. They talked to dozens of people, many of whom asked why Emerson was back in town and how long she was staying.

All her answers were vague.

But they held hands the entire time. Emerson rarely left her side. And when things finally started to wind down, when the crowd began to thin and people were saying goodbye, Emerson turned to her and said, "Can I come back to your place?" then waggled her eyebrows lasciviously.

Cassie couldn't help but laugh. "Well, you're awfully presumptuous, aren't you?"

Emerson leaned close to her ear and whispered, "Not presumptuous, just desperately wanting. I've been imagining taking that dress off you since the moment you walked into the kitchen."

Cassie's heart jumped to her throat, beating like a tribal drum, and a pang of desire hit low in her belly, warming her from the inside. Tugging Emerson's head back down to hers, she responded, "I thought the exact same thing about your dress."

After that exchange, they couldn't get out of there fast enough. As they made the rounds, said their goodbyes, and made it to the hall closet, Cassie said, "I hope you have a car because Frannie gave me a ride. If not, I'm afraid we're hoofing it."

"I have my mom's car," Emerson said. "Here." She held Cassie's coat for her, then they both changed from shoes to boots and tossed their shoes into Cassie's tote.

"Let me know when you're going back, and I'll take you to the airport," Cassie said, buttoning her coat, still slightly stung that she missed three hours alone in the car with Emerson.

Emerson hummed a noncommittal sound as she pulled on gloves. "Ready?"

The ride home was oddly silent, but not uncomfortably so. Emerson parked behind the store, waited for Cassie to come around the car, then grabbed her hand. Once inside, they began to climb the stairs. Halfway through the second flight, Emerson gave Cassie a look.

"Lotta damn steps."

"If only the landlord would put in an elevator," Cassie said in a dreamy voice.

"Fat chance."

Once all the way up and inside, Gordie was a wiggling, quivering mess of love at seeing not only his mistress, but company too. Emerson squatted down to allow him access to her face, which he proceeded to bathe with kisses.

"I missed you, too, buddy boy."

Cassie grinned at the display. "Let me take him out, and then we'll be in for the night." Hand on the doorknob, she turned back and arched a playful eyebrow at Emerson. "And don't you dare take off that dress. That's *my* job."

"Ooh, bossy."

Gordie was blissfully quick doing his business, and when Cassie returned to the apartment, Emerson was sitting on the couch obediently still in her dress.

"I made tea," she said sipping from a mug. She set it on a coaster on the coffee table. When she looked up, Cassie had crossed the room. She took Emerson's face in her hands, and kissed her. Deeply and thoroughly. When she finally pulled back, they were both breathless.

"Wow," Emerson said.

"I have wanted to do that since I first laid eyes on you at the party." Cassie held out her hand. "Come with me."

Emerson took the hand and followed Cassie into the bedroom.

While waiting for Gordie, Cassie had formulated a plan. She needed to come clean with Emerson, talk to her about everything that had gone on in her head for the past month, find out what Emerson's plans were, if they had any kind of a future together.

Because if they didn't, Cassie needed to deal with that.

But first and foremost, she needed to deal with Emerson and that dress. Her mouth literally watered at the sight. Bathed in just the glow from a small lamp on the bedside table, shadows stretched across Emerson's long form, but the green fabric caught what little light there was and made her look as though she was twinkling. Cassie stepped toward her, placed her hands on Emerson's hips, looked in her eyes.

"You were the most beautiful woman in that house tonight," she said softly, then slipped her hand around the back of Emerson's neck and pulled her in for a scorching kiss. As their lips fused deliciously and their tongues battled, Cassie tugged at the zipper on the back of the dress and slid it all the way down to Emerson's behind. Breaking free of the kiss, she reached for the neckline and pulled the dress off Emerson's shoulders as if peeling the wrapper off a delicate gift. Emerson slipped her arms from the sleeves and Cassie let the dress drop to the floor, a puddle of emeralds at Emerson's feet.

Cassie just stood there and absorbed the view. Emerson in a black bra, black panties, and nothing else was not a sight she would soon forget. Her long, lean form was breathtaking, all smooth skin and toned muscle. Even the scars on her knee were beautiful to Cassie.

The rest of their clothes came off quickly, and soon they were in the bed, under the thick down comforter, Cassie on top. She was determined to keep charge of this, wanting so much to have her way with Emerson, with Emerson's body. She kissed her, pressing her into the pillow, one small breast in her hand. She rolled a nipple between her fingers and was rewarded with a guttural moan from Emerson's throat.

"God, I missed you so much," Cassie whispered, moving to take the other nipple into her mouth. She ravished them both, first one, then the other, with lips, tongue, teeth, until Emerson was practically writhing beneath her. Cassie could feel fingers in her hair, gripping tightly, Emerson's breath coming in small gasps. Cassie took her time, lavishing attention on those beautiful breasts until she felt Emerson gently pushing her south. She smiled against warm skin, then let herself be directed, taking her time, using her tongue to taste every inch of softness across Emerson's taut abdomen.

Once she reached her destination, she positioned Emerson's legs so she had the best access possible and without preamble, she swiped Emerson's entire center with one pass of her tongue. Emerson's arms shot over her head and grabbed for the headboard as she gave a small cry, and Cassie smiled, then went to work in earnest.

It was just as she remembered, Emerson's unique musky tang coating her tongue. Warm and wet, welcoming, Cassie took her time, exploring, testing different spots, varying pressure. Emerson's hips began to rock, and Cassie clamped both hands on them, holding her as steady as she could while she tasted this exquisite creature beneath her. Eventually, she pushed Emerson higher, toward the precipice she strove for, and then tipped her over the edge. A long, soft keening came from Emerson's throat as she arched her back and pulled at the comforter. Cassie watched in awe as muscles tensed in orgasm, and she puffed up with pride knowing she was the one who caused such a reaction.

Catching her breath, Emerson reached down and tugged weakly at Cassie's shoulder. "Come here."

Cassie climbed up and lay across Emerson's flushed body so they were nose to nose. "Hi," she said softly, then kissed Emerson's mouth.

"Hey. Fancy meeting you here."

"Yeah, I was just in the neighborhood."

They smiled at one another. Cassie shifted so her full weight was no longer on Emerson, tucked her head under Emerson's chin.

"That was amazing," Emerson said after a few quiet moments.

"Yeah?"

"Yeah."

"I thought so, too."

"Well, don't get too comfortable. As soon as my heart stops pounding and I can feel my feet again, I will be turning the tables."

Cassie chuckled, but said nothing more, and Emerson seemed to feel the shift immediately. She moved her head so she could try to see Cassie's face. "Hey. What's wrong? You okay?"

Cassie nodded. "Mm hmm."

"That was convincing." Emerson waited, but when no more came, she turned so she was on her side and could look at Cassie directly. "Hey." She brushed hair from Cassie's forehead. When Cassie's eyes brimmed with unshed tears, Emerson's expression grew alarmed. "Cassie. What is it, honey? Talk to me."

"I just miss you," Cassie said in a whisper, then was immediately mortified by her own childish behavior. "Damn it." She swiped at a tear tracking across her temple. "I'm sorry. I promised myself I wouldn't do this." She sat up, snatched a tissue from a box next to the bed, blew her nose. When she ventured a glance at Emerson, Emerson was grinning. "What? This is funny to you?"

Emerson furrowed her eyebrows in an obvious attempt to look serious. "No. Not at all." Then she grew serious. "In fact, seeing you cry might be the worst thing ever." She tucked some hair behind Cassie's ear. "Tell me what you're thinking."

Cassie inhaled, blew it out. "I miss you, Em," she said again. "And I know you still have a life in L.A., and I know you're just here for a visit, and I am so incredibly happy to see you..." She let her voice trail off.

"But?"

"I was hoping you'd be here for good by now, but I worry you might not want to leave L.A., and I get that. Everything that needs to be dealt with here, you can do from there. And your life is there, really. I know that. I just…I'm so happy to see you and to be here in bed with you, but it's going to hurt even more when you leave again, and I don't know if I can take it." Fresh tears welled up and Cassie rolled her eyes with a frustrated groan.

"What if I didn't?"

"Didn't what?" Cassie blew her nose again.

"What if I didn't leave?"

Cassie blinked at her. "What does that mean?"

Emerson sat up, her back against the headboard, and pulled the covers up over her breasts. With a shrug she went on. "I don't know. What if I sold my car in L.A. and moved out of my apartment?"

"And lived where?"

She shrugged again and made a show of thinking about it. "Maybe here? I could help run the inn…I *do* own it after all, and my guests pay pretty well. Maybe I could get a part-time job at one of the slopes in the winter, maybe at the rehab center off-season. I think I'd do okay there."

Cassie blinked at her. "You'd consider doing all of that? But…why?"

Emerson studied her. "Because there happens to be a very sexy brunette in this town who helped change my point of view on things, helped me understand that it's okay to leave my past where it belongs: in my past, and to move forward, to reach for what I want."

"Really?"

"Mm hm."

"Would you live in your mom's place?" Cassie's eyes were wide, her questions quietly tentative.

"Yeah," Emerson said with a casual nonchalance. "I'd make a few changes, but I think I'd like it there. It's peaceful."

Cassie was nodding slowly. "It is." She picked at a thread on the comforter and was quiet for a beat. "Do you really think you could live here?"

"I do."

"When would this happen? Like, how much time would you need to do all these things?"

Emerson gazed off into the middle distance. "I don't know. I think…Wednesday?"

Cassie's head snapped around. "What?"

Emerson gave one nod. "Yeah. Wednesday."

"I don't understand."

"I will move in on Wednesday."

"Of next week?" Cassie was confused. "How is that possible?"

Emerson's grin widened. "Well, there's only one way it's possible. If I've already sold my car, if I've already moved out of my apartment, and if a moving truck full of my stuff is on its way and will arrive on Wednesday. Then it's possible."

"Oh, my god," Cassie said softly, blinking, absorbing. "Oh, my god." Emerson gave her some time. She didn't need much. She turned to Emerson and squealed, "Oh, my god!" then threw herself onto Emerson and kissed her as Emerson laughed.

"I wanted to surprise you, so I swore Mary and Jonathan to secrecy, but maybe that wasn't such a great idea," she said, her arms wrapped tightly around Cassie's middle. "You were so forlorn and quiet. I got worried." She made a face and poked

Cassie in the ribs. "Come on, I left seventy-five degrees and sunny for you."

Cassie playfully slapped at her. "I was forlorn and quiet because it was driving me crazy not talking to you about *us*. All those phone calls? When I never said anything about wanting you here? I was trying so hard not to add to your stress, but it was killing me. *Killing me.*"

Emerson kissed her softly. "Honey, you never add to my stress. You are my stress *relief.*"

"I am?"

"Definitely. Maybe we need to make a pact to be better communicators."

Cassie snorted a laugh. "I am all for that. Also, seventy-five and sunny on a non-stop basis is very, very boring." She kissed Emerson hard. "Variety is the spice of life, my sweet."

Emerson clasped Cassie's face in both hands and looked deeply into her eyes. They stayed that way for a beat before Emerson whispered, "I love you, Cassie."

Cassie's eyes crinkled with her grin, and she was sure she could feel her heart swell in her chest. Just as quietly, she said, "I love you, too," and the relief at finally saying those words aloud made her feel infinitely lighter, like she was floating on a cloud. Eyes locked, the two of them reveled in the moment.

Then, without warning, Emerson grabbed Cassie, who squeaked in surprise, and spun her. A blink of an eye later, Cassie was face-down on the bed, Emerson's weight on top of her, Emerson's fingers moving along Cassie's behind, then dipping between her legs and into the warm wet that waited for her.

Cassie groaned, pushed her hips up off the bed, closed the edge of the comforter in her fingers. "What are you doing?" she managed to ask around the pillow.

Emerson's lips close to her ear told her, "Variety is the spice of life, my sweet."

Cassie chuckled at the turnabout, but her chuckle turned into a delicious moan as Emerson's fingers hit the perfect spot.

All coherent thought was gone after that.

THE END